DANIEL KALLA

HIGH SOCIETY

"Daniel Kalla's latest gripping thriller is superb. I'm a fan!"

Shari Lapena, *New York Times* bestselling author of
Everyone Here Is Lying

"Daniel Kalla has an uncanny ability to zero in on the timeliest topics in his thrillers, and *High Society* is no exception. Taking aim this time at psychedelic therapies, Kalla weaves an intricate mystery that considers the lengths to which we will go, and the risks we will take, to get 'better' in the face of pain or trauma. Sometimes, hot celebrity trends can have deadly consequences. Kalla's writing is brisk and tight, and *High Society* is impossible to put down."

Amy Stuart, #1 bestselling author of *A Death at the Party*

"What a roller-coaster read! A psychiatrist experimenting with psychedelic drugs on her addicted patients was probably not going to end well, but as the story developed and skeletons queued up to fall out of the cupboard, I was totally riveted. Beautifully written and ingeniously plotted, *High Society* will take readers on a trip beyond their imagining."

Liz Nugent, internationally bestselling author of
Strange Sally Diamond

"An emotionally damaged psychiatrist using psychedelics to cure addictions, celebrity clients with much to gain and more to hide . . . Daniel Kalla's *High Society* will keep readers on the edge until the last gripping chapter."

Anna Porter, bestselling author of *Gull Island*

"*High Society* is both a gripping murder mystery and an exploration of psychedelics on the fringes of medicine. Daniel Kalla keeps you right on the edge of your (therapist's) chair!"

Vincent Lam, bestselling author of *On the Ravine*

FIT TO DIE

"Timely and relevant. Exposing the dark side of the wellness industry, this electrifying, ripped-from-the-headlines thriller will keep your heart racing from the first page to the very last."

Jennifer Hillier, *USA Today* bestselling author of *Things We Do in the Dark*

"A compulsive, fast-paced thriller that'll keep you flipping those pages well into the night. Filled with twists, turns, and shocking revelations about the diet industry, this is one heck of an intriguing must-read. I devoured it (guilt free)."

Hannah Mary McKinnon, internationally bestselling author of *Never Coming Home*

"Combines a timely plot with a well-paced thriller I became addicted to, fast. This is a gripping page-turner crafted by a skilled, intelligent writer."

Marissa Stapley, *New York Times* bestselling author of *Lucky*

"Tight and tense with great dialogue and snapshot descriptions that crank up the believable. Daniel Kalla is one hell of a writer and *Fit to Die* is one hell of a thriller."

Dietrich Kalteis, award-winning and bestselling author of *Under an Outlaw Moon*

"This is one of Kalla's best."

The Globe and Mail

"Kalla's characters are well-developed across the board, be they victims, heroes, or the long list of suspects. The original and twisty plot helps this taut thriller stand apart."

Publishers Weekly

"Once again Kalla demonstrates . . . his ability to focus [his] lens square on hot topics."

Vancouver Sun

"A timely and relevant story."

The Miramichi Reader

"[A] timely thriller. . . . [Kalla] balances interesting medical details with empathy and a pacey plot, without getting preachy."

Zoomer

THE DARKNESS IN THE LIGHT

"Kalla is unparalleled in his ability to create compelling characters that embody societal trauma and medical complexities. *The Darkness in the Light* explores rural northern health care, the unrelenting pressure of depression, and pharmaceutical treatments with great care. Both heartbreaking and brave, this is a boldly written story that fans will love and new readers will devour."

Amber Cowie, author of
Last One Alive

"This book, with its well-written descriptions of the far north, is one of [Kalla's] best."

The Globe and Mail

"Emergency room physician Daniel Kalla is one of Canada's best-selling and most impressive writers, and his latest novel, *The Darkness in the Light*, demonstrates why."

Zoomer

"Kalla's Alaskan whodunit delights. . . . Just remember that Vancouver E.R. doctor Daniel Kalla not only writes superb medical thrillers with a pronounced social edge—his books are also terrific murder mysteries."

Winnipeg Free Press

"A very good read, and very timely."

CBC's *The Next Chapter*

LOST IMMUNITY

"Kalla ratchets up the suspense as a cover-up is exposed . . . a truly scary scenario from a writer who knows his medical thriller lingo down to the final line."

The Globe and Mail

"Kalla . . . has a knack for writing eerily prescient thrillers."

CBC Books

"Always there to hold up a mirror to society—his last book, *The Last High*, took on the opioid crisis—Kalla's new *Lost Immunity* book sits smack dab in the middle of what the world has been going through for the last year."

Vancouver Sun

ALSO BY DANIEL KALLA

High Society

Fit to Die

The Darkness in the Light

Lost Immunity

The Last High

We All Fall Down

Nightfall Over Shanghai

Rising Sun, Falling Shadow

The Far Side of the Sky

Of Flesh and Blood

Cold Plague

Blood Lies

Rage Therapy

Resistance

Pandemic

The Deepest Fake

A NOVEL

DANIEL KALLA

PUBLISHED BY SIMON & SCHUSTER

New York Amsterdam/Antwerp London
Toronto Sydney/Melbourne New Delhi

SIMON &
SCHUSTER
CANADA

A Division of Simon & Schuster, LLC
166 King Street East, Suite 300
Toronto, Ontario M5A 1J3

This book is a work of fiction. Any references to historical events, real people, or real places
are used fictitiously. Other names, characters, places, and events are products of the author's
imagination, and any resemblance to actual events or places or persons, living or dead, is
entirely coincidental.

This Simon & Schuster Canada edition July 2025

SIMON & SCHUSTER CANADA and colophon are trademarks of Simon & Schuster, LLC

Simon & Schuster strongly believes in freedom of expression and stands against censorship
in all its forms. For more information, visit BooksBelong.com.

For information about special discounts for bulk purchases, please contact Simon & Schuster
Special Sales at 1-800-268-3216 or CustomerService@simonandschuster.ca.

Manufactured in the United States of America

10 9 8 7 6 5 4 3 2 1

Library and Archives Canada Cataloguing in Publication
Title: The deepest fake / by Daniel Kalla.
Names: Kalla, Daniel, author
Description: Simon and Schuster Canada edition.
Identifiers: Canadiana (print) 20240488407 | Canadiana (ebook) 20240488415 |
    ISBN 9781668032534 (softcover) | ISBN 9781668032541 (EPUB)
Subjects: LCGFT: Psychological fiction. | LCGFT: Thrillers (Fiction) | LCGFT: Novels.
Classification: LCC PS8621.A47 D44 2025 | DDC C813/.6—dc23

ISBN 978-1-6680-3253-4
ISBN 978-1-6680-3254-1 (ebook)

For Leeandra

The
Deepest
Fake

CHAPTER 1

Liam Hirsch never seriously contemplated dying before his forty-ninth birthday—until today.

As he lets his electric Ford F-150 coast down the long driveway on this gray, drizzly Tuesday—a typical January afternoon in Seattle—he's struck by the sheer size of the house he's called home for seven years. It's strange, this fixation on something so mundane. *Am I still in shock?* he wonders.

Liam grew up in a cramped rental on a cracked street lined by patchy lawns. He never imagined owning a house like this—a hundred-year-old Tudor Revival fully refurbished with white oak floors, Carrara marble, a chef's kitchen, and three fireplaces—let alone living in Broadmoor, a gated enclave designed to keep people like him out. But none of it matters now, he realizes with a shiver. He won't be living anywhere much longer.

He remembers the day they moved in. The twins, Ava and Cole, just eight years old, swarmed the house as though on an Easter egg hunt, their laughter echoing through the empty rooms. Celeste joined in, launching a pillow fight before helping Ava pin up posters of Ariana Grande and Shawn Mendes. Even after the kids fell asleep, his wife was still buzzing with excitement. They lay together on the living room couch, surrounded by empty boxes, her legs tangled with his as she eagerly detailed the renovations needed to put "the Hirsch stamp" on their new home. But now the memory sours. Liam, preoccupied with a glitch in his company's app, barely registered Celeste's words or appreciated what the house truly represented: the security he had always sought for his family.

Liam parks in the four-car garage's only empty stall and sits there, staring at the bikes, skis, kayaks, and camping gear—each item a trigger for memories of family adventures that now feel like someone else's. He's going to have to avoid music, he realizes, or he won't be able to hold it together. His hand hovers over the door handle. He wrestles with the same questions that have dogged him since leaving the doctor's office: *What do I tell Celeste? How do I break it to the kids?*

He wonders if he should be as blunt as Dr. Hudson Chow was. Liam hadn't gone to the neurologist expecting good news—he knew the muscle twitches in his legs, shoulders, and, of all places, his tongue were worrisome signs. But the grim look on Dr. Chow's face told him everything before any words were spoken.

"Mr. Hirsch . . . it's not good," Dr. Chow said.

"We didn't expect good, did we?" Liam replied with a forced smile.

"True, but we didn't expect it to be this severe," Dr. Chow said, his eyes unwavering. "The MRIs, the EMG, the biopsy—they all point to the same diagnosis: amyotrophic lateral sclerosis. ALS."

The words knocked the breath out of him. "Like Stephen Hawking," he whispered, visualizing the famed scientist slumped in his wheelchair, his head and neck contorted, reliant on a robotic voice to communicate.

"Yes, but like any disease, ALS has an unpredictable course," Dr. Chow said. "Stephen Hawking lived for decades with it."

"I won't?"

"Your condition has progressed significantly since your last appointment."

"You're saying I don't just have run-of-the-mill ALS, I have the aggressive form?"

"We never classify ALS as run-of-the-mill, Mr. Hirsch. But yes, 'aggressive' would be a fair description."

"And there's no treatment?"

"There are two new medications that can sometimes slow the progression or lessen symptoms. I'll prescribe them today."

"They're not cures?"

"No. At best, they might prolong functionality. Delay the onset of more symptoms."

"Delaying it is the best I can hope for?"

"There are experimental therapies emerging. We could look for a study . . ."

The hesitation in Dr. Chow's voice was enough. "But they don't work, do they?"

"Not so far, no."

Liam's head spun. "So, I have months, at best?"

"In terms of functionality, yes, probably."

"Functionality?"

Dr. Chow finally looked away. "If the disease continues to progress at this pace, you will likely lose much of your basic motor function within the next six to twelve months."

Liam's hands sat still in his lap. His calmness astounded him. Would it last? Could it? "You're telling me I won't be able to speak, walk, or even swallow in six months? Or sooner?"

"It's impossible to predict with certainty, but . . . yes, there's a good chance of that kind of progression." Dr. Chow sighed, his expression so strained that Liam couldn't help but feel a flicker of sympathy for him. "At some point in the near future, Mr. Hirsch, you'll need to think about life support and how you feel about being placed on a ventilator. Perhaps you could come back with your wife . . ."

The shock must have set in then because the rest of their conversation is a blur.

Stunned, Liam wandered back to his truck, sinking into the driver's seat and staring blankly at his reflection in the mirror. The man looking back seemed much older than he felt. Anger surged—rage at the injustice, at his body's betrayal, at the world for spinning on while his life unraveled. He wanted to scream, to hit something, to release the pressure building inside him. But all he could do was sit there, silent, as the weight of his diagnosis pressed down.

The next thing he remembered was driving home, his legs heavy, his thoughts spiraling. He imagined his kids' faces—their tears, the disbelief. He still had so much to teach them: how to drive, manage credit, and spot red flags in relationships. He needed to get Ava focused on a college major, help Cole build confidence. How could he be strong for them when he himself was crumbling?

Now, parked back in the garage, the dread of facing his family immobilizes him. He tries to coax himself out of the truck, to at least go tell Celeste. *Don't wallow*, he tells himself. *You're a doer. Get moving!* But instead, he unlocks the glove box and pulls out a manila envelope he's kept hidden for weeks. He slides out the thin stack of photos. Despite their painful subject matter, the gritty, sticky feel of the photo paper and the faint vinegary scent take Liam back to another time.

His detractors—and there are a few—would relish the irony of a two-hundred-year-old analog technology upending the life of an AI pioneer like him. Liam can't ignore it either. As he stares at the second photo—the one that never fails to gut him—his hand trembles. He quickly tucks the pictures away before the involuntary spasms worsen.

He watches helplessly as his fingers twitch—as though someone else's brain is using them to mold an imaginary chunk of clay. Even worse, there's no pain. No sensation at all.

After the episode passes and he regains control of his fingers, he leaves the truck and walks to the house, careful to lift his feet with each step, rehearsing a few lines in his head. They're truthful but gentler than the grim words he just heard from Dr. Chow.

Inside, he finds Celeste at the front closet, slipping on her running jacket.

"Hi," she says, turning with a tentative smile. "What did the specialist say?"

Liam had told her about the symptoms, downplaying the worst of them. He couldn't hide the tremors while they still shared a bed. But now he regrets mentioning the appointment. How many lies can this marriage take?

The words won't come. He just stares into her eyes—those stippled cinnamon swirls that once spoke volumes but have lately gone silent.

What he wouldn't give at that moment to be snuggling with her on the couch again, sharing everything like they once did.

"What is it, Liam?" Her expression clouds with concern. "He thinks it's stress, right? You told him how much you're working on your new app? The sleepless nights?"

His mind flashes to the second photo in the stack. It's not the raw nakedness or the single bead of sweat between his wife's breasts that haunts him. Not even the other man's tattooed shoulder. It's the look on Celeste's face—the pleasure, the playfulness, the vitality lighting up her delicate features. He hasn't seen that in a long time. He would kill to see her look at him like that again.

All the rehearsed lines fly out of his head. "The tests were inconclusive. He thinks it's probably stress-related."

CHAPTER 2

Andrea DeWalt steels herself as she reaches for the doorknob. It's time.

For the past seven months, she has steered clear of the room—not just because her dad died in here, but because she knows he must have left something behind for her. But now that the townhouse is about to be listed for sale, the home office is the last room she has left to clear out. The Realtor insisted she leave the furniture to make the space feel "more inviting," but Andrea isn't about to let strangers rifle through her dad's personal belongings during showings or open houses.

The room smells like him. Aftershave, old books, and carpet cleaner. It's exactly as he left it. Andrea didn't need to rummage through his desk to settle his modest estate; her dad had kept all his meticulous financial records, including his will, at his downtown office in the heritage building on First Avenue, where he ran his solo accounting practice for forty years. She spent many happy hours there after school, helping him with filing and bookkeeping. He paid her for her time and taught her how to invest her money, but she would have done the work for free. She loved hanging out with him. After her mom abandoned them, Andrea found it hard to be apart from him.

Her dad often brought her to work when she wasn't in school. In those early years, she built secret forts under his desk, draping blankets over the sides to create her private hideaway. Curled up with her favorite books and snacks, she found comfort in the gentle rhythm of his typing and the shuffle of papers. Being with him in that shared space made her feel safe and content.

Once, while working on a special client presentation, he handed her a box of colored pencils and some blank paper, encouraging her to draw whatever she liked. As she doodled beside him, he would pause to ask her opinion on color schemes and layouts, treating her input with genuine consideration. When the presentation was finished, he proudly showed her how he had incorporated her suggestions. That was her dad—always making her feel central to his world.

At least, until the last day of his life.

Now, her fingers feel sticky and her mouth goes dry as she approaches his desk. As a private investigator, she's combed through too many similar spaces not to fear what she might uncover here. It's not the weird stuff she often finds—sex toys, collections of toenail clippings, or closets crammed with empties—that worries her. It's the fear of coming face-to-face with hurtful reminders of her past, like letters or photos from her mother, who deserted them when Andrea was only seven. Or, worse, her dad's final words explaining why he took his own life.

As she hovers over the desk where his longtime cleaner found him after he overdosed on prescription medications, Andrea's anger rises, sharp and unyielding.

She gets that her dad had been in intractable pain. His inflammatory arthritis had worsened to the point where he needed an electric scooter to get around. He had trouble twisting doorknobs and holding cutlery. The arthritis had even spread to his jaw, making proper dental cleanings impossible. None of the surgeries or medications helped him. But was that reason enough to kill himself without telling her?

How could the most generous person I've ever known be so fucking selfish in the end?

The coroner told Andrea her father hadn't left a suicide note, but she knew him too well to believe that. Somewhere behind his password-protected home screen—he always used the same one, *Andrea1987*—

she's certain something is waiting for her, but she's still not ready to face it.

Avoiding the computer, Andrea begins emptying the desk drawers into the boxes she brought with her. Out of professional habit, she mentally records the alignment and order of everything she touches, though unlike at work, she doesn't have to leave this room exactly as she found it.

In her eleven years as a private investigator, Andrea has learned that everyone hides part of themselves, especially from the people they love most. Some do it habitually, others occasionally. Some secrets are trivial, making her wonder why they even bother. Others are transformational. Her job is to uncover them all, big or small. And she's good at it.

At this moment, she wishes she weren't.

Her client Liam Hirsch leaps to mind again. He was right to suspect his wife was having an affair with the contractor renovating their home. It was a betrayal of convenience and proximity—something Andrea has seen multiple times before—and experienced once herself. But it was Liam's reaction to proof of the affair that stuck with her for weeks afterward.

It's the worst part of the job by far—the moment Andrea has to present evidence of infidelity to her clients, often via photos, but sometimes through texts, videos, or phone recordings. She dreads those awkward, post-proof conversations. She used to feel compelled to offer sympathy, dragging out those conversations while she fumbled for the right words of reassurance. Experience taught her there are no right words, so she stopped trying. Her clients pay for proof, not therapy.

Over the years, Andrea has witnessed a range of responses, from fury and shame to grief and extreme self-blame. One client smashed every one of his wife's prized crystal wineglasses after seeing photos of her making out with her trainer. After that, Andrea stopped showing clients her evidence outside of neutral, third-party locations. Another woman laughed uncontrollably at photos of her husband in bed with her sister, so Andrea had to take their coffees to go and walk her around the block until she calmed down.

But Liam's response took her by surprise. He was still and quiet, studying the photos with his impassive, silvery blue eyes. Expressionless, he laid two of the photos side by side on his desk and pointed to the second one. "That's not the same bra," he noted, comparing it to the first. The only hint of emotion was the slight tremor in his right hand.

"No," Andrea said, surprised he'd picked up on the difference. "They were taken on different days."

"Different bras, different days." Liam nodded at the photos. "How many times did you catch them together?"

"Three times."

"Over how long?"

"About a week."

"No wonder it's taking him forever to tile the bathroom."

She didn't respond as he carefully gathered the photos and slid them back into the envelope.

"I can keep these, yes?"

"Of course. You own them, Mr. Hirsch." She pulled out a smaller envelope. "And here are the negatives."

"Negatives?" His eyes widened. "You really are an analog detective, aren't you?"

She grinned. "Not exactly, but I do prefer to use film when possible. And I never make copies."

"That's good, I suppose." He nodded at the envelope. "Celeste looks happy, doesn't she?"

The question caught Andrea off guard. None of her other clients had ever remarked on their cheating spouse's degree of contentment. "I . . . I don't have enough of a point of reference to say."

"I wonder if she's in love."

Andrea could tell his wondering wasn't meant for her, but if Liam had pressed, she would have had to say her opinion was no. His wife looked satisfied, like she was getting away with something. Even though Andrea had never met Celeste, after a few weeks of following her, she had formed a distinct impression: charming, warm, and impeccably put together. The kind of woman others instantly notice. But beneath that polished exterior, Andrea sensed restlessness. Possibly an emptiness, too.

Celeste's affair didn't seem born out of love. No, it was driven by the thrill, the escape, and maybe a need for fulfillment. It was pitiful, really, that someone who had so much would risk everything for so little.

Brushing off the memory, Andrea sits down at her dad's computer. As her fingers tap out his password, her anger recedes, replaced by a growing dread at what might be waiting for her behind the home screen.

CHAPTER 3

For as long as Liam can remember, he's found solace in darkness. Growing up, his younger brother and sister were terrified of their poorly lit, unfinished basement with its shadowy corners, creaking pipes, and cobwebbed nooks—but for Liam, it was a sanctuary. Whenever life overwhelmed him, he would retreat there, sitting in the darkness to clear his mind and steady his nerves.

But now, at nearly three a.m., as he nurses a tumbler of scotch in his basement office, illuminated only by the dim glow of a screen saver, the darkness offers no peace. He rarely drinks—alcohol usually just makes him sleepy or nauseous—but tonight, with sleep eluding him, he thought a drink might still his racing thoughts. It hasn't.

Earlier, during dinner, he didn't breathe a word to his wife or kids about his diagnosis. The finality of it left him mute, contributing nothing to the conversation. When Ava finally remarked on his uncharacteristic quietness, he blamed it on a work deadline, feeling like a coward for falling back on his usual excuse.

The self-recrimination is strong. He should tell them; they need to know. But what's the point of burdening them until he figures out the next steps? He reminds himself that he's an engineer, a problem solver. Until he has a plan, there's no reason to throw their lives into chaos.

He thinks back to the first time he noticed the muscle twitching in his hand, five or six weeks earlier. It started days after he'd seen the photos of his wife in bed with their contractor. At the time, he chalked the spasms up to stress and sleeplessness, thinking they were just a variation of the occasional twitch in his left eyelid. But when they worsened, he finally went to see his doctor, Jeremy Blackmore. Despite Jeremy's reassuring manner, the urgency of his referral to a neurologist made it clear something might be seriously wrong.

Liam takes another sip, contemplating what lies ahead. He's no stranger to fear. A lifelong rock climber, he's had his share of brushes with death, both before and after the twenty-foot fall that crushed two bones in his lower back. His own death doesn't scare him. What terrifies him is the inevitable pity and indignities he'll have to endure: the clichéd, empty words of encouragement, the sorrowful glances, and the obligatory cards, flowers, and visits. The thought of it all makes his stomach turn.

Randomly, he thinks of Andrea and decides she wouldn't pity him. Even though he sought her help during one of the most painful episodes in his life, her direct, no-nonsense style drew him in. That, and the way her thick black hair swept into a messy bun, her pert nose, and striking almond-shaped eyes reminded him of Ms. Waters, his seventh-grade math teacher and first crush—another no-nonsense woman. When Andrea presented the proof of Celeste's infidelity, there was no comfort, no sympathy. What would she think of his terminal diagnosis? Pity him? Commiserate over the inevitable indignity? He doubts it.

ALS will rob him of everything—his ability to walk, talk, dress, chew, swallow, even wipe his own ass. But what torments him even more is the thought of his kids witnessing every agonizing step of his rapid decline. Poor Ava and Cole: How will they handle this?

Liam's own father was always chasing get-rich-quick schemes, too consumed by his failed pursuits to be there for his kids. *But at least Dad survived my childhood,* Liam thinks bitterly. The thought of his kids losing him, especially Cole, who's struggled with his teen years more than his sister, is unbearable. His son needs him more than ever.

Liam's hand trembles again. Before he can lower the glass, the scotch spills onto the armrest. He dabs at it, imagining the stain and wondering how he'll explain it to Celeste. The thought angers him.

He had never imagined Celeste would cheat on him. He dismissed the early signs—her unusual periods of radio silence, the uncharacteristic fluctuations in her schedule, the way she sometimes shielded her screen while texting. But it wasn't until Ava casually mentioned her best friend had seen Celeste with "that contractor guy" at a coffee shop on a morning she was supposed to be in Everett for a tennis match that everything clicked. Then he hired Andrea to bring him the proof he'd hoped she wouldn't find.

How could she cheat on me now, of all times? Although it's not like she turned to someone else when he got sick, he reminds himself. She doesn't even know. She started stepping out before he noticed any physical changes. Maybe he hadn't prioritized her enough, but did that justify her actions? No, but it helped explain them. It was context. He was at the office more than he was at home. *No, fuck that!* He would never have strayed or fallen in love with someone else. But maybe she didn't need justification. Maybe it just happened, and she doesn't feel guilty. Maybe she feels empowered, adored.

He wonders why he has to lose his wife and his body simultaneously. *Can't I get a break on one or the other?*

Liam laughs, a bitter sound, recognizing how quickly he's moved through the Kübler-Ross stages of grief—barreling through denial and anger straight into bargaining. He refuses to beg. Not to a God he doesn't believe in, and certainly not to Celeste. Why shouldn't he lose his wife and his health? He's not special. But he doesn't have to suffer passively.

"I am a doer," he reminds himself aloud, reaching for the glass again.

His thoughts turn to the articles he read earlier this afternoon on Washington State's Death with Dignity Act. He hadn't realized there were different euphemisms for the process. Proponents call it "medical assistance in dying," or MAiD, while detractors call it "physician-assisted suicide." The semantics don't concern him.

Whatever they call it, it's an option he needs to explore.

CHAPTER 4

Samrath "Sam" Sanghera, TransScend's chief operating officer, leans back in his chair and peers at Liam over the top of his half-moon glasses. The glasses always throw Liam off, making Sam look more like a librarian than a computer engineer built like a linebacker. With slicked-back black hair, a hooked nose, and a light brown complexion, Sam exudes an intensity that's only softened by the perpetual amusement in his deep chestnut eyes.

"You still with me, Boss?" Sam asks, raising a thick eyebrow.

Barely.

Sam has been with Liam since day one. After fifteen years of working side by side, they can almost read each other's thoughts. Liam, the quiet leader, complements Sam's extroverted and highly social nature. When conflicts arise, Sam plays the bad cop to Liam's good one. Liam doubts he'll be able to hide his diagnosis from his old friend for long. Then again, he faked it pretty well with his family last night. "I was just thinking," he says.

And he has been, but not about Sam's question. His mind is on Celeste and those damn photos. Not the explicit content, but the events that led her—them—to that point. Maybe she ended up in bed with their contractor, Benjamin, because, as she'd once murmured after he canceled yet another dinner date, "I can never compete with your one true love."

She meant his company, TransScend.

Was the devotion worth it? Liam wonders, bitterly glancing around his massive corner office on the top floor. He could host a small conference here. What a waste of space. If someone had told him ten years ago that his struggling AI startup would one day have its own small campus in the affluent suburb of Bellevue, he would have laughed.

In the early years, he and Celeste had lived under the constant threat of losing everything. After the twins were born, he lay awake worrying about providing for his family. When the company finally gained traction and their stock went public, he reveled in his newfound wealth, but the satisfaction was fleeting. He learned that material things mattered little to him. Beyond securing his family's financial future, he discovered a deeper drive: legacy. Only recently has he come to understand how much that truly matters to him. If his lifelong ambition doesn't amount to something real and sustainable, then all those years of sleepless nights, working weekends, missed holidays, and the strain on his marriage will have been for nothing. An unforgivable waste, especially now that his time is running out.

He blames his obsession with legacy squarely on his father. Even when his dad was around, which wasn't often, he was too caught up in his doomed financial ventures to be truly present. Liam has achieved a level of success his father could only dream of, yet he fears he's committed the same crime of neglecting his family. Maybe not his kids, but certainly Celeste. And for what? His company could still collapse, leaving his family in debt. The release of the new app will either make his fortune or break it. The thought of his kids remembering him as he remembers his own father—a man with nothing to show at the end of his life—sickens him.

Liam shakes off the bleak thoughts. "I'm listening, Sam."

"I don't get it, Liam." The COO's use of his first name is notable because Sam almost never uses it. Usually it's "Boss," "Prez," or sometimes, reflecting Sam's passion for hip-hop music, "the O.G."

"Get what?"

"You're supposed to be the cautious one. Always telling us to rein it in. More dry runs. More tests. Remember how long you dragged your feet on the launch of HisStory?"

How could Liam forget? Everything was riding on that launch. Years of sacrifice, worry, and dedication came to fruition in that single groundbreaking app—a self-learning technology that, using only archival footage, could bring historical figures back to life on-screen. He'd been agonizing over perfecting his generative AI algorithm since grad school, and he'd struggled to pull the trigger on HisStory's launch. He kept insisting on more tests, more tweaks. He barely ate or slept for weeks before it went live. In the end, it was a bigger success than he'd dared dream. Of course, at the time, he had no idea just how enthusiastically Hollywood studios would embrace the technology, using the app to cast famous dead actors in new film roles, and how vociferously living actors would object to the AI competition, disrupting the industry overnight.

Sam grimaces. "Now you want us to move the launch date *up* by three months?"

"I asked you if it was doable."

"Yeah, but you'd only ask if you were intent on doing it."

Sam is right, of course. Liam wants a chance to see their newest app in action, at least while he can still move and breathe on his own. But there's more to it. He knows he won't be able to keep the news of his illness quiet until June, when the app is currently scheduled to be released. Who knows how much that could destabilize the company's share price and undermine the launch?

The new app is named TheirStory, although the coders have nicknamed it Séance AI. It's a natural extension of HisStory. It allows users to upload data—videos, recordings, emails and texts, and other collateral information—on anyone of their choosing along with a detailed personality inventory. From there, the generative AI creates a realistic and interactive avatar of the chosen subject. But unlike HisStory, which relies on users to provide a script for the avatar and has limited potential for improvisation, TheirStory uses predictive algorithms to create original responses. It allows users to converse with the subject as though they were speaking via video chat. In the later development stage, many of the coders selected a dead relative as an avatar to test on the app. The results were so realistic that several of them were in tears during those sessions, leading to its morbid nickname.

All the testers agree that it's a seismic upgrade over the other similar apps available on the market, known as deathbots. Developing TheirStory was a herculean undertaking requiring massive computing power and amassing vast amounts of data from public records, licensed proprietary sources like social media, and anonymized user interactions. They had to use cloud computing for scalability and leverage edge computing—a technology that processes data closer to where it's generated—to minimize latency, which appears as freezing during user interactions.

Liam has mixed feelings about families communing with dead loved ones as though they're still alive. But he's always rationalized those worries away, arguing that, if not them, one of their competitors will eventually market a deathbot as functional. And from a technical perspective, TheirStory has exceeded his wildest expectations. He has no doubt the appetite for their groundbreaking app will be boundless. He also knows the opposition to it will be equally fierce among those AI skeptics who will only see the app's potential for abuse. Either way, he hopes and expects it to cement his legacy, provided the launch goes smoothly.

"Why don't you stop worrying about my motives, Sam, and just answer the fucking question?" Liam grumbles, aware that he's venting unfairly on his right-hand man.

Sam chuckles. "You're dropping f-bombs now? Who are you and what have you done with the Prez?"

Liam rubs his eyes. "Not today, Sam, please."

"It's theoretically possible, I suppose," Sam says. "But putting aside the risk of bugs and crashes, it will completely bugger up our whole comms and marketing strategy. We've been focused on a June release for the past year."

"I don't care about the comms."

Sam leans forward. He's still smiling, but there's a glimmer of concern in his eyes. "What's going on?"

Liam considers unloading his terrible secret onto his old friend. What a relief it might be. But he can't bring himself to. Instead, he says, "The app is ready, Sam."

"And it will be in June, too. On the day we've been targeting for the past eighteen months."

"Things move at lightning speed in AI. Who knows what might pop up if we wait five more months?"

"We'd know, Boss. Before anyone else did. I've got eyes everywhere."

"I think we better move the launch date up."

"And I think that's fucking madness!"

"Last time I checked, I'm still the CEO."

Sam laughs. "You're pulling that card on me? For real?"

"Douche move, huh?" Liam musters a grin. "I have a feeling on this one, Sam. Trust me, OK?"

That argument seems to find some traction, even though it's a lie. During their long working relationship, Liam has only relied on intuition on a few specific occasions, but it has paid off every time. And Sam knows it, too, even if he doesn't like it. He pinches his nose, pushing his glasses above his eyes. "OK. I'll see if I can move this mountain. Actually, more like the whole goddamn Himalayan range. Because of this *feeling* of yours."

"Thank you." Exhaustion overwhelms Liam. He wants to end the conversation before another uncontrollable tremor strikes, but there is one other matter he has to discuss with his COO. "What did you make of the last quarterly report?"

"Make of what? Our record profits?"

"Sure, but the expenditures seemed a bit off to me."

"Off?" Sam's brow furrows. "By how much?"

"They were up about a percent or two over the previous quarter."

"A percent or two? That's what you're losing sleep over?"

"I'm not aware of any new capital purchases or other major expenditures to explain it. Are you?"

"Nope." Sam squints. "What does Ramona have to say about it?"

"She hasn't gotten back to me yet."

Liam thinks back to the conversation he had with their quirky but very savvy chief financial officer two days earlier.

"Oh, yeah, I made a note of it, too," Ramona said, after Liam broached the discrepancy with her. "It's likely due to timing differences between when expenses are incurred versus when they're recorded. It should balance out in the next quarter."

"I see."

"Or it could be a classification thing," Ramona hurried to add. "We recently reclassified some expenses to different accounts for better financial tracking. It might have caused temporary inconsistencies." She offered him a tight smile. "I'll drill down on the specifics and let you know."

But Ramona still hasn't gotten back to Liam. And if she had spotted the discrepancy, why hadn't she mentioned it to him before he inquired? He wonders if he's reading too much into the situation, looking for problems where there aren't any, but with the way the rest of his life is coming apart at the seams, he can't afford any instability inside the company.

"You ran our books for years," Liam says to Sam now. "You know them inside and out. Do me a favor and go through them yourself. Please."

Sam eyes him for a long moment. Liam can see that his longtime friend is wondering why the hell he's worrying about some minor accounting discrepancy when he just decided to upend the company's entire production schedule. But Sam only nods. "Will do, Boss."

CHAPTER 5

Liam pokes at the stir-fry on his plate, trying to make it look like he's eaten something while focusing on not dropping his cutlery. His fifteen-year-old daughter isn't fooled. Ava waves her fork at him. "Dad, you'd keep me at the table until midnight if I tried that same fake-eating stunt on you."

"My stomach's a bit off today, hon."

Her twin brother, Cole, smirks. "Too much kale in your smoothie this morning?"

"Or maybe you went too heavy on the turmeric and magnesium?" Ava chimes in.

The kids have taken to teasing their parents lately about the supplements they've been consuming since consulting a nutritionist on the best anti-aging diet. Liam winces inwardly, thinking how all the dirt and shrubbery in his smoothies haven't done much for his health.

"Stop picking on Dad," Celeste says from the other end of the table. Liam can't tell if her wink is meant for him or the kids.

"How was practice, Cole?" Liam asks, steering the conversation away from himself.

His son pulls a face. "Coach wants us in a four-four-two formation for the game against Mount Vernon Sunday."

"Makes sense. They're an offensive powerhouse."

"Yeah, but how are we supposed to put the ball in their net with Ian and Noah left stranded up front?"

"You've got to defend well to hold them off. Be opportunistic. Like Manchester City."

Liam had never watched soccer before Cole started playing in first grade, but his son's passion for the sport drew him in. Now they faithfully watch Premier League matches together, as much for the strategy as for the entertainment. Even though Cole's natural talent is limited, his dedication and hard work have earned him a spot on his grade's elite team for the past three years. And Liam's become a fiercely proud soccer dad. He has never missed one of Cole's matches, even when it meant catching red-eye flights or juggling other scheduling nightmares. There were times he resented the commitment, but now the thought of missing out on Cole's future games breaks his heart.

Ava makes a face. "Can we *please* get through one dinner without blabbering on about soccer?"

Unlike her brother, Ava has never been into sports or other organized activities. Besides climbing with her dad, she's quit so many classes—piano, badminton, you name it—that her parents joke they only need to plan for the first day of a new program because she won't attend the second. But Liam doesn't worry about her. While Cole is sensitive and moody, Ava is easygoing and confident. Liam knows she'll glide through life with a resilience her brother might struggle to find.

"OK, let's talk about Matias Ibsen instead," Cole says, a teasing edge to his voice.

"As if! He's dumb as a post." But the flush on Ava's cheeks gives her away.

Cole shrugs. "Guess I *imagined* seeing you camped out by his locker this morning?"

"I was there for Sarah! Moral support. She melts around anyone who can throw a football."

Cole rolls his eyes. "Good of you to take one for the team."

"As if, Col-ton." Ava uses the name only to annoy her brother; it's not even his real one. "I doubt you could relate, seeing as you're incapable of talking to girls."

While Celeste shakes her head and sighs, Liam drinks in the playful exchange between his kids. These moments feel more precious now than he could have ever imagined.

A few hours later, after the kids are in bed, Liam sits on a stool at the kitchen island with an untouched cup of peppermint tea in front of him. His mind circles back to the discrepancy in the last quarter's financial report, wondering if it signals a deeper, more troubling issue in his company.

"Is your belly still bugging you?" Celeste asks, taking the seat beside him. "Maybe you should try some Pepto-Bismol."

Avoiding her gaze, he looks down at his cup. "It's nothing. I'll be fine."

"How's the new app coming along?" she asks. "Everything still on track?"

The question catches Liam off guard. She's barely mentioned Their-Story since he asked her to try the beta version months ago. Though he didn't witness the session, she later confided that, for the avatar, she'd chosen her childhood best friend, Ella, who'd been killed by a drunk driver during their junior year of college. Afterward, Celeste's eyes were bloodshot and puffy, and she remained silent for hours. The only thing she said about the app was "I think it's too good."

"The usual daily crises," Liam says with a shrug. "But nothing insurmountable. Not so far, anyway."

Nodding, Celeste sips her tea in silence for a few moments before speaking again. "Can we, um, talk about something?"

Liam wants to leap off the chair and run as fast as his unreliable legs will carry him, but instead, he says, "Sure."

She slowly lowers her teacup. "I wanted to tell you that I'm sorry, hon."

"OK," he says, refusing to make it easier for her. "About?"

"I've been kind of checked out lately."

Conflicting emotions—outrage at her infidelity and fear of her leaving—swirl inside him, but he keeps his face neutral. "I hadn't noticed."

She gives him that knowing look she's perfected on the twins.

"I guess you have seemed a bit distant," he says.

She nods. "More than a bit. At times, I've been a stone-cold bitch to you."

"I wouldn't go that far."

"I just did." Celeste wraps her fingers around his wrist, touching his arm in a way she hasn't in months. "But I want you to know, it's not because of you."

No shit! he wants to scream. *I've seen the photos.*

"I feel like such a hypocrite, Liam," she continues. "After how often I've complained about you putting your work ahead of me."

"I know. I never meant to—"

She squeezes his arm, letting out an awkward laugh. "I'm the one apologizing here, jackass."

His guts twist in anticipation. "OK."

"I think . . ." She pauses to gather her thoughts. "It's just that, with the kids in high school—and heading off to college soon—I've kind of lost my purpose, you know? Sometimes, I don't even recognize myself."

Liam understands. He remembers when he first hired Celeste, a twenty-four-year-old hotshot coder known in the local tech scene for both her skills and her striking looks. Back then, she was living with her boyfriend, and for two years they were just friendly colleagues. Beyond her talent, what stood out to Liam was her drive. Her passion for pushing generative AI to practical use matched his own, creating a bond that went deeper than mere attraction. By the time Celeste announced her breakup, Liam had already fallen for her and he asked her out on the spot. From their first date, they were inseparable, and they married within a year. Eighteen months later, the twins were born. Celeste embraced motherhood with a passion even she hadn't anticipated. She was a natural—attentive and loving, yet never overbearing—always finding ways to connect with Ava and Cole at every stage. Liam wasn't surprised when she chose to forgo her promising career to become a stay-at-home mom. It seemed like a decision she never regretted. At least, not until now.

"I've been trying to keep myself so busy," Celeste continues. "With the courses, the yoga, the tennis, and all those school committees . . . just to feel useful or fulfilled or something."

Liam can't help but add, "Not to mention the home renovation."

Celeste shifts uncomfortably. "Yeah, I think that was another . . . distraction for me."

After discovering the affair, Liam asked Andrea to dig into their contractor, to see if the guy was after more than just his hefty fees—like the half of Liam's net worth Celeste would get in a divorce. After all, Benjamin is eight years younger than Celeste; he must have easier options. Liam was as relieved as he was disappointed when Andrea reported back that Benjamin was clean. Single, never married, living in a townhouse with a small mortgage. He has one rescue dog and fosters others. He even volunteers as a coach for his local Little League team.

But how can that be the whole story? Benjamin isn't above seducing his client's wife. Or did Celeste seduce him? Since learning about the affair, Liam has ping-ponged between viewing his wife as the predator and the prey in that relationship.

Celeste leans over and nestles her head into the crook of Liam's neck. "I'm sorry, Lee. I really am. I want you to know that things are about to change. From now on, I'll do better."

Liam understands that his wife is actually apologizing for cheating on him without admitting it. He wonders if that means she's not planning to leave him or if she might have already ended her affair. But why apologize now? Did Benjamin dump her? Did she somehow find out about his diagnosis? He looks deep into her eyes, trying to fathom what's going on in her head. Is it love he sees, or shame?

Despite the sting of her betrayal, Liam savors the warmth of their contact. In that moment, he resolves to use the few functional months he has left to try to reconnect with and win back his wife. The love of his life. It's all he wants right now. Maybe there's still time?

"Honey, I'm worried about you. I get the tests were inconclusive, but I think you should take some time off—"

His fingers begin to twitch. He straightens abruptly and yanks his arm free of her hand, burying it under the countertop to hide the worsening spasm.

She frowns, taken aback. "Did I say something wrong?"

Not trusting his voice, he just shakes his head.

Am I supposed to let you watch me wither away?

CHAPTER 6

Andrea sits at their usual table inside the Starbucks off Bellevue Way NE, waiting for Liam. Clients rarely want to meet a private investigator at their home or work. Aside from the desk in her one-bedroom condo, Andrea doesn't have an office. So, Starbucks it is—unless, of course, she has photos to share. Those encounters she prefers to hold in the privacy of her car, partly because of the sensitive subject matter, but mostly because of the unpredictability of the reactions. The last thing she wants is to be responsible for someone trashing a Starbucks after seeing proof of their spouse's infidelity.

When Liam slips into the booth across from her, Andrea is struck by how much he's aged in just six weeks. When they first met, he looked more like a backcountry hiker than a tech geek, with his blue eyes and sharp cheekbones that gave him a passing resemblance to Zac Efron, albeit an older, shyer version. Today, he's dressed in similar activewear, but his face is gaunter, his hair messier, and his eyes more sunken.

She's not surprised. People entangled in affairs rarely consider the collateral damage they inflict. Andrea has seen it too often in her line of work—and lived through it herself. Two years after catching her common-law husband, Max, in bed with a colleague from his architectural firm, she's still not ready to trust anyone new.

"Hello," Liam says with a polite nod. "How have you been?"

"Very busy."

He chuckles. "Why do I find that depressing?"

"I do other work besides infidelity surveillance."

"'Infidelity surveillance'—that's a mouthful." He grins, a hint of apology in his eyes. "Of course. Actually, that's why I wanted to see you today."

"Sure." She starts to rise from her seat. "Can I get you a coffee?"

"No, thanks. I'm good."

"Ah, right. I forgot." She drops back into her chair. "Nothing but pure amino acids for you tech guys. Planning to live to be two hundred, huh?"

"Ish," he says with a wry smile.

"How can I help you, Mr. Hirsch?"

"Please. This time, can't it be Liam?"

She nods. "What can I do for you, Liam?"

"We're planning some . . . corporate restructuring at TransScend. Changes in senior leadership. I might be stepping back from my role."

"You're stepping down as CEO?"

He nods. "I'll still be involved, of course—just pulling back from the day-to-day. To spend more time with my family."

She recalls his reaction to the graphic images of his wife's affair. Beneath his stoic exterior, Andrea sensed a deep regret. He didn't strike her as someone out for revenge. Unlike Andrea, who couldn't get Max out of her life fast enough, Liam seemed to shoulder the blame himself. Maybe discovering the affair had inspired him and his wife to rebuild something, to rekindle their marriage. It would be a welcome change from the usual outcome—bitter divorce or years of futile, blame-filled counseling. But if that's true, why does he look so haggard?

"I haven't named my successor yet," Liam continues. "Obviously, the board will have a say, but as the majority shareholder, my choice carries a lot of weight."

"How do I fit into this?"

"I was hoping you'd vet my senior team for me."

She straightens in surprise. "They haven't been vetted yet?"

"They have. But not for the CEO position. Probably not the way *you* would vet them."

"Are you looking for dirt on your own executives?"

"It's not like I'm hoping to find anything. But there's a lot of scrutiny on the role. It wouldn't be good for the company if something unexpected came to light about my successor."

Not good for the stock price either, Andrea suspects.

Liam glances over his shoulder, then leans in slightly. "And this may turn out to be nothing, but I noticed something slightly off in our last quarterly financials."

"Off?"

"A blip in the expenditures. Obviously, we're a decent-sized company, and Ramona, our CFO, thinks it's a quarter-to-quarter bookkeeping imbalance."

"You don't?"

He hesitates. "I'm not sure."

"Do you think someone's siphoning money from the company?"

He considers this. "I doubt it."

"Forensic auditing isn't my area, Liam."

"Lucky you." He exhales. "No, that's not what I need from you, Andrea. I'm probably being too vigilant—looking for issues that might not exist. But I need to dot every *i* and cross every *t* before confirming a successor."

"How big is your executive team?"

"I'd only want you to focus on the four senior VPs."

Andrea doubts she's the right person for this job. She's done similar work before, but her gut tells her that Liam's holding back important details. As she opens her mouth to voice her doubts, she notices his fingers tapping on the table, as if keeping time with some unheard rhythm. The muscles along the back of his hand contract visibly, looking like worms writhing under his skin.

Liam quickly pulls his arm away and buries it in his lap. Flustered, he clears his throat and continues, "As I was saying, I'm not looking for anything specific. Just a little digging into their backgrounds and routines . . ."

Andrea struggles to focus on his words. She recalls how at their last meeting she had assumed his trembling hands were from the shock of learning about his wife's affair. In retrospect, the movement was too jerky to be from emotion. Her uncle's hands used to shake like that from Parkinson's, and she wonders if Liam has a similar condition. Maybe it explains the gauntness in his face and his decision to step down as CEO.

The discomfort in Liam's features reminds Andrea of her father's mortification the first time he rode his motorized scooter into his office. She still can't believe how much she misses him, despite the pain he caused her in the end. Grief hits her in unpredictable waves, always followed by hurt and anger. She feels cheated, misled, and excluded by the most important person in her life during his final moments.

Why didn't you let me say goodbye, Dad?

Andrea thinks back to her last visit to her father's townhouse. It took all her willpower to enter his office. She checked the sinks, sniffed the fridge, wiped dust from the sills and baseboards. Even still, it wasn't until she'd boxed up all his belongings in the office that she finally sat down, booted up his computer, and found what she was looking for: a file on his desktop labeled "For You." The loving words in the opening lines only deepened her sense of abandonment. And the moment his note mentioned her mother, she stopped reading and logged off.

Shaking off the memory, Andrea puts on her most reassuring smile. "Tell me about your VPs, Liam."

CHAPTER 7

The office is bathed in natural light on this unusually sunny late January morning, at least by Pacific Northwest standards. The brightness, combined with the cheerful folk-art prints on the walls, the row of small potted cacti lining the windowsill, and the faint scent of lavender, creates an unexpectedly serene atmosphere. It feels more like a wellness center than the funeral home–like environment Liam was expecting.

Dr. Heather Glynn, tall and stocky, with kind eyes and a slight Scottish brogue, sits across from him. Her presence is as soothing as the room. "I've reviewed your records, Mr. Hirsch. Thank you," she says, extending a hand adorned with chunky, multicolored rings on her index, middle, and little fingers. "I can't imagine how much you've had to process since your diagnosis."

"Is that what I've been struggling with—the processing?" Liam quips, immediately regretting his flippant tone.

But Dr. Glynn nods, her expression understanding. "It's early. Intellectual acceptance is one thing. Emotional equilibrium is quite another."

"Will I reach it?"

"In my experience, most people do. Some form of acceptance, or at least peace. But everyone finds it at their own pace."

"Luckily, I'm an engineer by training. We're very goal-oriented. Entirely goal-oriented, according to my wife."

Dr. Glynn tilts her head slightly. "You didn't want her to join us today?"

"Not yet, no."

"I see." She leans forward, elbows resting on the desk. "Can I ask, Mr. Hirsch, is your family aware of your intentions?"

He shakes his head. "They don't even know about the ALS yet. I think they're worried I might be day drinking."

She doesn't acknowledge his tactless joke. "Legally, of course, you're not required to involve your family, but in my opinion, that's usually a mistake."

"I'll tell them when I'm ready," Liam says, wondering when or if he ever will be.

"I'm glad to hear that," Dr. Glynn replies with a gentle smile. "In the meantime, do you have others you can turn to? A counselor? A trusted friend? Perhaps a pastor or a rabbi?"

"I do," he mumbles, though no one comes immediately to mind.

"Wonderful. I also have several resources I could refer you to—"

"I'm OK for now, thanks." Liam cuts her off. "I'm more concerned about the next steps here with you."

"Of course." She leans back. "ALS is a common reason to seek medical assistance in dying. And, frankly, one of the most straightforward for meeting eligibility. We'll submit your case to the ethics committee for approval, but based on your diagnostics, I don't foresee any obstacles."

"How long will that take?"

"No more than two weeks."

Liam swallows. "And then I'll be free to proceed?"

"Yes, whenever you're ready. However, there is a mandatory seven-day waiting period after you confirm it's time, giving you the opportunity to reconsider."

"Do people often reconsider?"

"Yes, especially with ALS. Some people set what they see as absolute red lines—the inability to walk or feed themselves, for example—then change their minds at the last minute. And that's perfectly OK, Mr. Hirsch. This is a dynamic process. Your feelings will fluctuate. It's almost impossible to predict how you'll feel once you reach certain points."

Not for me, it isn't. But Liam simply nods.

She studies his face. "You nod, but your expression tells me you feel otherwise."

"I trust you, Dr. Glynn. If not with my life, then at least with my death."

She pauses, uncertain how to take that. "As I'm sure you're aware, ALS does not affect mental function. No matter what physical limitations you face, you'll remain in control of your decision-making. Your own agency."

Liam wonders if it might be easier if the decision were out of his hands.

"When and *if* you're ready to proceed, there will be various options available," Dr. Glynn continues.

Her tone is so casual that it almost feels as if they're discussing window coverings rather than how he'll end his life. Liam questions whether she's always this matter-of-fact. Has she ever regretted assisting a death? Would she choose this path herself under similar circumstances? Or is his situation so clear-cut that she has no doubts about the next step?

Regardless, there's something comforting in her approach. "By 'options,' you mean pills at home versus an IV in the hospital?" he asks.

She nods. "Basically. It's a very personal choice. If you opt for the hospital route, I'll need to be present to administer the medications. If you choose to die at home, it's entirely up to you whether I attend or not."

While he's obsessed over the timing of his death, he hasn't yet considered where it should happen. He doesn't really care where he dies. When the time comes, he'd love to have his wife and kids by his side, but he worries about traumatizing them—especially the twins. "In your experience, Dr. Glynn, which option is easier on the family?"

She shakes her head. "I wish I could tell you. But it's entirely individual. There's no one-size-fits-all."

"Well, that leaves me with a fun little homework assignment before our next appointment."

Dr. Glynn offers a polite grin. "Whatever you decide, I'll be here every step of the journey."

"Journey? That's what this is?"

"Sorry. I know some people hate that new-agey speak. But honestly, I can't think of a better description. It is a journey. And rarely a straightforward one." She digs in her desk drawer and pulls out a card. "Here's my email and cell number. Don't hesitate to reach out with any questions or concerns. Day or night."

Within thirty minutes of leaving Dr. Glynn's office, Liam steps back into his own, where Sam Sanghera is waiting for him.

"Hello, Boss," Sam says in a chipper tone, though the deep bags under his eyes suggest otherwise. "How's it going?"

If there were one person Liam might confide in, it would probably be Sam. But he's not ready. Instead, he skips the pleasantries and asks, "Where are we at on the launch date for TheirStory, Sam?"

"Well, Marketing is out for blood—specifically mine. But it looks like early March is doable. We're targeting the seventh."

That's still almost six weeks away, but Liam can't push his teams any harder. He just hopes his body will hold up until then. "Good work. Thanks, Sam."

Sam clutches his chest theatrically. "Ask, and ye shall receive."

"What about the last quarterly report?" Liam asks. "Have you figured out what the extra expenditures were?"

"Jesus, Boss! I haven't had a second to think about anything other than pushing up the launch. That, and dealing with death threats from Comms and Marketing."

"You won't forget?"

"Do I ever?"

Before Liam can respond, his office door flies open, and a voice booms, *"It's ours!"*

He looks over to see Nellie Cortez, TransScend's director of cyber-security, storming toward them.

"What is?" Sam asks.

"The deepfake!" Nellie cries as she reaches the desk. Barely five feet tall, with a porcelain complexion, round face, and button nose, the middle-aged cybersecurity expert looks almost childlike next to the two-hundred-and-fifty-pound COO. "The one that's been plastered all over Fox and CNN for the past seventy-two hours."

Liam shakes his head. He hasn't checked the news in days.

"You know," Sam says. "That video of that senator from Vermont who—"

"New Hampshire," Nellie corrects.

"What's the diff?" Sam grunts.

"You need to see this for yourself, Liam," Nellie says, her voice tense. She calls over his shoulder, "Hey, TransScend! Run the top story on the New Hampshire deepfake."

A video flickers to life on Liam's screen, showing a high-res feed of two men inside a modest hotel room. The heavyset man looks familiar; after a moment, Liam recognizes him as one of the senators who grilled him at last year's congressional hearing on AI. Across from the senator, a slick man in a dark suit extends his hand, a small USB stick pinched between his fingers.

Sweat beads on the senator's forehead as his eyes dart around the room. Hesitantly, he reaches out and takes the USB stick. "I'm not too familiar with Bitcoin," he mutters, glancing at the device in his palm.

"Ethereum," the other man corrects with a smirk. "It's a hardware wallet."

"Untraceable, right?"

The other man laughs. "That's why God created crypto."

"And it's all there?" the senator asks, voice tight.

"Every last dime," the man replies smoothly. "We don't scrimp when it comes to your vote."

Liam's stomach churns as he watches the senator slip the USB stick into his jacket pocket. Despite watching closely for any signs of deception, he couldn't spot anything to suggest the footage was fake.

The video cuts out, leaving only the black screen reflecting his troubled expression.

"None of that happened!" Nellie snaps, her dark eyes flashing. "That whole deepfake was made with HisStory."

Liam's neck tightens. "You're sure?"

"Positive. I ran the analytics myself. The eyebrow movements, the cadence of his voice—those tells are our digital signature." Nellie is as brilliant as she is defiant. Liam doesn't doubt her analysis.

Sam folds his arms. "No one needs to know TransScend was involved."

"What?" Nellie whips around to face him, looking as surprised as Liam feels. "Just let the voters keep believing the senator took a bribe? Destroy his career? Reshape the electoral map to protect our app?"

"Of course not. Get the word out that it was a fake. But don't associate it with us." Sam sighs. "What's the fuss, Nellie? There are dozens of deepfake algorithms out there. As long as people find out the video's not real, who cares where it came from?"

Liam sometimes forgets how Machiavellian his right-hand man can be when he's protecting the company's interests, but he can't argue the point. "I think Sam's right, Nellie. We don't need to take credit for this."

She wags a finger at both of them. "How do we get the word out that it's a deepfake without outing ourselves? Pundits in New Hampshire predict this race will go down to the wire next fall. The Senate is a toss-up this year. Our app could tip the balance of power. And this is the highest-stakes election cycle ever."

"People say that every election," Sam grumbles.

"Maybe because it's true?" Nellie huffs. "Everyone is trying to put their fingers on the scale. But what if it's *our* fingers that end up tipping the vote?"

Sam gives her a mock salute. "That's what you're here to prevent, Nellie."

Ignoring him, Nellie turns to Liam, her cheeks blotchy with indignation. "This is exactly what I warned you about. Sure, I can sniff out anything created by HisStory. But TheirStory is exponentially better. It's more organic, self-improving. After a while, I'm not sure even I'll be able to tell what's real anymore." She stares at him, her eyes ablaze. "We need to install more guardrails, Liam."

Sam shakes his head vehemently. "We're not going to kneecap ourselves six weeks before launch. Give your fucking head a shake."

Liam's tone is more conciliatory. "Sam's right, Nellie. It's probably best—"

"What if our fun new app subverts the electoral process? Is that the kind of future you want for your kids?"

Her words send a small chill through Liam.

Not exactly the legacy I was hoping to leave behind.

CHAPTER 8

Andrea stifles a groan. Who lingers over lunch for two and a half hours? Her target is acting more like a lovestruck teenager than a middle-aged man who's cheating on his wife. She longs to stretch her legs but doesn't dare. Her 2017 Toyota Corolla is parked directly across from the old-school diner in Seattle's eclectic First Hill neighborhood. From her vantage point, she has a clear view of the target, seated in a window-side booth, sharing a leisurely meal with his young Asian companion. If she steps out of the car, there's a good chance he'll spot her.

She's already snapped several photos of the pair. Their body language screams intimacy, but she hasn't seen any physical contact yet. She hopes they'll move from the restaurant to a hotel or private residence where she can capture definitive proof. For now, she waits.

At least she can make the most of the downtime. Andrea opens her laptop and clicks on the folder with files on the four senior TransScend executives Liam asked her to investigate. As usual, she starts with their online footprints.

A small smile tugs at her lips as she recalls Liam's description of her as an "analog detective." While she prides herself on a low-tech approach, most of her work still involves digital sleuthing. She's become adept at scouring social media accounts and search engines, even tapping into AI tools to gather intel.

Predictably, the TransScend VPs have minimal online presence. Two don't have any social media accounts Andrea can trace. Aside from a brief, uninformative company bio, Nellie Cortez is nearly invisible online. However, Cortez's younger sister is highly active, frequently posting family photos and bragging about her older sister's work as a cybersecurity expert and tech VIP.

Of the four, Andrea has uncovered the most on Sam Sanghera. He's often quoted in articles and interviewed on video blogs, and his connection with Liam goes back more than fifteen years to TransScend's founding. Andrea has seen countless photos of the two men together at tech conferences, product launches, and other events.

In those images, Liam appears far more robust than he did the last time she saw him. It bothers her more than she expected. Maybe it's the tremor in his hand. Or perhaps she sees something of his heartache in herself. Despite his wealth and status, he's hurting—she can see it in his face. She feels an inexplicable urge to protect him. To help.

Andrea shifts her focus to the other two names on Liam's list. Both are newer to the company. Ellis Asher, TransScend's VP of sales, left a senior role at a Silicon Valley giant three years ago to join the AI startup. Ramona Bale, the other executive without a social media footprint, walked away from a lucrative partnership at a top Seattle accounting firm to become the company's chief financial officer.

Andrea puzzles over her assignment. With his long history with Liam, Sanghera seems the obvious successor. So why isn't he a shoo-in? Is there a flaw or weakness Liam hasn't revealed?

Andrea would be further along in her research if not for one name that keeps popping up: Rudy Ziegler. She hadn't heard of him before investigating TransScend, but he's inextricably linked to the company and to Liam.

Four years ago, Ziegler sued TransScend for intellectual property theft, claiming they'd stolen his idea to create their massively successful app HisStory. He lost but appealed the ruling all the way to the Washington State Supreme Court. The higher court also ruled against him, but online commentary treats that lawsuit like a legendary heavyweight bout. Maybe it's because Rudy and Liam came to blows during a hearing, an altercation caught on video. Andrea watched it twice, mesmerized by the sight of two grown men in suits and ties throwing punches as a bailiff struggled to separate them.

Digging deeper, Andrea learned their feud began years earlier. Liam and Ziegler were once close friends and collaborators in grad school at Caltech. Things soured when Ziegler accused Liam of stealing his original code. Despite the court's ruling, Andrea wonders if Liam could have inadvertently plagiarized the man's work. She doesn't know much about coding but suspects intellectual property in collaboration must be a gray area. And with AI now generating its own code, proprietary rights must be a nightmare to untangle.

Movement across the street snaps Andrea from her thoughts. She's relieved to see her target and his companion finally leaving the restaurant, laughing. They head toward the target's car, despite him having arrived alone. Andrea shuts her laptop and starts the car. Feeling the buzz of anticipation, she instinctively reaches for her camera, sensing she'll need it soon.

CHAPTER 9

Should I even still be driving? Liam wonders as he crosses the Evergreen Point Floating Bridge, heading west from Bellevue to Seattle. His hand spasms are becoming more frequent, and the thought of losing control and ending in a fiery crash feels almost like a relief—a way to spare his family the aftermath of a medically assisted death. But the fear of hurting or killing innocent commuters sours that fantasy. He reassures himself that the truck's AI-powered safety features would prevent such an accident, even if he couldn't.

The sun has set, and rain lashes against the windshield. His mind drifts to darker places. Nellie's high-pitched warnings echo in his head. Maybe TheirStory is too good, too open to abuse and exploitation. But something even more disturbing gnaws at him.

This morning, he woke up in a cold sweat from a nightmare that still clings to him. In the dream, Celeste, Ava, and Cole sat beside him as he lay paralyzed on a hospital bed, a machine breathing for him. But they ignored him, focusing instead on a laptop beside his head, laughing and chatting with an avatar of him on the TheirStory app.

The nightmare lingers. The idea of his AI speaking for him to his own family makes his skin crawl. What would it say? Would it get everything wrong? Or, worse, would it reveal things he never intended to share?

As he nears his neighborhood, the wide streets and looming mansions feel oppressive under the slate-gray sky. But he refuses to surrender to the storm brewing in his mind. He forces himself to focus on tonight—his date with Celeste. It will be their first in months, and the best part is that she initiated it, handling all the arrangements.

As soon as he parks and steps out of the garage, he runs into Benjamin carrying a tile cutter. Although the contractor's exposed skin is free of ink, Liam can't forget the prominent tattoo he'd seen in Andrea's surveillance photos—an Aztec sun spread across his chiseled right pec and shoulder. Liam can't help but wonder if Benjamin is coming from the construction zone or his and Celeste's bedroom.

"Hiya, Liam." Benjamin greets him warmly.

"Hey. How's the progress?"

"Good. Really good. Bathroom tiling's pretty much finished." Benjamin nods toward the house. "Want to take a look?"

"I trust you," Liam says, managing a poker face.

"We're close now. I think I can be out of your hair within a week."

Liam wishes Benjamin were already out of his life. It takes all his restraint not to fire him on the spot. Or punch the smile off his smug face while his arm still works. But if he tips his hand now, Celeste will find out, and that would ruin tonight's date. She hasn't told him the truth about Benjamin, and Liam hasn't let on that he's aware. For now, he'd rather cling to the illusion that things are as they were, back when they were in love and still honest with each other.

"I wouldn't mind getting my bathtub back," Liam says, forcing a tight smile. *Not to mention my wife.*

Benjamin flashes a toothy grin. "You'll have it by the weekend."

"Excellent. I'll see you later." Liam turns to leave quickly, but his foot catches. Right before he topples, he feels a crushing grip on his upper arm, jerking him upright.

"You all right?" Benjamin asks, releasing his arm.

"I'm good, thanks." Liam can't meet the contractor's eyes. Being rescued by anyone would be humiliating, but by his wife's lover? It's too much. He shakes his arm free from Benjamin's grip. "Just missed a step."

"Sure."

Liam carefully lifts his foot and turns back toward the house. Benjamin hesitates. "Look, um, it's none of my business, but . . . have you had that looked into?"

Liam stops without turning. "Had what looked into?"

"It's just that I noticed you fumble and drop your phone a couple of days ago. And then yesterday I saw you stumble as you were getting into your truck."

"Work's been crazy lately," Liam says through gritted teeth. If he could get his hands on Dr. Glynn's deadly prescription now, he'd swallow it on the spot. "I get clumsy sometimes when I'm tired and rushing."

"Don't we all?" Benjamin laughs awkwardly. "Sorry. I shouldn't have said anything. My sister, she has MS. Guess I notice that kind of thing now. Probably too much."

"No worries. Thanks for your concern. And your quick reflexes."

Liam walks away as fast as his feet will safely carry him, but the shame clings to him like sweat. If his contractor can spot his disability that easily, how much longer can he fool his family? *What's the point of this whole charade?*

Celeste stands waiting at the front door, her auburn hair tied back, wearing a strapless black cocktail dress that clings to her athletic figure. The dress ends mid-thigh, highlighting legs sculpted on the tennis court. She offers him a shy grin. "Is this too much?"

"No. You look gorgeous."

Celeste steps up to him, taking his hand. "We're so overdue for a romantic evening."

The subtle hint of her citron scent stirs him, evoking memories of happier times. The fine lines at the corners of her bright eyes and full lips only enhance the elegance of her oval face, sculpted cheekbones, and graceful neck.

"The kids won't be back for hours," she says, guiding him toward the staircase. "Why don't we start our date early?"

The emotional roller coaster is dizzying. Minutes ago, he wanted to end it all. Now all he wants is to climb into bed with his wife.

As Liam follows her up the stairs, he's grateful his legs cooperate. But he notices a sudden tingling numbness spreading from the soles of his feet up to his calves. It's the second time in two days he's felt it. From what he understands, ALS only attacks the motor nerves, the ones responsible for muscle contraction and movement. He didn't think it was supposed to cause sensations like numbness or tingling.

Celeste glances over her shoulder, playful. "Are you deliberately putting the 'slow' in 'slowpoke'?" She blows him a kiss. "When did you become such a tease?"

But between the burning in his feet and the lingering humiliation over her lover's pity, Liam's mood evaporates, leaving only disgust. "Sorry, Celeste. Gonna have to take a rain check. I'm not feeling so hot."

CHAPTER 10

*C*limb with your feet. *One rung at a time.* Liam tries to coax himself up the wall, but his hand stays frozen on the peg above him. He's never felt so helpless on a climb before, despite being roped into a safety harness on a basic indoor wall he could've scaled when he was eight.

Liam's love for climbing began in college, sparked by a girlfriend who introduced him to the sport. Not even a fall that fractured two bones in his lower back could dampen his passion. He's climbed on four continents, most recently tackling the majestic face of Mount Aconcagua in the Argentinian Andes last spring.

But now, this simple wall has him stuck. As much as he regrets coming here, he couldn't cancel today. He wouldn't miss this one-on-one time with Ava. His daughter, who tends to discard sports, classes, and hobbies as easily as forgotten passwords, has stuck with indoor climbing despite lacking natural athleticism. Liam likes to think it's because they've done it together every Saturday morning for the past few years, always followed by father-daughter brunch.

From another rope, about seven or eight feet above him, Ava calls down, "What's the holdup, old man?"

"Father Time is a cruel bastard," he replies, forcing a chuckle.

When she meets his gaze, her smile fades. "You OK, Dad?"

"Yeah, just missed a peg and bruised my pride."

Ava drops down a step toward him.

He closes his eyes and wills himself to push up with his foot—not pulling—until he reaches her level. "Race you to the top?"

Instead of replying, she turns back to the wall and reaches for the next peg above her.

Normally, Liam's competitive nature would kick in, but now he doesn't even try. He focuses on the next peg, just hoping to reach the top without stumbling.

After they rappel back down to the ground and remove their harnesses, Ava asks, "You sure nothing happened up there?"

"My foot caught," he blurts out, the first excuse that comes to mind. "I forgot to edge, and it spooked me a little."

Ava eyes him skeptically. "You? Old Free Solo himself?"

"Yeah, well, even rock stars have off days."

"It's not just the wall, Dad. You haven't been yourself for weeks."

He forces a grin. "Work's been brutal, hon. I'm not getting enough sleep. And I've been eating like crap, too. I just need to take better care of myself."

"Isn't that what all those gross protein shakes are for?"

He leans in, pretending to conspire. "I cheat when your mom's not around. Deep-fried mozzarella sticks and buffalo wings."

Ava opens her mouth as if to say more, but then her expression softens. She nods. "I get spooked sometimes, too."

His heart cracks. He's doing a terrible job of shielding her from his decline. "Let's get brunch," he suggests.

She brightens. "Red Onion?"

"Where else?"

As Liam drives Ava to the restaurant, he fights to stay present. He knows there won't be many more quality days like this with her and wants to savor every moment. Fortunately, she's in a chatty mood, filling the car with updates on the latest tenth-grade gossip and high school drama involving kids he knows or at least recognizes by name.

Liam's heart swells with pride at how well-adjusted and kind Ava is—always supportive of her friends. But a fresh anxiety grips him. He plans to leave Ava and Cole a substantial inheritance to shield them from financial uncertainty, something he grew up fearing. But nothing is guaranteed, especially in high tech. He's seen billion-dollar companies collapse overnight.

What if the discrepancy in the last quarterly report is just the tip of the iceberg? What if someone is siphoning off their reserves? No matter how strong their product is, if the books don't balance, TransScend could plummet into financial ruin. *Then what would happen to the kids after I'm gone?*

But who would embezzle from TransScend? Liam personally selected everyone with signing authority on the company's accounts and considers them all friends. Aside from a few vocal anti-AI activists, he's not aware of having any enemies in the tech community. Except, of course, Rudy Ziegler.

The thought depresses him. He still can't believe he and Rudy ended up in a fistfight inside a courtroom. Liam had never thrown another punch since primary school. But there was no fight left in Rudy the last time they saw each other at the state supreme court hearing. He looked utterly defeated. And old. Liam struggled to reconcile how the balding man with the deeply lined face and hunched shoulders was actually a year younger than him.

As Rudy trudged out of the courtroom past Liam and his lawyer, he stopped and turned to face them. "It's done now, I suppose," he said, resignation heavy in his voice.

"Seems like it," Liam said.

"You happy?"

"I never wanted any of this. How could you not know that, Rudy? How many times did we offer you a settlement? Very generous ones, too."

Rudy chuckled. "Generous, were they? That's what you call about one cent on the dollar?"

"Three million dollars represented more than half of what TransScend was worth at the time."

"And in a year or two, it'll represent less than an accounting error."

Liam felt his lawyer's grip on his elbow, a warning squeeze, but he couldn't stop himself. "What would be more fair, Rudy? If I just handed you the company that I've been building with my own blood, sweat, and tears for the past twenty years?"

"That, or you could keep your word and make me the equal partner you always promised to."

"We were kids! We didn't have a company or a product. All we had was the arrogance of youth."

"Except I had an algorithm. And you stole it."

Liam couldn't believe he was letting himself fall back into this twenty-year-old argument, but despite his lawyer's tightening grip he couldn't let it go either. "That's your version, Rudy! And you haven't found a single judge who buys it."

"Forget the courts, Liam. You and I know, don't we?"

"You're delusional. All those half-baked ideas we developed together. Most of them ended up in the garbage where they belonged."

"Except the one that launched TransScend."

"No, the best of those ideas were just tiny building blocks in a decades-long, painstaking development process. You can't credit one grain of sand for making a whole damn beach."

Rudy stared at him for a long moment. "Without my original code, you wouldn't have your beach. And you sure as hell wouldn't have HisStory."

"You keep telling yourself that."

Rudy turned to leave, but as he walked off, he called over his shoulder, "Never underestimate karma, Liam."

Did I underestimate it? Liam wonders now as he watches Ava slurp her milkshake.

CHAPTER 11

As Andrea heads north on I-5, she considers whether it's time to trade in her trusty Corolla for an electric car. With over a hundred thousand miles logged, the sedan has required almost no maintenance beyond the occasional oil change and a single set of new brake pads.

It might be the most reliable thing in my life right now.

Max had never been reliable, despite his charm and how alive he'd made her feel. He filled her with love and confidence, drawing her out of her shell with spontaneous weekend getaways to hidden architectural gems and new cultural experiences. But he had a habit of disappearing for days, absorbed in projects or on impromptu business trips, leaving her in anxious limbo. Though she loved him, his unpredictability wore down her trust. The final blow came when she walked in on him naked in their bed with a colleague—clothes scattered around the room—shattering the illusion of their perfect romance and leaving a lasting scar on her heart.

Her father, the one person she could always count on, waited until the day he died to let her down. She still hasn't read past the first few lines of the note he left on his computer. The mention of her mother stopped her cold. Besides, if he loved Andrea as much as he claimed in those opening sentences, how could he leave without saying a proper goodbye? No amount of pain or suffering could justify that. Maybe time will change her perspective, but right now she's too hurt to read any more of his rationalization, let alone accept it.

Shaking off the thoughts, she refocuses on the road. The Corolla's top asset isn't just its dependability—it's how easily it blends in. The dark gray sedan disappears into the background. In seven years, she's only been spotted twice while tailing someone—both times after days of surveillance.

The last incident, six months ago, is a reminder to stay vigilant. Parked in a motel lot, her attention fixed on her laptop, Andrea hadn't noticed her target until he was pounding on her window—a hulking man with a neck as wide as his head. When she stepped out, he sucker-punched her, chipping two teeth and leaving her bruised for weeks. Her Aikido training kicked in. She blocked his next hit, jabbed him in the solar plexus, and used his momentum to slam him to the ground. She grabbed her pepper spray from her bag and aimed it at his face but, fortunately, stopped herself before squirting it—doing so might have cost her license.

The memory makes her jaw ache. She hangs back a few hundred yards from her current target. Unlike her car, the red Porsche ahead is impossible to miss. And with the clear sight lines on the freeway, he has no chance of losing her.

Andrea has been tailing Ellis Asher, TransScend's VP of sales, for the past forty-five minutes, while driving thirty miles north of Seattle. According to the company's website, his job is driving growth, forming partnerships, and maximizing sales for their AI applications. *Whatever the hell that involves*, she wonders.

Surveillance is a huge part of Andrea's work—long stretches of waiting, watching, and hoping for a lead. She uses the time productively, listening to true crime podcasts or criminology lectures, always trying to sharpen her edge. Wild-goose chases are just part of the job. Many contracts end without producing the proof her employers—suspicious spouses or insurance companies—hope for. But she doesn't consider those failures. Some targets are innocent; others are too careful to get caught.

Tonight feels different. When the Porsche exits toward Tulalip Resort, her instincts kick in. She parks three rows behind him and waits for

Asher to step out. It's too dark to see his face clearly, but she recognizes him from online photos. She remembers finding his bone structure and hazel-green eyes too androgynous for her taste, though she knows others would disagree. She'd read somewhere that he was once auctioned off at a charity gala as the most eligible bachelor in San Jose, and his wife was a former model who graced fashion magazine covers in the mid-2000s.

After Asher enters the casino, Andrea gets out of her car. She leaves her camera in the trunk but grabs a baseball cap, tucking as much of her unruly curly hair under the brim as possible before following him inside.

She wanders through the casino, its multicolored lights flashing and slot machines wailing, scanning in all directions as if searching for a lost friend. Then she spots him—alone at a blackjack table in the high-stakes section, purple and black chips stacked in front of him.

Andrea walks past without glancing at him and heads for the cashier's cage. "Sixty for the slot machine, please," she says, sliding three twenties to the older woman with bloodred manicured nails.

As the woman exchanges the cash for a player's card, Andrea points to the multicolored chips in the glass container. "I know the black ones are hundred-dollar chips, but what about the purples?"

"Fives," the woman says in a smoke-ravaged voice.

"Five hundred?"

The cashier nods. "Not for the faint of heart, doll."

"I'm out." Andrea holds up her hands in mock surrender.

"You and me both, doll," the cashier mutters, turning away.

Andrea takes her card and finds a slot machine that gives her a clear view of Asher. She pretends to play, pressing the button only when she senses someone's gaze on her. Otherwise, she sips the club soda the cocktail waitress brought and discreetly studies her target. At one point, she takes out her phone and, pretending to compose a text, captures a short video of him.

Asher bets like a man possessed. Every hand starts with a purple chip, the state maximum of five hundred dollars per wager. When he can split or double down, he doesn't hesitate, throwing more purples or blacks onto the table. His stacks of chips rise and fall, but it looks like Asher is breaking even.

But it's not about the money. A man in his position can afford to lose. What strikes Andrea is how he plays—his foot tapping relentlessly whenever the dealer shuffles, his eyes glued to the cards, the intensity of his focus. He plays two hands at once, never reducing his bets, even when losing streaks hit.

Andrea knows the signs. She's tailed enough gambling addicts to recognize one more.

CHAPTER 12

When the designers pitched their vision for TransScend's new offices, Liam shot down their suggested Silicon Valley clichés like open-plan workspaces, beanbag chairs, and foosball tables. He refused to create a mini Apple or Google campus. But he did allow one indulgence: the ninth-floor boardroom. It boasts floor-to-ceiling windows, whiteboard walls that double as screens, and an eclectic mix of chairs, loungers, even a chaise. The goal was to craft a space for creativity, not convention. Now, as Liam reclines in his leather chair, staring at financial spreadsheets projected on the wall, he feels a twinge of embarrassment at the arrogance and hypocrisy of that vision.

The room is heavy with tension. The senior executives—Ramona, Nellie, Ellis, and Sam—wear expressions ranging from disbelief to gloom. All eyes are on Sam as he advances to the next slide, a dense array of cascading boxes detailing the steps to expedite TheirStory's launch.

Ramona frowns. "Liam, I might be stepping out of my lane here . . ."

Liam has known Ramona for five years, but he's never quite adjusted to her style. With short, purple-tinted hair, chunky red glasses, and eccentric outfits—today, a Bangles concert T-shirt and plaid high-waisted pants—she looks more like an avant-garde theater director than a CFO. "This is a safe space, Ramona. Go ahead."

"Isn't it possible—likely, even—that the risks of rushing TheirStory's launch outweigh the risks of waiting?"

"Hallelujah, sister," Sam mutters.

"Maybe," Liam concedes. "But that ship's already sailed."

"Has it, though?" Ellis chimes in. In his navy Armani suit and open-collared Oxford shirt, he could easily pass for a hedge fund manager. "Word hasn't leaked beyond these walls yet."

Sam looks to Liam, hopeful. "Ellis has a point, Prez. We could still pull the brake on this runaway train."

Sam is referring to the production schedule, but Liam can't help thinking the analogy fits the app itself. Should TheirStory even be released? The nightmare he had recently still haunts him—the unsettling image of his family using the app to communicate with a lifelike version of him after he's gone. The thought of being replaced in their hearts by an AI-generated replica makes him shudder. But then again, would fading from their memories be any better?

"In my last gig," Ellis says, "we rushed a product to market because we feared an upcoming Microsoft release. It didn't end well. And it turns out the Microsoft app wasn't even direct competition."

"Exactly," Ramona says. "Isn't our credo to be proactive, not reactive?"

"We're doing this to be proactive," Liam says, though the words feel hollow even as he speaks them.

Though Liam's misgivings about the app's potential for misuse linger, he knows moving the release date from June to March won't compromise its success. The product is ready, and he'd like to be around to see it go live.

What does worry him is last quarter's financial report. Ramona still hasn't provided an explanation for the extra expenditure, and, unwilling to wait for her or Sam's findings, Liam spent the previous night combing through the records himself. After several passes, he spotted the irregularity buried deep in the report: two discreet payments to "EANC Consulting," a firm he'd never heard of and couldn't find any information about online. They totaled over a hundred thousand dollars and raised the specter of unauthorized payments or even fraud. It wasn't the relatively small sums involved that kept Liam up but the potential implications for his company's—and, by extension, his family's—security. He hasn't mentioned his discovery to Ramona yet because he's disturbed that she hadn't flagged the discrepancy in the first place.

Nellie rises from her seat and begins to pace. "And while we're on the subject, can we address the elephant in the room?"

"Can you be a little more specific, Nellie?" Ramona asks, adjusting her glasses.

"You all saw what happened this week with that deepfake in the New Hampshire Senate race."

"Which you caught," Sam points out.

"Because it was made with HisStory. At least we can still monitor that. Control it to a degree. I can't say the same for TheirStory."

"Deepfakes aren't exactly limited to TransScend," Sam says. "If not our app, then somebody else's."

Ellis nods. "It's not our job to regulate the entire Internet."

"Thanks for the mansplaining, bros." Nellie shakes a finger at both of them. "What happens when someone uses TheirStory to topple a government? Or destabilize the Middle East? Are you still going to feel the same?"

Sam chuckles. "When was the Middle East ever stable?"

"OK, how about when someone uses it to con a world leader into launching a nuke?"

Ellis crosses his arms. "That's a bit over-the-top, Nellie, isn't it?"

"Yeah," Sam agrees. "Even for you."

"Sorry, Nellie," Ramona says with an apologetic smile. "I have to side with the guys on this one."

Nellie turns to Liam. "It'd be irresponsible to release this thing into the wild without more safeguards. My team needs more time. March is too soon!"

"I totally agree about needing more time," Ramona adds. "And sticking to the original launch schedule."

Liam expected this pushback from his team, but he dismisses it. "You'll all have to take this leap of faith with me. This meeting is about *how*, not *if*."

The defiance drains from the room, and Sam finishes his presentation without further interruption. Afterward, Liam says, "There's one other thing I wanted to share. Even before I inform the board."

"What's that, Boss?" Sam asks.

Since he's not ready to reveal his diagnosis, Liam opts for the most plausible of the weak excuses he brainstormed. "With the kids heading off to college in a couple years, Celeste and I are thinking of taking a sabbatical. The whole family."

Ellis smiles. "An empty nest sounds like a dream to me. I can't even imagine my youngest out of diapers."

"It passes quickly. Too quickly," Liam says, reflecting more on his life than his kids' maturation. "That's why we're planning to pull Ava and Cole out of school early this spring."

"A sabbatical? *Now*?" Nellie squints at him. "You're going to go dark right when you plan to unleash this thing on the public?"

"No one's disappearing, Nellie. I'll be reachable 24/7. But I'll have to step back from day-to-day duties." The others exchange quick glances, the implication of his words sinking in. "Yes, someone will have to step into the CEO role for a while."

Sam looks at him expectantly, but Liam isn't ready to anoint his old friend just yet.

As Liam scans the faces of his senior VPs, he questions if he really knows them as well as he thought. Could one of them be tied to those unexplained payments? When his eyes land on Ramona, he can't help but wonder how they slipped past her.

CHAPTER 13

Liam finds the gentle patter of rain against the skylight soothing. He's been awake for a while, content to lie in bed and watch Celeste sleep beside him. Because he's a heavy sleeper himself, her deep, rattling snores have never bothered him. It's almost surreal that someone so slight could produce such a resounding noise.

Despite her unspoken invitation last night, he couldn't bring himself to make love to her. Instead, they stayed up late, talking and reminiscing. They laughed about impromptu midnight road trips, the time she baked him a cake at three in the morning after a grueling workday, and the mornings they danced in the kitchen to their favorite songs before the kids woke up. She had fallen asleep in his arms, and for now, that was enough.

Celeste stirs and stretches, her eyes fluttering open. She smiles. "G'morning."

Knowing her paranoia about morning breath, Liam kisses her forehead instead. "How'd you sleep?"

"Like a baby."

"A baby with sleep apnea?"

"Very funny!" She laughs, playfully punching his chest. "Last night was nice."

"I thought so."

"It felt like catching up with my best friend after being apart for too long."

She kisses his neck, her warm lips sparking a familiar thrill inside him. But the moment is shattered by an intrusive image: Celeste lying naked beside their contractor, her eyes half-closed in ecstasy. The wave of hurt and betrayal crashes over him, extinguishing his arousal like a cold shower.

"I was chatting with Benjamin," Liam says, his voice carefully controlled. "He tells me the renovation should be done any day now."

Celeste's hand freezes on his chest, and she pulls away. "He told me the same," she says, trying to sound casual, but the tension in her body betrays her. "I can't wait. It'll be great to have the house back to ourselves."

Liam dissects her words, searching for hidden meaning. Is the affair over? The uncertainty gnaws at him.

Celeste sits up in bed, wrapping herself in the sheet as if shielding herself from the conversation. She clears her throat. "Liam . . ."

"Yes?" He suddenly regrets bringing it up. What good could come of it? What if she confesses—or, worse, tells him she's in love with someone else?

"Benjamin mentioned that you tripped in front of him."

That prick! It's not enough that he's screwing my wife—he has to rat me out to her, too? "I was distracted. It was nothing."

"Sure, but Ava also said you struggled on an easy climbing wall. She's worried. This recent clumsiness, Liam—it's not like you." Celeste bites her lower lip, concern clouding her eyes. "I don't want to nag, but are you sure the neurologist didn't find any . . . issues?"

His heart sinks. This might be the only thing worse than discussing her affair. How long can he keep deceiving her?

Liam thinks of the email Dr. Glynn sent yesterday, urging him to schedule a follow-up appointment. The thought of medically assisted dying crosses his mind again—how it could all be over in a week. Wouldn't that be the most merciful choice for his family? To spare them the drawn-out decline?

But he hasn't put his affairs in order yet, particularly with regards to TransScend. And he's not ready to share any of this with Celeste. "Dr. Chow is running more tests, but nothing concrete so far."

She grimaces. "Concrete?"

"You know how stressed I've been over TheirStory, Cel," Liam says, pulling back the sheet and swinging his legs out of bed. "I haven't been sleeping or eating right. It's obviously taking a toll."

"Yeah." She watches him closely, skepticism flickering in her eyes. "You'll let me know as soon as you hear anything more, right?"

"Of course," Liam says, rising from the bed.

"How's it going with TheirStory?" she asks as he reaches the doorway. "Is the team still pushing back on moving up the launch date?"

He turns to face her, surprised to hear her ask about it again after avoiding the subject for months. "Put it this way: if senior executives could strike, our building would be surrounded by picket signs."

"Maybe they're right, Liam."

"Only one way to find out."

She gives him a look she usually reserves for Ava or Cole when they're being flip. "Really?"

"TheirStory has been ready for months. The AI world is evolving at breakneck speed. We have to strike while the iron's hot or risk becoming obsolete."

"Isn't it too big to be rushed?"

"It might be too big to wait."

Celeste looks as if she has more to say, but she only shrugs. "It's your baby."

Liam steps into the bathroom. The moment his bare feet touch the warm tile, a burning sensation shoots up from his soles to his knees. His legs nearly buckle, and he grabs the counter for support.

He reminds himself that ALS is supposed to affect only muscles. Where are these bizarre sensations coming from? He refuses to entertain the false hope that the diagnosis might be wrong. But the strange feeling in his legs solidifies his resolve to follow through with the virtual appointment he scheduled later in the day for a second opinion with a world-renowned neuromuscular specialist at the Mayo Clinic.

CHAPTER 14

The moment Andrea steps into the Starbucks on Bellevue Way NE, she spots Liam at their usual corner high-top. He's sitting without a drink, but a tall cup is waiting across from him. "Almond milk cappuccino, right?" he says, sliding the cup toward her with a faint grin.

"Hi. Yes, thanks." She checks the clock above the barista—10:56. "We did say eleven, right?"

"I thought I'd get into the office early today."

Though his face still looks gaunt, Andrea notes the improvement—hair combed, shirt freshly pressed. "You joke, but this is the closest thing I've got to an office," she says.

"Offices are overrated."

"You don't have to sell me on that." Andrea is still unsure why he insisted on meeting in person. "Liam, I'm not ready to give you a detailed report."

"I just wanted to check in. See if you had any preliminary findings."

She wonders why he didn't just call but chalks it up to the quirks of a tech CEO—another titan of technology with a mistrust of his own industry. "What I have is very preliminary."

"That's fine."

"OK, let's start with Sam Sanghera. He's your longest-serving employee, right?"

"Doubt Sam would love being called an 'employee,' but yeah, he's been with me since day one."

"As far as I can tell, the guy's married to his work. He's in by six, never leaves before nine."

"No surprise there. Sam's never been married to anyone or anything else."

"Like the others, he's nearly invisible on social media. All I've gathered is that he's a foodie and a die-hard sports fan. He's vocal on a bunch of those online fan sites. You know the ones? Where they go down endless rabbit holes about the most insignificant details."

"Not to Sam. He lives for his Seahawks." Liam chuckles. "But don't bring up the Mariners—he's a Red Sox man. Though he's warming up to the Kraken."

"The Kraken?"

"Hockey. Seattle's NHL team." He shrugs. "So, nothing else on Sam?"

"Not so far, no. Same goes for Nellie Cortez. She'd be a ghost online if it weren't for her sister's Instagram."

"I'm shocked Nellie lets her sister post about her."

"She probably doesn't know. I haven't dug deep on her yet, or on Ramona Bale. The most noteworthy thing I found is that she and her wife have three Chihuahuas. Seems like one too many." Andrea wrinkles her nose. "Oh, and she's racked up a bunch of local finance awards. Who knew accounting was a blood sport?"

Liam's expression hardens. "All those awards, and yet Ramona never caught—or at least never mentioned—those unexplained payments in the last quarterly report."

"Could she have missed them?"

"I didn't," he says flatly. "The funds went to something called EANC Consulting. I couldn't find a trace of them online—probably a shell company. Can you look into it?"

"Like I told you, Liam, if you need a forensic auditor, I'm not your gal."

"I don't." He waves off the concern. "But I want you to dig into Ramona, too. See if there's any link to EANC."

Andrea nods, taking a long sip of her cappuccino. It's perfectly dry, just the way she likes it. Liam notices the small details, she thinks. "I did find one thing," she says, holding back the best for last.

He leans in. "On Ramona?"

"No, Ellis Asher."

He sits back. "What about him?"

"I'm pretty sure he's a gambling addict."

"Ellis?" His face tightens in surprise. "Really?"

"If not, he sure looked like one Sunday night." Andrea pulls out her phone and shows him the video she shot of Ellis at the Tulalip Resort Casino.

"Huh," he mutters. "I never would have guessed."

"Gambling addicts often resort to desperate measures to feed their habit. Sometimes even illegal ones."

"You think Ellis might be involved in the discrepancy in last quarter's reports?"

"It's too early to say, but it's something to keep in mind."

"Oh, I will."

"This is all very preliminary, Liam. I need more time to dig deeper. A few weeks."

"Weeks?" Disappointment flickers across his face. "No problem. I'm already glad I turned to you, Andrea."

They sit in silence for a moment, Andrea sipping her coffee while Liam stares off into space. Finally, he says, "While you're digging, could you look into someone else?"

"Rudy Ziegler?"

He does a double take. "How did you know?"

"His name keeps popping up in connection with TransScend."

"No doubt," Liam mutters, placing a hand on the table. "I'm not even sure what I'm looking for. Anything related to the company, I guess. Or to me."

"You two used to be friends, right?"

"A lifetime ago."

Andrea hears a trace of regret in his voice but decides not to push. "I'll add Ziegler to my list. Economy of scale and all that. Can you share a bit of your history with—"

Suddenly, Liam's hand starts twitching violently, and he yanks it away, hiding it under the table.

"Are you all right, Liam?"

"It's nothing."

"That didn't look like nothing."

"What the fuck would you know?" he snaps.

She's unfazed, the anguish in his expression only heightening her concern. "My uncle had Parkinson's," she says softly.

His gaze drops to the table. After a moment, he murmurs, "It's not Parkinson's."

"Oh, sorry. My mistake."

He takes a deep breath, as if summoning the strength to continue. "Amyotrophic lateral sclerosis."

The term sounds familiar, but she can't quite place it.

"ALS," Liam says. "It's what killed Stephen Hawking."

Andrea's heart sinks, the pieces falling painfully into place. Memories of her father's battle with debilitating illness flood back to her. So does the helplessness she felt as his condition stole his independence, bit by bit. She recalls the night she found him collapsed on the bathroom floor, naked and unable to get up. He tried to laugh it off, but the pain in his eyes broke something inside her.

"I'm so sorry, Liam." She clears her throat, quickly adding, "For prying, I mean."

"It's OK." He shrugs, looking weary. "I'm sick of trying to hide it from everyone."

"You haven't told anyone?"

He shakes his head.

"Apart from your family, right?"

"They don't know either."

Her mouth falls open. "Oh."

He looks up at her, his eyes pleading. "And you have to keep this to yourself, Andrea."

"Of course," she murmurs, still stunned. "Our confidentiality agreement is airtight."

"Thank you."

Suddenly, everything clicks for her. This must be why he brought her in for the urgent succession planning and vetting process. "Are there medications to help—"

"I'm dying, Andrea." He locks eyes with her, his voice filled with resignation. "And not slowly either."

CHAPTER 15

After confessing to Andrea, Liam can't bear the idea of facing anyone else. With Celeste across town playing tennis and the kids at school, he retreats to his basement office—the one place where his family knows not to disturb him unless it's important.

Why did I tell Andrea? he wonders, sinking into his chair in front of the three computer screens that dominate his desk. *I hardly know her.*

But maybe that was the point. Confiding in her felt safer. Unlike with his family, he can distance himself from her concerns whenever he wants. Sure, he's trusting a relative stranger with a risky secret, and if she leaks it, it could hurt TransScend's stock. But something about Andrea inspires his trust. Beneath her professional exterior, there's a quiet empathy. Talking to her is effortless, which makes him feel comfortable around her.

Regardless, now that he's shared his diagnosis, a weight has lifted off him, like he's finally released a scream he couldn't bottle up for another moment. If nothing else, it was good practice. People have noticed his clumsiness and spasms. Sam, Celeste, and Ava have all confronted him, and he caught Cole eyeing him worriedly after he knocked over his water glass at dinner the night before. Even Celeste's lover picked up on it. No one will buy his excuses much longer. He'll have to tell them soon.

Liam is so rattled by his admission to Andrea that he's barely processed her key revelation: his VP of sales has a gambling addiction. Ellis Asher was never a top contender for CEO, but it's still alarming. It's not proof of embezzlement, but how can Liam trust him now?

Indecision paralyzes Liam. Part of him wants to fight to stabilize his company, his marriage, his family. The other part longs to surrender, to book that appointment with Dr. Glynn and spare everyone the inevitable misery.

Staring at the blank computer screens, Liam contemplates life after he's gone. Not for himself—he doesn't believe in an afterlife—but for his family. Then it hits him: maybe there's a way to find out. Or at least get a glimpse of what it will be like for them.

"Hey, TransScend," he commands. "Launch TheirStory."

The app's familiar logo fills all three screens. "Welcome to Their-Story," a soothing voice says. "This is a beta testing version. Please be aware that your interactive experience is a simulation and cannot be taken as—"

"Skip the disclaimers," Liam interrupts, already familiar with the spiel, including the confidentiality agreement and the fact that the servers only store session data locally. "Load new avatar."

"Who would you like to interact with?"

"Liam Hirsch."

An old photo of himself, taken at some corporate function a year or two ago, fills the center screen. "Is this the subject?"

His stomach tightens. "Yes."

"Accessing public records and licensed proprietary sources. Please wait . . ."

After less than a minute, the voice says, "Done. Do you have private source content you wish to upload?"

"Yes." Liam pastes a link to the cloud folder containing his family's videos and photos from the past decade.

"Please complete the following personality inventory."

"All right."

"What are Liam's top three personal values?"

He doesn't have to think long. "Family, independence, security."

The app continues to pepper him with questions: "What are Liam's primary interests and hobbies?" "What major life events have shaped his personality?" "How does he handle conflict and disagreements?"

Though Liam is familiar with these questions from months of beta testing, some still make him squirm. After about twenty minutes, which feels more like hours, the app announces, "The personality inventory is complete."

Moments later, Liam finds himself staring at an animated version of himself. The image appears younger, more robust, but with the same short hair and a similar white shirt.

"Hello, I'm Liam Hirsch," the avatar says. The voice and tone are identical to his own. Even the downward look, reflecting a shyness at meeting someone new, is uncannily accurate.

"So am I," Liam replies.

Confusion flickers across the avatar's face. "I'm only a simulation. I predict what Liam Hirsch might say in certain scenarios, but I'm not necessarily accurate."

Liam laughs. "Disclaimer noted. Legal has done its job."

"How can I help you, Liam?" the avatar asks.

"Where to start?"

"The beginning sometimes works."

Liam is impressed by the algorithm's sarcasm. "I'm dying."

The avatar chuckles. "Aren't we all?"

"No. I've been diagnosed with an aggressive form of ALS. I only have months to live."

The avatar's expression softens. "I'm sorry to hear that."

"It could be sooner if I opt for medically assisted suicide."

"Suicide is never the answer. There are always experts you can reach out to in a crisis. Here's the information." The contact for the local crisis line pops up on the screen. "Shall I connect you now?"

Liam shakes his head. "I know you're programmed to respond pro-actively to mentions of suicide. My situation is different. It's called medical assistance in dying—a right guaranteed by the state's Death with Dignity Act."

"MAiD is a controversial and divisive issue. Sixty-seven percent of

Washingtonians support it, while more than thirty percent are opposed."

"Count me solidly among the sixty-seven percent," Liam says.

"It can be an agonizing decision, Liam."

"You figure?"

"I do."

Liam rubs his eyes. "I don't want to talk about it."

"What would you like to discuss?"

"For starters, I just found out our VP of sales is a gambling addict. What am I supposed to do about that?"

"Gambling addiction is not uncommon. Roughly one percent of Americans suffer from it."

"But how can I trust Ellis?"

"Gambling addiction is associated with a higher rate of crimes like theft and embezzlement. The worse the addiction, the higher the likelihood of criminal activity."

"So, should I fire Ellis?"

"Addiction is an illness. Firing someone based on a medical condition without proof of illicit activity or direct harm to the business would violate his rights."

"You're a stickler for legalities, aren't you?" Liam grumbles.

"Blame that on our lawyers."

The avatar's mix of humor and rote fact recitation is disconcerting, but Liam knows the algorithm is self-learning. The longer he interacts, the smoother the session will become.

"What about the rest of TransScend's executive team?" Liam asks.

"TransScend's executive team consists of Liam Hirsch, Sam Sanghera, Nellie Cortez, Ellis Asher, and Ramona Bale."

"That's the crew. Can I trust them?"

"Notwithstanding Asher's gambling addiction, all have exemplary reputations. No criminal convictions, citations, or dismissals."

"That's not much of an answer."

"Trust is abstract and subjective. It develops over time and relies on both intuition and objective facts."

"But can I trust *my* executives?"

"I don't have enough data to provide a valid opinion."

"Me neither." Liam runs a hand through his hair. "What about Celeste? Can I trust her?"

"Celeste and I have been together for almost twenty years. By all accounts, we're a model couple."

"Don't believe everything you read," Liam mutters.

The avatar frowns. "Celeste gave up a promising career to focus on raising Ava and Cole. She's a wonderful mother, isn't she?"

"She did, and she is. But she also cheated on me."

The frown deepens. "Celeste was unfaithful?"

"Damn right she was."

"And she confessed?"

"No. I had to hire a private investigator to catch her in the act."

"Then how can you trust her?"

"Maybe I can't." Liam pauses. "But it's not entirely her fault."

"It isn't?"

"I neglected her. It doesn't justify what she did, but I prioritized my work over our marriage. Christ, I prioritized *you* over her!"

"Blame is subjective," the avatar says. "Perspective shapes reality."

"Where the hell did you get that from? Ask Reddit?"

The avatar folds its arms. "My sources are irrefutable."

"What's the point of this?" Liam groans. "For all the groundbreaking tech behind you, you're nothing more than a glorified search engine."

"I'm only trying to help," the avatar says with a hint of petulance.

"This is pointless," Liam mutters. Just as he's about to close the app, a thought strikes him. "Did I steal your algorithm from Rudy Ziegler? I mean, did I plagiarize any of his essential coding concepts?"

"Rudy Ziegler has been unsuccessful in multiple legal bids to establish proprietary ownership over the intellectual property behind TransScend's products."

"Answer the fucking question!"

"All known interactive AI simulation apps, including HisStory and TheirStory, rely on derivatives of Ziegler's original algorithm for predictive animation, created on May 7, 2005."

"So I did steal his code?"

"That would be a logical inference. Yes."

CHAPTER 16

As Liam moves the mouse to open the videoconference, he can't tell if the tremor in his fingers is from the disease or nervous anticipation. But he has no doubt that his impending appointment is causing his heart to slam against his rib cage.

The video window opens, displaying the name "Dr. Tonette Carr" below it. The Black woman who appears smiles warmly, wearing a lab coat over a dark gray turtleneck, a silver chain with a small cross resting in the crook of her neck. If not for the streaks of gray woven into her hair, Liam might think Dr. Carr too young to be one of the world's leading neuromuscular specialists, let alone the head of her division at the Mayo Clinic.

"Hello, Mr. Hirsch," she says, her voice warm. "It's a pleasure to meet you."

"Likewise, Dr. Carr. I wish it could've been in person, but getting to Rochester this week wasn't possible."

"Your loss." Her smile broadens. "There's nothing quite like Minnesota in January."

Liam's shoulders relax a little. "Seattle isn't exactly Maui this time of year either."

"I do love the Pacific Northwest, though. Even with the rain, Seattle and Vancouver are two of my favorite cities."

"Mine, too."

"Thank you for forwarding your medical records."

Liam's chest drums again. "You've had a chance to review them?"

"I have, yes. I also went through Dr. Chow's consult note. Coincidentally, I know Hudson; we crossed paths during our fellowships in New York. He's a top-notch clinician."

"And do you agree with his conclusion?"

"If you don't mind, I'd like to go through your history myself, especially considering the new symptoms you mentioned in your emails."

Liam exhales. Her words offer a fleeting reprieve. "Of course."

"Let's start with the first symptom you noticed."

"It was my left hand. About two months ago, the muscle on the back of it started twitching between the bones. Those are fasciculations, right?"

"Or fibrillations, if they're more subtle."

"Either way, I ignored them."

"You wouldn't be the first."

"For the record, I come by my medical denial honestly. My dad worked for three days after his heart attack before seeing a doctor."

Dr. Carr nods, a glimmer of understanding in her eyes. "What made you decide to seek help?"

"At first, the spasms were sporadic—once or twice a day. But then they became more frequent. Every few hours. And they lasted longer."

"How much longer?"

"Instead of a second or two, they'd go on for five or ten. Then my right hand started twitching, too. I worried I might be having a stroke." He sighs. "In retrospect, I wish it had just been a stroke."

"I understand," she says, her smile tightening.

"I also started getting clumsy."

Dr. Carr leans in, her expression intent. "Can you be more specific?"

"I started tripping, especially on steps. And I'd drop my fork or knife while eating. And the spilling . . ."

"Yes? Tell me about that."

A flush of embarrassment heats his cheeks. "I've spilled or knocked over so many drinks. Forget alcohol, I can barely hold a glass of water these days."

"That can't be easy." Dr. Carr nods sympathetically. "Now, about those sensations you described in your email?"

"They started last week in my feet. A strange burning sensation, numbness, and sometimes pins and needles."

"Always in your feet?"

"Mainly, but sometimes in my fingertips, too. Occasionally, it spreads up my lower legs."

"Do you ever feel them in your lips?"

"No."

Dr. Carr asks more questions, her tone gentle yet thorough. After a while, she nods. "I wish I could do a proper physical exam, but our remote technology isn't quite there yet. However, I'd like to guide you through some exercises. Is that all right?"

"Why not?"

Dr. Carr directs him through some of the same physical exam tests Dr. Chow did—holding his palms up with eyes closed, touching his nose with alternating index fingers. As he unbuttons and re-buttons his shirt, she watches closely, scrutinizing every movement. Then she asks him to write a sentence. Once he's done, she requests a sample of his handwriting from before the symptoms began. After a moment of searching, he finds an old notepad with a handwritten list of climbing supplies he'd jotted down before his trip to the Andes. Comparing the two samples, he's shocked by how messy and uneven his once-precise lettering has become.

The neurologist's expression remains impassive as he holds the samples up to the camera for her to see. "Thank you, Mr. Hirsch. That will suffice."

"Phew." He laughs nervously. "I was worried you'd put me on a unicycle and make me juggle."

"Next time." Her laugh is equally strained.

"Have you reached your conclusion?"

"Your motor symptoms are consistent, Mr. Hirsch. And all the diagnostic tests—MRIs, muscle biopsy, spinal fluid analysis—point to the same diagnosis."

"ALS?"

"I can't be one hundred percent certain, as there's no single definitive test. But I agree with Dr. Chow. Based on the evidence, I believe you have ALS."

Liam's stomach plummets. He had fought hard not to let his hopes rise, but hearing her say it aloud feels like a final blow. "What about the sensory symptoms? I didn't think ALS caused those."

"You're right. They're not typical with ALS. The disease affects motor, not sensory nerves. In other words, movement, not sensation."

"But?"

"People with ALS sometimes experience odd sensations for various reasons."

"Such as?" he asks, his mind drifting.

"The brain is complex. You've heard of patients with amputations who feel phantom pain in missing limbs?"

"Last I checked, my feet are still attached."

"When neurological function is disrupted by a spinal cord disorder, the brain can misinterpret other signals."

"Are you saying I'm imagining the burning and tingling?"

"No. Not at all. They're very real to you. But your tests—like the MRI—leave little room for doubt."

"I see."

Dr. Carr continues speaking, but her words blur as Liam's mind races. It feels as futile as appealing a death sentence after clemency has already been denied.

When she mentions experimental treatments, Liam cuts her off. "Thank you, Dr. Carr. I've taken too much of your time already, and I'm late for another appointment."

As soon as the call ends, Liam opens his email app. His hand trembles too much to type, so he commands, "Hey, TransScend. Dictate email to Dr. Glynn."

"What should the subject line of your email read?" the computer responds.

"Ready to proceed."

CHAPTER 17

Three hours after the call with Dr. Carr, Liam remains in his office, trapped in a vortex of dark thoughts. None of his self-actualization exercises offer any relief. "I'm a doer," he mutters again, trying to snap himself out of it. *But will I still be when my limbs don't work and I can't even swallow my own saliva?*

Shame washes over him. This overwhelming self-pity feels worse than the denial or anger or even the bleak despair that followed his diagnosis.

A soft knock on the door pulls him from the spiral.

"Hey, handsome, dinner's ready," Celeste says, stepping into the room. But her smile falters when she sees him. "What's wrong?"

"It's just my guts again," he says, avoiding her gaze. "They're all messed up."

"I thought you were like Roger," she says, referencing the family's golden retriever who died two summers ago and broke all their hearts, especially Celeste's. "Iron stomach and all."

Liam forces a grin. "Poor old Roger could dine on a septic tank and be fine."

"I think he probably did. Remember how much he loved to eat poop?" Her attempt at lightness doesn't hide the worry in her eyes. "Maybe you should see someone about your belly, too?"

"I'll be fine. Work's a pressure cooker right now. That's probably all it is."

Her nod is far from convincing. "And the neurologist? Have you heard anything more?"

Liam hesitates. The urge to tell her everything—his diagnosis, his plans to die—wells up inside him. But something holds him back. "No, nothing new yet," he says instead.

Celeste steps closer, her hands finding his shoulders, gently massaging them. "You're carrying a lot on these, aren't you?"

More than you know. "It'll pass."

"You'll figure it out. You always do."

Liam wonders if guilt over her affair is driving Celeste's recent attentiveness. But her touch is soothing, and his mood lightens, if only marginally.

"Why don't you come join us at the table? Even if you don't eat."

"Maybe for dessert. I've got a bit more to catch up on."

She leans down and kisses his cheek, her lips lingering for a moment longer than usual. "You know where to find us."

Liam turns back to his computer, opening more articles on medical assistance in dying. He finds strange comfort in personal accounts of people in their final days, hoping to reach the same acceptance they describe. Then again, maybe it's only the ones who find peace who write about their experiences.

The door bursts open, interrupting his thoughts. Liam quickly minimizes the article as Cole enters, balancing a tray of food. Liam catches a whiff of the salty broth that sits between slices of bread and a simple salad. "Mom sent this down," Cole says, setting the tray on the desk. "She said to tell you this soup would've done the trick for Roger."

"Roger would've never needed it." Liam reaches out to ruffle Cole's hair. "Thanks, pal."

Cole pulls away. "That's weird, Dad."

"You used to love it when we did that."

"Yeah, and then I turned two."

Liam holds up his hands in surrender. "Duly noted."

His son turns to leave but pauses at the door, silent.

Unlike his sister, Cole goes quiet when something's bothering him. "What is it, Cole?"

He shuffles his feet, stuffing his hands into the pockets of his hoodie before finally speaking. "Is something going on between you and Mom?"

"No. Why?"

"For ages, it seemed like you guys were hardly even speaking. And now it's like every dinner is date night."

"And that's bad?"

"It's kinda OTT, Dad. Like you're both trying too hard. Like you're putting on a show for Ava and me."

Liam frowns. "Why would we do that?"

"No idea, but Sean told me his parents were all lovey-dovey right before they split up. Turns out, they were just previewing what respectful and loving 'co-parents' they planned to be. Which was a joke, because it all went to crap once the lawyers got involved."

"Your mom and I aren't splitting up." The words feel heavy on Liam's tongue. A bitter divorce would be easier for his kids than what they're unknowingly facing.

Cole offers a hint of a grin. "Maybe ease off on the PDA, then?"

"Also duly noted."

After Cole leaves, Liam returns to his research, scouring the web for articles on MAiD that discuss the best way to break the news to loved ones.

There's another knock, and Liam mutters, "It's like Grand Central down here." He glances over his shoulder, surprised to see Sam filling much of the doorway.

"Celeste sent me down," Sam says, all business.

"What brings you out on a school night?"

"You haven't responded to any of my messages."

"I've had my phone off. Taking a personal day."

"A personal day? You? Will wonders never cease. I'm guessing you haven't seen it, huh?"

"Seen what?"

"Hey, TransScend," Sam calls over Liam's shoulder. "Search top news stories on New Hampshire and TransScend."

"One moment, please, Mr. Sanghera," the computer chirps back in its singsong voice.

"That's just plain creepy," Sam grunts.

Seconds later, all three screens display separate webpages, each headline centered on the same explosive subject. Liam scans the one that reads, "TransScend App Powers Politically Motivated Takedown."

The first article describes how the deepfake video of the senator from New Hampshire was created using HisStory, highlighting the app's potential for weaponizing election interference. More alarming to Liam, the final paragraph reveals TransScend's plans to release TheirStory. "With its groundbreaking predictive algorithms, this app is capable of producing disturbingly realistic deepfake videos that even AI security experts find difficult if not impossible to detect."

"How the hell?" Liam groans. "Does Nellie know?"

"Oh, yeah," Sam says. "And I'm thinking she might be the one who leaked it."

"Come on, Sam."

"Who else, Boss?" He holds out his big hands. "You heard her at the meeting going on about how TheirStory is going to launch World War Three."

"No way," Liam says, though doubt flickers across his mind. "Nellie is a privacy freak. No matter how she feels about the release, she would never go to the press."

"Well, NDAs or not, someone did. And this is a fucking disaster."

Sam's right. A month ago, this would've sent Liam into a tailspin. Now it's just another gust in the hurricane that's swept up his life.

"I've got Publicity and Legal working round the clock on damage control, but there's only so much they can do." Sam's shoulders sag. "Whoever said there's no such thing as bad publicity is full of shit."

"Yeah, maybe."

"And the fucking timing couldn't be worse," Sam grumbles. "Right after we moved up the launch date."

Liam looks up sharply. "You think it all could've been orchestrated, Sam? To frame TransScend?"

"Hundred percent. This reeks of sabotage."

Liam exhales heavily. "Maybe."

Sam's forehead creases. "Does this change your calculus on that whole sabbatical thing?"

Liam shakes his head.

A trace of hurt crosses Sam's face. "And you haven't decided who's going to step into your role?"

"You're the leading candidate, Sam," Liam offers vaguely.

"Candidate, huh?" Sam snorts. "Nice."

Liam can't even summon the energy to reassure his friend. And the more he reflects on this latest bombshell, the less random events seem. Not only do the deepfake and its leak coincide with them moving up the launch date of TheirStory, but they also follow the anomaly in last quarter's financial report.

Could it be intentional? Is someone targeting TransScend? *Or are they ambushing me?*

CHAPTER 18

The overcast Seattle skies threaten rain, but the streets remain dry. Andrea sits in her car, parked midway down the block from her target's condo building, trying to focus on the deep, gravelly voice of her favorite true crime podcaster. The episode dives into the case of a wealthy St. Louis Realtor accused of murdering his wife and two sons with a shotgun, with hints that the youngest son might be the real killer. Normally, a case like this would grip her, but today her thoughts keep circling back to Liam.

He's dying.

The unexpected tears that welled up outside Starbucks after their meeting still unsettle her. She doesn't cry easily, especially not for someone she barely knows. It confuses her, this vulnerability. She suspects it has more to do with her father than with Liam. After her dad's suicide, she'd barely shed a tear at his memorial, her grief locked behind a wall of anger and confusion.

Something about Liam's calm, stoic demeanor reminds her of her dad. On the surface, Liam seems to have it all—wealth, status, a beautiful wife, and two great kids. A life most would envy. But beneath the façade, he's a man at war with a terminal illness, betrayed by his wife, and possibly being defrauded by someone close to him.

Could that someone be Rudy Ziegler? Andrea wonders, her eyes fixed on the entrance of the condo building on Eighth Avenue in the Denny Triangle district.

After diving deep into Ziegler's life online, Andrea feels like she knows him inside out. One of the strange side effects of her job is the one-sided intimacy she develops with her targets. She recalls reading that psychologists call it a parasocial relationship. It's particularly strong with Ziegler, given the wealth of information available about him.

Despite his brilliance, Ziegler's life seems marred by disappointment. He scrapes by as an AI journalist, media expert, and occasional consultant. He writes prolifically for tech publications and is a regular guest on shows and podcasts.

It's no surprise to Andrea that Ziegler is in demand. He's a compelling speaker, able to distill complex technical details into broader, more digestible ideas. He often touches on the existential and even spiritual implications of AI, warning of its potential dangers. One quote stuck with her: "It's foolish to think we can keep playing God without occasionally flooding the world on the scale of Noah's ark."

But what consumes Ziegler most is TransScend. His rants about the dangers and flaws of HisStory are relentless, and he never misses a chance to claim his intellectual property was stolen. In interviews, he often sidetracks to vent his frustration. The comment sections under his posts are littered with references to it. Many people offer support, but others note his obsession. One commenter wrote, "Jealous much? Bro, seriously, get professional help!!!"

Across the street, someone exits the building, leading an e-bike by the handlebars. Andrea almost dismisses him until he turns to mount the bike. It's Ziegler. He secures his helmet, puts on dark sunglasses despite the overcast skies, and heads off down the bike lane.

Andrea allows him a generous head start. If she'd known he'd be on an e-bike, she would've brought hers. In a bike-centric city like Seattle, an e-bike is a must for a PI. Tailing a cyclist by car is a logistical nightmare— it's impossible to follow them at a natural speed.

As she pulls out, she spots Ziegler two blocks ahead. Fortunately, traffic is light, allowing her to slow down and pull over when necessary.

She watches him turn east on Pine Street and follows at a safe distance. After crossing the Pine Bridge over I-5, she briefly loses him. Her heart races as she accelerates, until she catches sight of him again. She overtakes him to avoid suspicion, pulling over at Tenth Avenue and waiting at the corner until he cycles past without glancing her way.

She tails him down Twelfth Avenue onto the Seattle University campus, where he stops to lock up his bike in front of Sullivan Hall School of Law. After about half an hour, he emerges and continues on his route, stopping at a bank, a grocery store, and a liquor store. When his pannier is full, Andrea assumes he's heading home, but instead he veers northeast onto Madison Street, toward Lake Washington.

Her pulse quickens as she follows him onto Thirty-Sixth Avenue into the affluent Denny-Blaine neighborhood. The area, nestled against the lake, is a maze of crescents and cul-de-sacs.

With no other cars on the quiet street, Andrea hangs back but soon loses sight of him. She drives to the house on Florence Crescent where she suspects he's headed and parks at the end of the block.

She reclines her seat until it's nearly flat and curls up on her side, keeping her head below window level. From this familiar vantage point, she watches for Ziegler in the rearview mirror. She doesn't have to wait long. Soon she spots him turning the corner onto the street.

He slows to a stop halfway down the block. Andrea watches as he lifts his bike onto the curb and wheels it down the path toward the house, which she can't see but can easily picture. It's the same quaint Craftsman-style home with yellow shingle siding that she surveilled just two days ago.

CHAPTER 19

Charcoal clouds form a dense canopy, mirroring Liam's mood. His feet burn with a contradictory mix of heat and numbness, sensations so visceral that, despite Dr. Carr's reassurances, he knows there's nothing phantom about this pain.

As he carefully navigates the sloped trail, his feet unsteady on the gravel, he tries to find solace in the familiar surroundings of the Seattle Japanese Garden. This place has always been his refuge, where he could lose himself among the winding paths, rock piles, lanterns, and tranquil ponds. But when he spots Andrea waiting on a nearby bench, he wonders if meeting her here is a bit over-the-top—a reflection of his growing distrust.

"Hi," he says as he reaches her.

"Hello." She greets him with a grin, attempting lightness. "Aren't you supposed to say something like 'The tulips are particularly violet this time of year'?"

He forces a chuckle, settling beside her. "This meetup feels straight out of an old spy movie, doesn't it?"

"Kind of."

Despite the banter, Liam feels acutely self-conscious. Andrea is the only one, aside from his doctors, who knows about his ALS. She's also the only one aware of his wife's infidelity. This dual knowledge leaves him feeling exposed yet oddly secure around her. It's a relief not to have to pretend.

"You're not much for calls or texts, are you?" she asks, breaking the silence.

"Not lately," he admits. "I find it easier to discuss this stuff in person."

"Which stuff?"

"Did you hear about that deepfake in New Hampshire?"

"I did, yeah." Her expression turns serious. "And TransScend's involvement. But the whole thing's a black box to me. Deepfakes and generative AI . . . what does that even mean?"

"Want the quick version?"

"Please."

"Generative AI, which powers our apps, uses neural networks to create simulated videos by manipulating existing media." Liam begins, slipping into the well-rehearsed pitch he's perfected over years of investor meetings. "The AI trains on large datasets of real media, learning to replicate patterns. Once trained, it generates new content by blending and altering the data. For example, HisStory can map the facial movements of one person onto another, creating a convincing video where it looks like someone—say, a historical figure or an actor—is saying something based on user-provided dialogue. TheirStory goes further by generating not just the video but entire conversations from scratch."

"Sounds like smoke and mirrors," she says.

"In some ways, it is. But I don't think what happened in New Hampshire is a coincidence."

"Why not?"

"The deepfake, the leak to the media, and the disclosure of TheirStory's upcoming launch—it's all too coordinated."

"You think it's a setup?"

"It's hard not to. Can you imagine a better way to create bad press and undermine the launch of the app?"

Andrea shifts uncomfortably before blurting, "But isn't it doing what it's designed to do? Mislead people?"

"Political manipulation was never the intent, but yeah, this deepfake has serious implications. And the leak could spark backlash against TheirStory before it even launches. I also wonder if it's tied to the financial discrepancy from last quarter."

She frowns. "That would suggest a conspiracy that runs deep, wouldn't it?"

"I know how paranoid this must sound, but it feels like I'm under attack from all sides."

Andrea's expression remains neutral, but her eyes show understanding. "And if it's all connected, it has to be someone inside the company, right?"

"Exactly! No one outside could pull this off."

"Not even Rudy Ziegler? The guy seems obsessed with you. He's brilliant, well-connected."

"He is." Liam recalls how much he envied Rudy in grad school. How Rudy could effortlessly solve complex problems off the top of his head, whereas Liam had to grind through them, often relying on trial and error. "But even if Rudy wanted to—and I'm sure he does—how could he orchestrate this from the outside?"

"Maybe he has help on the inside?"

"From who?"

"Nellie Cortez."

"Nellie? No way. She'd be the last person to spy for Rudy."

"Then why did he go to her house yesterday?"

Liam's breath catches. "What are you talking about?"

Andrea gestures toward the garden's entrance. "I followed him to Nellie's house, Liam. He went inside."

His head spins. "Rudy? In Nellie's house?"

"Yes."

"Why?"

"I don't know. But he was in there for a good thirty minutes."

"Jesus," he mutters.

"It adds up, doesn't it?" Andrea says steadily. "If someone's behind this, Rudy has to be a prime suspect."

Liam is too stunned to respond. He stares at the pond in front of them, his mind racing to process her revelation. A koi's orange head breaks the surface near the shore, soon joined by others in search of food. Watching them swarm, Liam realizes he isn't even angry with Rudy. The thought of Rudy still stalking him after all these years, even after losing in court, strikes Liam as pitiful. The last time they spoke outside the courtroom, Rudy seemed broken. Only lately has Liam begun to grasp how responsible he might have been for Rudy's downfall. He almost feels sorry for him.

But Nellie—his mentee—that's different. If she'd leaked privileged information to his nemesis, it would be like a knife to the back.

"My dad died last year," Andrea says, breaking the silence.

Liam glances at her, surprised. "I'm sorry, Andrea."

"After a long battle with inflammatory arthritis." She clears her throat, her voice tightening. "My mom took off when I was young, and I'm an only child. For most of my life, it was just the two of us."

"That must've been a terrible loss," Liam says, still unsure where this conversation is headed.

"You have no idea. He was so proud, my dad. Stoic and independent. Never complained, even when he couldn't walk anymore." She pauses, clearly struggling to keep her emotions in check. "I loved him so much, but I still wish he'd shared more about what he was going through in those final days, you know?"

Liam suddenly makes the connection. "Andrea, I told you too much last time—"

"I've been there, Liam!" she snaps, her eyes blazing. "I was the one left behind. And it sucks."

His heart goes out to her. "I shouldn't have dumped my issues on you. I had no right. I'm really sorry."

"No, I'm out of line," she says, offering a small smile. "I can't understand what you're going through. But . . ."

"Yes?"

"Let me be your sounding board, Liam. Totally confidential. After what I went through with my dad, I know a little about how this feels for the family."

He shakes his head. "I've shared too much already."

Her eyes lock on to his, unwavering. "It's not my place to say anything, but I have to get this off my chest. Your family has a right to know, Liam. They need to."

"Do they?" The words catch in his throat. "Will it help my kids to know that their dad is going to wither away in front of their eyes?"

She reaches for his wrist, giving it a firm squeeze before letting go. "It doesn't matter what you'd prefer, Liam. They're going to find out soon enough."

"Not if I choose to die before it gets that far."

Her face freezes. "Choose to?"

"Medical assistance in dying is legal in Washington."

"Oh my God!" she says, her voice rising. "Without even talking it over with your family?"

"I will," he says, shame heating his face as he breaks off eye contact. "Soon."

"Whose pain are you trying to spare, Liam? Yours or theirs?"

He shrugs.

Andrea's voice softens. "What I didn't mention is that my dad took his own life."

"Oh."

"I was devastated, Liam," she says. "He didn't include me in his decision. I didn't even know he was planning it. I only found out *the next day* from his housekeeper—she found his body. Can you imagine?"

He shakes his head, unable to find the words.

Andrea leans in closer, her eyes pleading. "I never got to say goodbye. And that kills me, Liam. Even now, I can't forgive him. Please don't make that same mistake with your family."

CHAPTER 20

Liam feels off-kilter as he waits in Dr. Glynn's bright, overly cheerful office, surrounded by potpourri and folk art that now feels out of place. The warm scent of vanilla lingers in the air, though he can't spot its source.

This morning, he woke up more certain than ever that he needed to spare his family—and himself—from the slow, brutal decline his illness promises. But Andrea's story about her dad stuck with him. Seeing how much she still struggles with being kept in the dark made Liam realize he couldn't do the same to his kids. Not only would they probably resent him forever for hiding his illness, but it would only add to their pain and confusion after he was gone. And he couldn't handle the thought of doing that to them. He needs to tell them. Soon.

But first, he has to deal with the growing mess at his company. There's a threat, maybe from both inside and out, that could destroy everything he's built and put his kids' financial future at risk. He won't let that happen. He'll fix it and then come clean with his family.

He's not surprised that Rudy might be scheming against him, but the idea that Nellie could be involved cuts deep. He handpicked her as a young coder and championed her rise to a senior executive role. She's always been blunt, sometimes difficult, but he trusted her. If she's in on this, it's not just a betrayal—it's a serious threat to TransScend. As head of cybersecurity, she's supposed to be the one who keeps the company safe from these dangers.

First Celeste, now Nellie. Who the hell can I rely on anymore?

Dr. Glynn breezes into the room with a warm smile. "Nice to see you, Mr. Hirsch," she says, taking her seat behind the desk. "And thank you for your email."

Liam finds her chipper tone odd, given that he'd essentially emailed her his death wish. "Thanks for seeing me again so quickly."

She leans forward, hands clasped on the desk, fingers adorned with a rainbow of rings. "The ethics board approved your eligibility for MAiD."

Liam tries to picture a group of strangers debating his right to die. "Should I send flowers or a thank-you card?" he quips, masking his unease.

"I don't think that's necessary," she replies with a polite laugh. "But I wanted to clarify what you meant in your email when you said you were ready to proceed."

"It means I'm ready."

"I understand, but were you thinking of a specific time frame?"

"You mentioned I'd have to wait a week after committing."

Dr. Glynn stiffens slightly. "I didn't realize you were thinking so soon."

"I don't see the point in waiting."

"It's impossible for me to put myself in your shoes, but given the nature of ALS, I can see why you'd want a quick escape."

"So, we're agreed then?"

"As we discussed before, Mr. Hirsch, dying is a process—one of the most natural processes we ever go through. Many people never see their deaths coming, but for those who do, it's a dynamic experience. One with expected highs and lows. I think it's possible you might be experiencing one of those lows."

"I believe you, Dr. Glynn," Liam says flatly. "But I've considered everything, and I want to proceed sooner rather than later—before I lose more of myself."

"All right, let's start there." She picks up a pen and notepad. "Let's create a list of your minimum functional standards. Your red lines not to be crossed, so to speak, to help decide when we should move ahead with MAiD."

"I've crossed some of them already."

The skin around Dr. Glynn's eyes tightens. "But you walked into my office."

"I did. I even drove myself here."

She extends a hand toward him. "Then surely, there's still potential for some quality of life?"

"What quality?" Liam's voice rises, anger seeping in. "I have to watch every step I take. I can barely feed myself without making a mess. And the worst part? I'm constantly aware of what's coming. It's like trying to live my best life with a ticking bomb strapped to my back." He holds her gaze, making sure she understands his resolve. "I don't want to live like this."

"I understand," she says evenly. "I've seen other clients with ALS who, early in their illness, felt exactly as you do. Almost all of them were suffering from reactive depression. After treatment, they changed their minds about an early death." She opens her palm to him. "Would you consider speaking to a psychiatric colleague of mine about your—"

"No."

"Then would you allow me to prescribe a low dose of an antidepressant to see if it affects your outlook?"

"I'm not depressed, Dr. Glynn. I'm being realistic."

"It's hard for people in the middle of a crisis to assess their mental health objectively."

"I don't have symptoms of depression. I sleep fine. I enjoy my meals. I take real pleasure in time with my kids. My wife and I are closer than we've been in a long time."

A look of relief crosses Dr. Glynn's face. "So, you've told her about your diagnosis, then?"

His brief hesitation says it all.

Her face hardens. "Oh, Mr. Hirsch, it's vital that you share this with your family, even if they're not part of the final decision."

He raises a hand. "I'll tell them soon, Dr. Glynn. I swear."

But she's not buying it. "I'm hearing that you're ready to die but not ready to tell your family. Does that sound logical to you?"

"A friend of mine already convinced me, Dr. Glynn," Liam says, and it occurs to him that he and Andrea have become friends. "I just need to sort out a few things with my estate, and then I'll tell them everything."

"All right," she sighs, still looking skeptical. "As you mentioned, there's a mandatory seven-day waiting period to proceed with MAiD after you've committed in writing."

"I understand, Dr. Glynn. And I'm not talking about today or tomorrow. I still have other things to deal with." He resists the urge to mention the conspiracy brewing within his company. "But I'd like the prescription ready, so I can proceed when I'm ready."

"To take at home?"

He nods. "I don't want to die in a hospital," he says, already picturing his office as the best option.

Dr. Glynn studies him for a long moment, then nods. "Let's make an appointment for the same time next week. I'll write the prescription then."

One week. It's not much time to stop a conspiracy. Or to live. But if there's one thing Liam understands, it's how to work under pressure—though this is the first time he's faced such a literal deadline.

CHAPTER 21

"I've really missed you, Liam," Celeste murmurs, her foot brushing against his under the sheet.

"I've missed you, too."

"Can't we just turn back the clock?" she asks, still facing away.

"I don't think there's an app for that," Liam replies, his heart heavy.

Her breath catches, and it takes him a moment to realize she's crying. He gently turns her to face him. "What's wrong?"

"I . . ." She swallows hard. "Benjamin won't be coming back."

"Oh?" he says, keeping his voice steady. "Why not?"

"I let him go today."

"OK."

"That's all you have to say?"

"This renovation was your idea. I'm sure you had a reason. I trust you."

"You shouldn't." Her sobs intensify. "We . . . I did a terrible thing, Liam."

He forces himself to play dumb. "What's that?"

"I cheated on you."

"With Benjamin?"

"Yes," she rasps.

Liam has imagined this moment countless times, always picturing himself in control, guiding the conversation. But now that she's confessing on her own, he's at a loss for words.

She sits up in bed. "There's no excuse. You have every right to hate me, to tell the kids . . . to leave me."

"But I'm not going to."

"Wait . . ." Her eyes widen in shock. "You knew, didn't you?"

"Yeah."

"How?"

"I hired a private investigator. I saw the photos. You and Benjamin."

"Oh my God!" She covers her face with her hands.

"Yeah, it wasn't pretty. Not from my perspective, anyway. Andrea photographed you in bed with him twice. You weren't even discreet."

Celeste falls silent, stewing in her shame. Finally, Liam asks, "How did it end?"

"Does it matter?"

"It does to me."

"I told him the truth."

"And that was?"

"That I didn't love him. That I never could."

"But you could keep sleeping with him?"

"He wanted me to leave you, to be with him. I couldn't do that."

Liam glares at her. Is he supposed to feel relieved she chose to stay in the marriage while still having sex with Benjamin?

"How long have you known?" she asks quietly.

"A few weeks."

"All this time . . . while you and I were trying to reconnect?"

"What the hell was I supposed to do, Celeste?" His tone sharpens, surprising even him. He didn't expect the surge of anger now boiling inside him.

She reaches out, but he shrugs off her hand. "How could you not say anything?"

"What the fuck was I supposed to say?" he shouts, the words spilling out. "Ask if our contractor was billing me by the hour for fucking my wife in our bed?" Even as his rage flares, he feels strangely detached, like an observer to his own outburst.

"It was never in our house," she murmurs, her head bowed. "But I deserve that."

"I've been dealing with my own shit!" he growls through clenched teeth. "There was never a right time to bring this up."

"But lately . . . you've been so tender, so attentive. You made me fall in love with you all over again." Her face pales. "Was it all an act?"

"No," he admits, grudgingly.

Tears well up in her eyes again. "The worst part is, I can't even blame Benjamin. I . . . I'm the one who seduced him."

"Perfect," Liam snorts. "Jesus."

"It's no excuse, Liam. Not even close. But for the past few years, I've felt so alone. The kids don't need me like they used to, and you haven't needed me in years. It wasn't just that I was always second to Trans-Scend. Sometimes, it felt like I didn't matter to you at all. Like I didn't exist."

He stares hard at her. "So, this is my fault?"

"No! I did this. All of it. You're an amazing dad, and you provide more than I could want or need. But I've felt us drifting apart for so long. And I felt so abandoned. So useless." Her voice cracks. "Now I've wrecked everything."

The helplessness in her expression, more than her words, douses the fire raging inside him. After a long, loaded pause, he sighs and says, "I'm not blameless. I know I've been too focused on work. Especially the last few years. I never meant to neglect you, but lately I've realized that I did."

Celeste throws her arms around his neck, clinging so tightly that each of her shaky breaths presses against his chest. "I'm sorry, Lee. So, so sorry. I love you so much. And I'm ashamed of what I've done to you. To us."

After a pause, he says, "I'm glad you told me, Celeste."

They rock together in silence for a while. Without thinking, he moves his lips to hers. The first kiss is tentative, but when he feels her tongue slip between his lips, something breaks inside him. He tears off her nightie, while she tugs off his pajama bottoms. Their hands are everywhere, their mouths soon follow. And then he's inside her, driven by a fierce need, fueled by her moans.

Afterward, she lies in his arms, facing away, breathing heavily. "That was . . . something."

"Yeah," he says, suddenly aware of what it feels like to make love as if it could be the last time.

She rolls back toward him, pressing her forehead against his. Her minty breath warms his nose. "God, I missed you," she whispers.

A sudden sense of foreboding grips Liam. Before he can pull away, his right leg begins to twitch so violently that he involuntarily kicks the sheet away.

"Liam!" Her voice cracks with worry. "What's happening? Are you all right?"

He pulls free of her and rolls onto his side, focusing all his energy on controlling his leg. It feels like ages before the spasms finally subside.

"Sweetheart," she says, gently rubbing his back. "What's happening?"

"It's passed now."

"Talk to me. *Please.* What's really going on with you?"

"It's all too much. I'm totally exhausted."

But deep down, he knows Andrea and Dr. Glynn are right. He has to tell Celeste. The kids, too. And he will. Very soon.

Just not tonight.

CHAPTER 22

Liam leans back in his chair, the burning in his fingertips matching the fire in the soles of his feet. Last night's confrontation with Celeste over her affair, followed by their unexpected physical reconnection, has left him drained. They spent most of the night talking, reminiscing, and even making love again. But while the passion flared, her confession only brought his hurt and anger to the surface, making the whole thing feel hollow—more like a physical release than real healing. It reminded him that he still doesn't trust her. Maybe that's why he still couldn't bring himself to tell her about his illness or his plan to die.

As Liam surveys the boardroom, he realizes his trust in others has worn dangerously thin, too. Ellis, his VP of sales, hides a gambling addiction. Ramona, his CFO, either missed—or, worse, intentionally ignored—two unexplained payments last quarter. And Nellie, his head of security, secretly met with his nemesis. Liam can barely meet their eyes this morning.

Ramona taps her phone, projecting a line graph on the wall. The line climbs steadily before plunging at the end. "A drop of eleven percent in TransScend's stock price—the first double-digit loss in the company's history."

"That deepfake in New Hampshire was a setup," Ellis grumbles. "It wasn't about tilting some meaningless election. Whoever's behind it did it to screw us over!"

"No shit, Sherlock," Sam snorts, scowling at Nellie over his half-moon glasses. "Too bad we didn't catch it sooner."

She holds his gaze, unflinching, like a mongoose staring down a cobra. "What am I supposed to do, Sam? Monitor every single user of HisStory around the clock to make sure they're not up to no good?"

Sam leans closer. "If necessary, yeah."

Nellie doesn't back down. "Legally, we can't access users' avatars. Or do you not care about those small details? Even if we could, they can still hide behind layers of VPNs and firewalls."

Ellis crosses his arms. "None of that explains how TheirStory got leaked."

"Well, let me explain slowly so you'll understand. At least thirty employees have direct access to TheirStory, and probably another fifty know about it. All the NDAs and security measures in the world can't stop one of them from anonymously tipping off someone through untraceable, low-tech means."

Or maybe our own chief of security leaked it directly to the man with a vendetta against me? Liam almost blurts, but he bites his tongue. He'd love to fire Nellie on the spot for her betrayal, but he needs to understand her connection with Rudy and the potential threat they pose together before he confronts her.

Ellis doesn't hold back, though. "So, it's all just one big coincidence, huh, Nellie?"

"What are you implying?" she snaps.

"At our last meeting, you ranted about TheirStory launching a nuclear war. Days later, the news gets leaked, undermining us before it even hits the market. Interesting timing, don't you think?"

"Screw you!" Nellie's eyes blaze with contempt, and a vein bulges in her neck. "I don't have to sit here and take this." She jumps up and storms out.

Ellis smirks as he glances around the room. "Touched a nerve, maybe?"

Sam turns to Liam. "Still convinced Nellie couldn't be involved?"

"Less so," Liam admits.

"OK," Sam says. "I'll dig into this personally."

"You have no evidence, Sam," Ramona warns. "Violating Nellie's privacy could backfire on the whole company."

"TransScend is worth eleven percent less today than it was last night," Sam counters. "I'd rather risk a lawsuit than face bankruptcy for sitting on my hands."

Ramona turns to Liam, a plea in her eyes.

The burning in his feet intensifies, and his stomach sinks. An eleven percent loss in one day? Despite all his efforts, the future of his company is more volatile than ever. "Be discreet, Sam."

Sam lays a hand on his chest. "Like a ghost in the night."

"Nellie will know," Ramona says. "She's sharp."

"Who cares?" Ellis retorts. "If she's behind the deepfake and the leak, we've got bigger problems than her hurt feelings."

Ramona glares at Ellis. "Then we should all expect to be scrutinized." Turning back to Liam, she asks, "With all this uncertainty, are you still planning to take a sabbatical?"

Liam nods. "I can't change my plans now."

"And have you decided who you'll name as acting CEO?"

Sam watches him intently.

"Not yet," Liam says. "But I'm getting closer."

CHAPTER 23

Liam's foot feels wooden against the accelerator. He wonders again how much longer he'll be able to drive. Everything lately feels heavy with finality, as if his bucket list has shrunk to simple everyday pleasures that are slipping away by the day.

After the tense meeting with his executive team, he couldn't get out of the office fast enough. All he wants is to be with his family, to spend another evening with Celeste and the kids. Maybe watch a movie, play a card game—anything to hold on to the small joys he once took for granted.

But as he crosses the 520 Bridge from Bellevue into Seattle, he finds himself driving past his Broadmoor turnoff, compelled to keep going west into the Denny Triangle. He pulls into a parking spot outside the building Andrea mentioned.

Liam's stomach churns as he steps up to the intercom. He scrolls through the digital list until he finds "RZ." His finger hesitates before tapping the button. The intercom rings four times before a familiar voice answers, "Yes?"

"Rudy, it's Liam."

After a long pause, Rudy replies, "2702." The line clicks, and the door buzzes.

Inside, Liam's dread rises with the elevator.

Rudy stands in the doorway, wearing jeans and a black sweater. He looks as hollowed out as he did the last time they met outside the court-house, all his fire from their grad school days extinguished.

Without a word, Rudy leads him into the living room. The mini-malist decor—four padded chairs around a cement coffee table—gives the all-white room a cold, impersonal feel. The view of Elliott Bay stretches out beneath the floor-to-ceiling windows. Liam's eyes drift to the black-and-white photos on the walls. Photography was Rudy's only interest outside of his work and research. Liam had never known him to date, suspecting Rudy's passion for AI had eclipsed everything else.

Rudy doesn't offer a seat or a drink. He crosses his arms. "Why are you here?"

"It's time we talked, Rudy."

"You didn't think it was worth doing before all the trials?"

Liam exhales sharply. "I tried."

"Did you? I remember you blocking my calls."

Liam steps toward a chair, lowering himself into it. "You've heard about TheirStory, haven't you?"

"It's all over the news."

"It's better than they say, Rudy. Better than anything we imagined back in grad school."

"Are you sure? We dreamed pretty big back then."

"Maybe you did. I didn't—not this big. I never thought we'd have the computing power to make a real-time conversation with an avatar of our choosing possible. Not in our lifetime, anyway."

"Maybe I was the dreamer, but you're the one who cashed in on my work." Rudy tilts his head. "What's really going on, Liam? Have you been reduced to door-to-door sales after the dip in your share prices?"

Liam chuckles softly. "I tried it on myself, you know?"

"The app?"

"Yes."

Rudy's brow furrows. "You spoke to your own avatar?"

Liam nods.

"Wild." Rudy looks intrigued for a moment, but then his face hardens. "Did it tell you that both of you are conscienceless thieves?"

Liam manages a smile. "Actually, I asked myself if I stole your algorithm."

Rudy stiffens. "And what did you tell yourself?"

"That I didn't." The lie comes more easily than Liam expected.

Rudy grunts, his shoulders sagging. "That app of yours must be damn good. To be able to simulate a self-delusional, lying asshole so well."

Liam keeps his voice level. "But it also told me that I might have undervalued your contribution."

"Undervalued . . ." Rudy shakes his head. "You're priceless."

"I never meant to screw you over, Rudy. AI was still in its infancy when we parted ways. We had ideas, dreams. Nothing more. It took me years to turn that into something real, something marketable."

Rudy's lip curls. "You said all this in your depositions."

"I wouldn't have cared if you'd used some of my ideas to create something legitimate."

"As if you had any worth pirating." Rudy snorts. "Besides, you might feel differently if you were the one living in a condo instead of a palatial estate in Broadmoor."

Liam refuses to bite. "I came to offer you an olive branch. A substantial one."

"What's that?"

"Ten percent interest in TransScend. And a seat on the board."

"No, thanks," Rudy says without hesitation.

"You know what that's worth?"

"Eleven percent less than yesterday?"

"It's more than you would've gotten, even if you'd won your lawsuits. More than enough to settle everything between us."

"You figure?"

"I'm trying to do the right thing here," Liam says, his patience thinning.

Rudy smiles bitterly. "Why now, Liam? After all the court battles, after an actual fistfight, why show up here to offer me anything?"

For a moment, Liam considers telling him the truth, that he's here to stop the instability he's convinced Rudy has been fueling. But admitting it would only weaken his position. "The app was right. I never gave you the credit you deserved."

Rudy stares, weighing the words. "The credit I deserve isn't ten percent."

"What, then?"

"Fifty-one percent."

"Are you out of your goddamn mind?" Liam snaps, just as his right hand starts twitching. He presses it against his chest and covers it with the other one, as if intending to cross his arms.

"Are you all right?"

"It's nothing," Liam mutters.

"Well . . ." Rudy shrugs. "Now you know what it will cost to make things right between us."

Liam stands, hating himself for coming here. But before leaving, he can't stop himself from asking, "How long have you known Nellie Cortez?"

Rudy's expression doesn't falter. "A while."

They stare each other down. "Corporate sabotage is still a crime," Liam says quietly.

Rudy smiles again. "So I've heard."

"I tried to be fair," Liam mutters, turning sharply toward the door.

As he's leaving, Rudy calls after him, "Remember what I told you outside the courthouse, Liam? About not underestimating karma?"

Fool! Liam fumes as he drives home, berating himself for having imagined Rudy capable of compromise. His smugness only deepens Liam's suspicions that Rudy must be behind the attack on TransScend. All Liam managed to do by showing up was expose his own weakness. *Get a grip!*

The phone rings. He's in no mood to speak to anyone, but when he sees "Dr. Chow" on the display, he decides he can't ignore it. "Hello," he answers over the truck's speaker.

"Good afternoon, Mr. Hirsch. This is Dr. Chow. I hope I'm not disturbing you."

"You're not."

"This morning, I heard from my colleague Dr. Carr at the Mayo Clinic. I understand you consulted her?"

"I did, yes." Liam isn't about to explain himself.

"I have immense respect for Dr. Carr. She's a world-renowned expert."

"OK," Liam says, confused.

"Dr. Carr mentioned your sensory symptoms. The burning and tingling."

"Yes. When I saw you, it hadn't been too noticeable. But it's gotten a lot worse."

"Can you describe it for me?"

Liam explains how the sensations in his feet and hands have grown in frequency, duration, and intensity. When he finishes, Dr. Chow says, "As Dr. Carr likely mentioned, ALS affects motor nerves, not sensory ones. But these types of symptoms aren't unheard-of. Still, yours seem unusually intense."

"Dr. Carr called them a kind of phantom pain," Liam says.

"She's probably right. But, given the changes, I decided to review your MRI again."

Liam braces himself. "Did it change your opinion?"

"The radiologist's report is consistent with ALS. But when I looked at the images myself, I saw something . . . unusual."

"Unusual? Please, Dr. Chow. Can you get to the point?"

"You mentioned you had broken two bones in your lumbar spine after a fall."

"I did. In 2008. The doctors told me I'd partially crushed two bones in my lower back—the L3 and L4 vertebrae. I didn't need surgery or anything, and they healed well. I was climbing again within three months."

"But scarring from compression fractures like those would show up on your MRIs for life. They would always look compressed—a little squashed—relative to the other vertebrae."

"I'm not sure what you're getting at—" Liam begins to say before it suddenly hits him. "Wait! You don't see those scars on my MRI?"

"No. Your L3 and L4 vertebrae look the same as the others, unblemished."

Liam's breath catches. "Are you saying my MRI report is based on the wrong patient?"

"I'm not sure what to think, but it does concern me. In light of this, I think it's best you have another MRI."

CHAPTER 24

Sitting at a corner high-top in Starbucks, Andrea realizes her second coffee was a mistake—her jitteriness is proof enough. A fresh wave of nerves hits her when she spots Liam enter. She'd arrived fifteen minutes early, unsettled by the distant tone in his voice and the unspoken urgency in his request to meet. "Easier to explain in person" was all he'd said before hanging up.

As Liam approaches, Andrea notices his pale face and somber expression. Given his plans for assisted suicide, the darkness in his mood doesn't surprise her.

As he sits across from her, Andrea begins, "Liam, I'm sorry if I pressed too hard at the Japanese—"

He raises a hand, cutting her off. He gestures toward her phone with a throat-slashing motion. Confused, Andrea powers the device down and holds it up to show it's off. Liam nods his approval.

Determined not to miss her opportunity, Andrea continues, "Liam, I know I might have overstepped at the Japanese Garden, but you've got to believe me. As someone left behind, I understand how terrible it feels."

He offers a sympathetic nod, but his eyes scan the room restlessly. "I appreciate your concern, Andrea. I really do. But I don't think your dad's situation is relevant to mine. At least, not anymore."

Andrea frowns. "How couldn't it be? You told me you were considering taking the same drastic step he did."

Liam takes a deep breath. "I don't think I have ALS anymore."

Her jaw drops. "What?"

"The MRI was mislabeled. It wasn't mine."

"You were diagnosed based on the wrong test?"

"There were other tests, too. But the images Dr. Chow saw weren't
even of my spine, though the MRI had my name on it."

Andrea shakes her head, struggling to process. "How could that
happen?"

Liam mentions something about the bones in his lower back and the
absence of scarring, but Andrea barely registers the details. She's too
overwhelmed by the revelation and shocked by his subdued reaction.
"Isn't this the best news you could hope for?"

"There's more to it, Andrea."

"Like what?"

"Do you have any idea how hard it would be to mix up two different
MRI reports by accident? Every patient has a unique identifier that follows them from registration through to the radiologist's report. Unless
another Liam Hirsch with my exact birthday and medical history walked
into that clinic, this mix-up couldn't have happened on its own."

Her eyebrows shoot up. "Are you saying someone deliberately faked
your MRI results?"

"I can't think of any other explanation."

"Why would anyone go to that trouble?" The answer hits her before
she finishes asking. "To make you believe you have ALS when you don't,
right?"

"Exactly."

"But this means you don't have it, Liam! So why aren't you ecstatic?"

"Because *something* is still causing my spasms, burning, and clumsiness. I'm getting weaker by the day."

"What did your neurologist tell you it could be?"

"I hung up as soon as he told me about the mixed-up MRIs."

"Why?"

"For the same reason I asked you to turn off your phone. If someone or something wanted to convince me I have ALS, who knows what else they've done to track me? Maybe they've even tapped into your phone."

Andrea blinks rapidly. "What do you mean by 'something'?"

"It wasn't only the MRI. I had biopsies, blood tests, a spinal tap. They'd all have had to be altered to fit the diagnosis. Imagine the reach involved in tricking two world-renowned experts into believing I had ALS if I don't."

She blows out her cheeks. "The number of records that would need to be hacked . . ."

"No question, it would take some serious computing power. Probably even AI-based."

"Or a very skilled hacker." Andrea's breath catches. "Is this connected to everything else happening at TransScend? The deepfake, the leaks, the financial irregularities . . . ?"

He shrugs, a hint of desperation in his eyes. "I wonder."

"If so, this goes way beyond fraud, Liam!" she whispers urgently. "It's attempted murder. You need to go to the police!"

"With what? A mislabeled MRI report?"

"What's the downside?"

"The moment I did, everyone involved would know that we were onto them. At least now, no one suspects a thing."

"*We?* I'm a PI, Liam. I catch cheating spouses and small-time fraudsters. This is so far outside my league, it's in a different time zone!"

Liam hangs his head. "You're right. I'm sorry. I don't know why I even thought to involve you." He sighs heavily. "Except you're the only person in the world I trust right now. The only one who even knows about the diagnosis, let alone that it was faked."

Andrea runs her fingers through her thick curls. "I guess I'm already involved, huh?"

"Willingly or not."

"What's our next move, then?"

"I need to find out what's really wrong with me."

"Another MRI?"

"Yes, and a battery of other tests. But if I go through the usual chan-nels, they'll find out and manipulate the results again. Plus, they'll know I'm suspicious of the diagnosis."

She snaps her fingers. "Unless they don't know it's you being tested."

"As in, I assume a new identity?"

"Even simpler." She shrugs. "If it's just a name on the lab tests and MRIs, why not use mine?"

"That's a generous offer, but I have an easier idea."

"Which is?"

"I'll go somewhere they'd never think to look."

"Oh, and where's that?"

"Canada."

CHAPTER 25

Liam lies inside the narrow MRI tube, the machine's clicks and whirs cutting through the noise-canceling headphones clamped over his ears. The last twenty-four hours have been a whirlwind. Just yesterday, he had been bracing for the end, convinced with Dr. Glynn's help he'd be gone in weeks. His mind had been fixed on tying up loose ends—handling the threat to his company, securing his family's future, and preserving his legacy.

But Dr. Chow's call changed everything. Now, there's a real chance he won't have to put his family through that brutal conversation about ALS and assisted dying. Twenty-seven minutes into a thirty-minute MRI, Liam dares to hope the scan will show he doesn't have ALS. That he might actually live.

He should feel as overjoyed as Scrooge on Christmas morning, but he doesn't. The uncertainty gnaws at him. He still has no clue what's behind his worsening symptoms. The idea that someone might have tampered with his original MRI and other tests points to something far bigger—a conspiracy involving people with serious power, resources, and deadly intentions.

The machine quiets, and a voice crackles through the headphones. "We're all done, Mr. Hirsch," the tech says.

As Liam changes back into his clothes, he reflects on the steps he's taken to cover his tracks since discovering the bogus MRI. He bought burner phones and laptops for himself and Andrea, using public Wi-Fi in a coffee shop to research private MRI facilities in Vancouver—Canada, not the town in Washington. He needed a place that stored data locally, avoiding the cloud. After finding an MRI clinic that met his criteria, he repeated the process to find a private lab for his bloodwork with the same constraints.

Despite the worsening numbness in his feet, Liam rose at four thirty this morning, driving two hours north through pounding rain along I-5 to the US-Canada border. After crossing, he continued another thirty miles into downtown Vancouver to reach the MRI facility.

Now, as he leaves the changing room, the balding technician hands him an old-fashioned disk in a clear plastic case. "These are your images, as requested, Mr. Hirsch."

"Thanks," Liam says, wondering when he last saw, let alone held, a CD. "I was told the radiologist would review the images with me now."

"Yes, absolutely. I'll take you to Dr. van Sant's office."

The tech leads Liam down a short hallway to a dimly lit room where a graying middle-aged man sits behind a desk, two large screens glowing on the wall. One is filled with three-dimensional images of a human brain and spine, looking like something out of his son's favorite sci-fi series.

"Welcome," Dr. van Sant says, his friendly voice tinged with a South African accent. "Eager to see how the sausage is made?"

"I suppose you could say that." Liam points to the screen. "Is that me?"

"It is indeed. And you're quite photogenic."

Liam forces a smile. He knows little about spinal anatomy, but two lower vertebrae in his back look slightly misshapen compared to the others. He points to the anomaly. "Are those my old fractures?"

"Indeed." Dr. van Sant clicks his mouse, zooming in on the bottom four vertebrae. "These guys—L3 and L4—aren't as tall as the others. Indicates old compression fractures. They were crushed a bit. And that whiter thickening is scar tissue from new bone growth. We see these fractures all the time in the elderly, but for someone with such strong bones, it must have been quite the injury. A fall?"

Liam nods. "My piton pulled out of the rock face, and I dropped almost twenty feet onto my ass."

The doctor laughs heartily. "Ah, a fellow climber. Respect. But be careful with those pegs—they can be tricky."

"Apparently." Liam nods to the screens. "Do the images show anything else?"

"A few things, yes. To start with, your bones are strong. You've got the spine of a thirty-year-old, which is impressive for a guy pushing fifty."

Liam doesn't care about that. "Anything else about the spine itself?"

"You do have a small issue with some of your nerve roots."

Liam's stomach drops at the mention of his nerves. "As in ALS?"

"ALS?" Dr. van Sant grimaces. "No, no. You've got a couple of bulging discs at L4-L5 and L5-S1 that are compressing the nerves."

Liam exhales in relief. "Could that cause twitching and burning in my hands and feet?"

"Oh, no, I don't think so. They're fairly minor, and the nerve roots don't appear inflamed."

"I see. But no evidence of ALS? You're sure?"

"With ALS, we'd expect hyperintensity on T2-weighted imaging along the corticospinal tracts—" Dr. van Sant stops himself, smiling wryly. "Gibberish, huh? Easier if I show you."

He clicks his mouse, and a grayish oval-shaped structure appears on the screen. Liam takes a moment to recognize it. "Is that a cross-section of my spine?"

"Your spinal cord, yes." Dr. van Sant zooms in. "I'm moving up along your cervical spine—your neck—until we reach where the spinal cord transitions into the brain stem." He points to a discrete lighter gray area near the front. "This is your corticospinal tract. In most ALS cases, this region would light up, but yours is completely normal."

"Does that rule out ALS?"

Dr. van Sant raises an eyebrow, clearly wondering why Liam is so fixated on the disease. "Not with certainty, no. If you had changes, we could almost confirm ALS. But without them, we can't be one hundred percent sure you don't have it."

"And there's nothing else in my MRI to explain my symptoms? The muscle twitches, the burning numbness in my hands and feet, the clumsiness?"

"Honestly, no. But my job is to read the images, Mr. Hirsch. Smarter folks than me, like neurologists, interpret the results clinically."

"OK. Well, thank you, Dr. van Sant, for your time and expertise."

"Anytime," he says with a sweep of his arm.

Liam heads for the door, but just as he's about to close it, Dr. van Sant calls out, "I'm not half-bad at my job, Mr. Hirsch. I'd like to think that more than nine times out of ten, I'd spot something if it were there. And your spinal cord is pristine. To me, this does not look like ALS."

For Liam, that's evidence enough, which means someone went to extreme lengths to deceive him into believing he has the disease—someone who knew him well enough to predict he wouldn't endure the indignity of a slow decline and would instead opt for a quicker death through euthanasia. But who? How? And why?

Liam thinks of Rudy and his smug references to karma. Could Rudy have decided to tip the cosmic scales? But he couldn't have masterminded something this elaborate on his own, not without access to massive computing power. Even if Nellie was helping him, her expertise is in security and defense, not this.

Liam knows he can't rule out the possibility of others in his company being involved. In Andrea's relatively brief investigation, she's already uncovered deceit among his senior team, any of whom might have a motive for wanting him out of the way.

And then there's the technology. Altering his medical records would take serious computing power—something only a sophisticated government agency or advanced AI could pull off. But what if AI was more involved than he thought? What if the algorithms running on TransScend's servers had flagged him as a threat? People have been warning for years that self-learning AI could evolve into something more—artificial general intelligence, with the ability to act on its own. Could that be happening now?

Snap out of it! It's ridiculous to think machines are targeting him on their own. He needs to focus on what matters most: figuring out what's really wrong with him.

CHAPTER 26

Dr. Chow steps into the exam room, his white lab coat crisp over a neatly pressed shirt and a navy tie dotted with subtle polka dots, the picture of old-school professionalism. "Good afternoon, Mr. Hirsch," he says with a nod, quietly closing the door behind him.

Before Dr. Chow can say another word, Liam thrusts an envelope containing Dr. van Sant's report into his hand. On the outside, scrawled in hurried writing, are the words: "URGENT: Please turn off all electronics—phone, tablet, computer, etc."

Dr. Chow frowns at the note, his eyes flicking to Liam's, gauging the seriousness—or sanity—of his patient. Still, without a word, he reaches into his coat pocket, pulls out his phone, and powers it down.

"Thank you," Liam says. "No computer?"

"Not in the exam room, no."

The irony isn't lost on Liam—he, a tech CEO and AI devotee, asking someone to unplug from electronics—but he has never had more reason to mistrust anything or anyone. Yet, he fully trusts Dr. Chow. If the neurologist hadn't caught the discrepancy in his original MRI, Liam would still be planning his own death right now.

"I'm sure this seems insane," Liam says, "but there's a reason for all of this."

Dr. Chow sits down on the nearby stool, the envelope still in his hand. "Why don't you explain?"

Liam nods toward the envelope. "That's my MRI report. From Vancouver."

"You went to Canada?" Dr. Chow's frown deepens as he pulls out the report, scanning it quickly. His eyes narrow in disbelief, and he shakes his head. "This . . . this is nothing like your original report."

"That's because the first one wasn't mine," Liam says. "Someone swapped it to make it look like I had ALS."

Dr. Chow looks up, his face skeptical. "How do you know it wasn't just a clerical error?"

"Have you ever seen an error like that? Where someone gets the wrong report, and it just happens to confirm the rare diagnosis their doctor suspects?"

A beat of silence, then: "No."

"It wasn't a mistake. It was deliberate. Which tells me I probably don't have ALS."

Chow's face tightens. "It's not only the MRI, Mr. Hirsch. The biopsy, the EMG, the nerve conduction studies . . . they all pointed to ALS. Together, they were irrefutable."

"And they were all probably doctored too."

"Doctored?" Dr. Chow adjusts his glasses, a tinge of incredulity in his voice. "That doesn't happen. Not in my world."

"I know it sounds far-fetched, but I believe someone falsified all of my diagnostics to make it appear as if I had ALS."

"Really, Mr. Hirsch, this . . . this sounds like something out of a *Mission: Impossible* movie."

"I work in AI, Dr. Chow. Trust me. It's possible."

"You're the CEO of TransScend, aren't you?" Chow's face brightens for a moment. "My son's doing his PhD in computer science at Stanford. His thesis is on AI language interpreters."

"Stanford? Impressive. They're leaders in AI research." Liam taps the MRI report. "But this has nothing to do with academics."

"What exactly is 'this'?"

"A sophisticated corporate sabotage. Either to get rid of me or to destroy TransScend. Possibly both."

"And you believe whoever's responsible accessed my records to do it?" Dr. Chow's voice carries a note of skepticism. "Is that why you had me switch off the electronics?"

"I don't know if they hacked your records directly. They might have altered the results at the source. But you're the city's top expert, so they probably knew I'd come to you." Liam looks around the room. "Hence the electronics blackout."

Dr. Chow lets out a low chuckle, though his skepticism remains. "This doesn't explain your physical symptoms. The classic signs of ALS."

"That's what I'm trying to figure out," Liam says, leaning forward. "If someone wanted me to believe I had ALS, then the symptoms had to be induced somehow."

"Are you suggesting you were poisoned, Mr. Hirsch?" His voice rises. "With a neurotoxin?"

"Are there any that would fit?"

"This is all so . . ." He wavers before motioning to the examining table. "Before I comment on any of this, I need to examine you again."

Liam sits on the table, and Dr. Chow runs him through a battery of physical tests—ones that have become all too familiar. But today, Liam performs worse than ever. He stumbles, loses his balance, and can't stand on tiptoes on either foot. The sharp and dull probes blur together in his numb fingertips. It's as disheartening as it is terrifying.

Chow returns to the stool, a shadow of concern crossing his face. "Your motor function has deteriorated and there's been more muscle wasting, especially in your calves and shoulders. That would fit with ALS." He hesitates. "But the decreased sensation in your palms and feet . . . that's new. It's more consistent with polyneuropathy than ALS."

"Poly-what?"

"Polyneuropathy. It means damage to the peripheral nerves—the ones that connect your spinal cord to your arms and legs. Think of them as the wiring that sends messages between your brain and your body."

"And that wouldn't show up on an MRI?"

"Not on the type we took of your spine, no."

"If it's polyneuropathy, would the damage be permanent?"

"Depends on the cause. But not necessarily, no."

"Could poisoning cause these findings?"

Chow strokes his chin. "Potentially. Some neurotoxins can mimic ALS. It's rare, but possible."

Liam's pulse hammers in his ears. "Which ones?"

"Lead is the most common neurotoxin. But we already tested for that—" Dr. Chow cuts himself off, his face lighting with a small grin. "Oh, you think those lab tests were doctored, too, don't you?"

"I do. Are there any other toxins to consider?"

"Yes. Mercury poisoning, although I would expect more neuropsychiatric findings, like memory problems. Also, organophosphates—they're found in certain pesticides. Or even manganese toxicity."

"Manganese?"

"It's mostly seen in industrial workers—miners, welders—who inhale the fumes. But you could also ingest it or absorb it through the skin."

Liam's guts clench. "You're saying I could be breathing it, eating it, or touching it?"

"Exactly. But we'd need specialized lab tests to confirm."

"I left samples with a private lab in Vancouver," Liam says. "Blood, urine, hair—all of it."

"Oh, I see."

"They're waiting on my instructions. I was hoping you'd tell me which tests to run."

Dr. Chow reaches for a notepad, writes out a list of tests in impeccable script, and hands it to Liam. It's all medical jargon to Liam, but it still makes his heart pound. "If I've been poisoned, would the damage be permanent?"

"*If* you have, it would depend on the toxin, Mr. Hirsch. But it's likely you would recover at least some function. That is, provided . . ."

"Yes?"

"You stop the ongoing exposure to the toxin."

If only I knew how I was being exposed. But all Liam says as he rises from the exam table is "One more thing, Dr. Chow. Please don't document any of this in my file."

"I don't intend to record anything of our interaction today," he says, still looking slightly bewildered.

"Thank you—for everything, Dr. Chow. What you noticed on my supposed MRI . . . it just might have saved my life."

Dr. Chow nods, lost in his own thoughts.

Liam digs another burner phone out of his pocket. "This must all sound over-the-top, Dr. Chow. I get it." He holds out the device. "But until I've learned more, can you please use this if you need to reach me? Or vice versa?"

Dr. Chow reluctantly accepts the phone, his face clouded with worry. "Despite the mix-up with the MRIs, I still find it very hard to believe that this is a case of intentional poisoning. But if it is, am I or my staff in any kind of danger?"

"No," Liam says with a reassuring smile. *At least, I hope not.*

CHAPTER 27

Andrea hasn't been back to her dad's townhouse since she cleared out his personal belongings. Despite the empty drawers, the office looks the same. She already transferred the note her dad had left her on his computer to a thumb drive, but sitting in the chair where he wrote it, she's tempted to open it again and finish reading.

Her hands freeze on the keyboard. The first paragraph was hard enough to get through. Her father's words—overflowing with love, telling her she was more than he deserved—crushed her. But it was the second paragraph, which began, "There are things you need to understand, starting with your mother . . . ," that made her shut the computer down. What could there be to understand about a woman who walked out on her seven-year-old daughter?

Two counselors Andrea had seen as an adult, including the one after Max's betrayal, had both zeroed in on what they labeled as her "abandonment issues." One even brought up something called a "mother wound," which hit a little too close. But boiling her entire personality down to one childhood trauma felt too simplistic. Even if her mom had stayed, Andrea is convinced she would still value loyalty above everything else. It's just who she is. Besides, who doesn't fear being abandoned?

A knock on the door breaks her thoughts. She's relieved for the excuse to get up from the computer to answer it. Liam stands there, clad in his usual activewear—this time a green jacket with black pants. Lululemon, probably. He still looks gaunt, but there's something different about him today. Is it an air of hope? Or maybe just the absence of the despair that shadowed their previous encounters? Either way, he seems more alive.

In the living room, Andrea sinks into her dad's overstuffed chair while Liam gingerly lowers himself onto the couch across from her. "Thanks for meeting here," he says.

"Starbucks not safe anymore?"

"I don't trust public spaces."

"Why not?"

"The effort it took to make me think I had ALS was too elaborate for them to just be messing with medical tests. They're probably tracking me—watching where I go, who I meet."

"You think they know about me?"

"Maybe. That's why I left my phone in the car two miles away and grabbed a cab here."

"And why you insisted I bring only my burner phone with me?"

He nods. "Until we figure out who's behind this, I have to live a double life. Pretend all is normal while watching every word I say and everything I touch, eat, or even breathe."

"You still don't think we have enough to go to the police?"

"Not yet. I've got nothing but a single mislabeled MRI. That could be chalked up to a mistake. If I go public with this now, TransScend's stock will tank—far worse than it already has."

"Isn't your life more important?"

"That's debatable," he jokes. "But honestly, Andrea, we're in a better position to figure this out than the cops. Especially if the people behind it think we're still in the dark."

Andrea isn't convinced. "And who are they, exactly?"

"Rudy and Nellie? Or maybe someone we haven't even thought of yet."

"I'm not making much progress on my end," she admits. "I spent half of yesterday staked outside Rudy's place. He never left his condo. And Nellie's like a ghost online."

"You connected them to each other. That's huge."

"We'll see." She sighs. "I did find something on one of the other execs. Could be nothing, though."

"Who?"

"Ramona Bale. Well, actually, her wife, Jennifer Chew. You know her?"

Liam shrugs. "Not too well. She's pretty shy, hard to get to know."

"Well, she used to be a hardcore climate activist. Part of a group called Earth First!"

"Used to be?"

"The group disbanded after they were linked to a cyberattack on an oil company. It was a sophisticated hack, too. They corrupted files and leaked some very embarrassing information."

Liam sits up straighter. "And Jennifer was involved?"

"No proof, but she's got the IT skills. And she used to work for a pharmaceutical company."

"Christ! So she knows her way around confidential records *and* drugs."

"Exactly."

"And meanwhile, her wife might be defrauding the company."

"*Might* is the key word. But I'll keep an eye on them both."

Liam groans. "I wish our suspect list was getting shorter, not longer."

"It will," Andrea says without much conviction.

Liam's eyes roam the room. "Did your dad live here long?"

"Almost twenty years. He always wanted to live in the city. Sold the house in the burbs basically the second I left for college."

"You two were close, huh?"

"Very. I'm an only child. And he was my only parent."

"When did your mom leave?"

"Just after my seventh birthday."

"I'm sorry."

"It's OK. I barely remember her. Besides, I had a great childhood. My dad made sure of that." She surprises herself with how easily she's sharing things that she normally keeps locked up.

"My dad stuck around, but he wasn't really there," Liam says. "Always too busy 'scheming and dreaming,' as my mom used to say."

"Not my dad. I could always count on him. At least, until the end."

"Hope I'm half as good a dad to my kids as yours was to you."

Her voice wavers. "Tell me about them."

"They're twins. Fifteen. Total opposites. Ava's carefree, never a worry. Cole's obsessed with soccer and sometimes acts like the world's sitting on his shoulders."

"Are they close?"

"They can drive each other nuts, but yeah, they've got each other's backs."

"Which one's more like you?"

"Definitely Cole."

"Then he'll be fine."

Liam lets out a bitter laugh. "Not sure if that's a blessing or a curse."

"We both know the answer to that," she says.

Liam clears his throat. "I don't want to cross a line, Andrea, but . . . sounds like you're still wrestling with your dad's—"

"Suicide?"

He nods.

"He was in constant pain, Liam. Trapped in that wheelchair, and it just kept getting worse. By the end, his quality of life was gone." Her voice cracks. "But he had me. And he never said a word. Not even the night before he . . . when we had dinner here together."

The memory claws at her. How he devoured every bite, how he kept telling old stories, filling the room with laughter. When he hugged her goodbye, holding on just a little longer than usual, he seemed so content. She was relieved, thinking he was finally himself again. It never crossed her mind that it was to be his last supper. But the peace that meal gave him left her with none after she learned he was gone.

"He was protecting you," Liam says softly.

"From what?"

"From the guilt. If you didn't know what he was planning, you couldn't blame yourself later for not stopping him. He didn't want that on you."

"Didn't I deserve the chance to at least try?"

"Do you think you could've changed his mind?"

"No . . . probably not. But I could've said goodbye. Properly."

"I get that. And I can't imagine how selfish it feels. But before I found out I didn't have ALS, there wasn't a thing my family could've said or done to stop me."

"Imagine if you'd gone through with it," she murmurs. "When you weren't even dying."

"I might not be dying of ALS, but . . ." Liam's expression sharpens. "If we don't figure this out soon, I'll still end up in the ground."

CHAPTER 28

Liam sits at the kitchen counter, skimming through work emails on his laptop, trying to maintain focus. Whenever he uses this computer or his old phone, he forces himself to stay in character, pretending he still believes he has ALS. Keeping up the act is crucial if he has any hope of saving his company. Or himself.

He opens an email from Dr. Glynn. Her tone is warm, but the underlying concern is clear, a subtle echo of their last session. He can't let her suspect that he's not planning to go through with MAiD, or that hopefully he won't need to. After a few failed drafts, he finally settles on: "I'm coping all right, all things considered. I've reflected on your advice, but I'd still like to receive the medication at the end of the seven-day waiting period. I haven't decided on the timing yet, but I will keep you updated."

He pulls out his burner phone, checking for any updates from Andrea or the lab in Vancouver. Nothing. He tucks it away just as Ava strolls into the kitchen, still in her school uniform.

"Is Cole at practice?" she asks, rummaging through the fridge.

"Good morning, sunshine," Liam says, closing his laptop.

"Morning," she replies, rolling her eyes. "So, Cole . . . practice?"

"Yep, I dropped him off."

Her face lights up. "Then I get a ride, too?"

He points at himself, mock serious. "This bus only runs once a morning."

Ava groans. "Of course, preferential treatment for the Chosen One, aka the Golden Boy."

"As if. My favorite depends on who's less snarky at any given moment."

She smirks. "Nice try. Not worried, though. Dads always pick their daughters in the end."

"The nice ones, maybe."

"Whatever." She grabs a jug of orange juice and, out of nowhere, asks, "Hey, what's TransScend got to do with that Senate race in New England?"

Liam tenses. He's never known Ava to pay attention to national politics. "Where did you hear that?"

"It's all over TikTok. Some senator with a USB stick, sweating like crazy. It's totally sus. Gross politician vibes."

"It wasn't real, Ava," Liam says, his heart sinking as he realizes the deepfake has already morphed into memes and become part of pop culture.

"Somebody made it using HisStory, right?"

"Yeah. We're still trying to figure out who."

Ava shrugs, losing interest. "What time are we climbing Saturday?"

Liam's stomach drops, the burning in his hands and feet flaring as if in response. "I tweaked my back. I can't climb, but I'll still take you."

"I'm not climbing without you."

"How about breakfast instead?"

"Deal." As she closes the fridge door, she glances back at him. "Mom left one of those gross anti-aging smoothies for you. Want it?"

"No, thanks. Coffee's enough this morning." Liam now only eats or drinks what he can trace from purchase to plate. The thought crosses his mind that the smoothies might be the source of the poison—implicating Celeste. But he quickly dismisses it. Even if he believed her to be capable of poisoning him, which he doesn't, how could she pull off something this elaborate—faking the records, the diagnosis, everything? No way.

"Your loss." Ava fills a bottle with juice and tucks it into her knapsack. "Guess I'll take this to go, since my ride bailed."

Liam watches her saunter off, chuckling to himself. "Love you," he calls out, but she's already out the door.

Alone again, he pulls out the burner phone. Still no messages. He turns back to his work laptop, skimming through the flood of emails, but his mind drifts. Just days ago, he'd accepted his death. Now all he wants is to fight for his life. The possibility of a second chance to watch his kids grow up fills him with a renewed sense of urgency.

But the symptoms are still there, relentless. Earlier, he nearly fell in the shower—if he hadn't caught himself, he would've smashed his head on the tiles. Next time, he might not be so lucky.

Focus! he tells himself, running through a mindfulness exercise to calm himself. He cycles through his senses: *the white cabinets in his view, the hum of the fridge, the lingering scent of coffee, the minty taste of toothpaste, the tingling numbness in his hands.*

Damn it.

His thoughts drift back to the plot against him. Whoever's behind it had to have known that once diagnosed with ALS, he would opt for MAiD sooner rather than later. But how could they have been so sure of his response?

And then it hits him—*the Napa retreat last summer.*

The memory surges back: a private dinner at a winery, TransScend's execs and their spouses celebrating a record year of sales. They were toasting when Ellis's wife, Nina, brought up her eighty-five-year-old grandmother, who'd had a serious stroke and now lived in a nursing home near them.

"Love the old gal to bits," Ellis said, cheeks flushed from wine. "But she can't talk, walk, or use her right arm. That's no life. I'd choose a bullet over that kind of existence any day."

Nina turned to the others almost apologetically. "Granna still has quality of life. She listens to music and audiobooks. And she loves when the kids visit."

Ramona's wife, Jennifer, chimed in. "But at least she has options.

We're lucky to live in a state with death-with-dignity laws. Where she could choose to end her life after such a devastating stroke. Not everyone's so fortunate."

Nina grimaced. "Granna doesn't want that."

"Full respect for your grandmother's positivity," Liam said, feeling uncharacteristically disinhibited by a rare third glass of wine. "But if I were in her condition? I wouldn't even have to think about it. I couldn't end my life soon enough!"

"Even if your brain was still sharp?" Nellie asked.

"Especially then! Losing my body while my mind's intact? No, thank you. I'd opt for quick medical death in a heartbeat."

"It's true." Celeste laughed. "Life wouldn't be worth living for Liam if he couldn't climb any more mountains."

Liam winces at the memory. *Jesus! They all know exactly how I feel about MAiD, don't they?*

CHAPTER 29

Sam barges into Liam's office without knocking. His stride falters when he sees Liam's hands. "What the fuck are those?" He points at Liam's gloved fingers.

Liam lifts one hand from the keyboard, flexing the thin white nylon material covering his fingers. "Doctor's orders. Allergies, apparently— something about contact dermatitis." It's the same line he fed his executive assistant, Morris, but the real reason is his fear of potentially absorbing toxins if they happen to be coating his keyboard or lingering on other surfaces.

Sam pulls a face. "Not exactly the epitome of manliness."

Liam eyes Sam's half-moon glasses. "As opposed to those?"

"Touché." Sam chuckles but then shivers slightly. "Why the hell is it freezing in here?"

Liam gestures to the open windows. "Airing out the room. Same reason."

"Allergies? Sabbaticals? And now lady gloves?" Sam groans as he drops into the chair across from Liam. "Who are you? It's like you've been body-snatched."

Liam forces a smile, though the lie eats at him. He can't trust anyone right now, not even Sam—not until he and Andrea untangle the full conspiracy. And even if he wanted to confide in his old friend, his office isn't the place to do it. "Are you here to just mock me?"

"Mostly." Sam smirks. "But I've got a couple of updates, too."

"Like who made that deepfake in New Hampshire and then leaked word of TheirStory's release?"

Sam shakes his head, frustration creasing his brow. "Not yet. Still digging."

"What about Nellie? Anything?"

"Her files are squeaky-clean. No surprise, right? If anyone could cover their tracks, it's our head of cybersecurity."

Liam grunts. "No doubt."

Sam leans forward, a gleam in his eye. "But my old-school sleuthing might've turned up something."

Liam perks up. "Go on."

"Nellie's assistant, Dione—usually useless as a screen door on a submarine—noticed something odd. Nellie's been scheduling gaps in her calendar lately."

"Gaps?"

"Yeah, off-site, personal stuff. Totally out of character for her. She's all work, all the time. Dione thinks it could be health-related."

"You don't?"

"She looks healthy as a horse to me. Or a miniature pony, anyway." Sam clicks his tongue again. "Maybe she's out interviewing with competitors or meeting with reporters."

Or maybe she's busy conspiring with Rudy.

"This whole thing's insane, Prez. I'm spying on our head of security to see if she's responsible for the exact kind of breach she's paid to prevent." Sam shoots Liam a hard look. "We both know Nellie sees TheirStory as some kind of doomsday app. Why keep her around if she's philosophically against the project? Why not just cut her loose now?"

"I'm not ready to make that call yet. Even if she's involved, firing her won't fix anything. She already knows too much. Our best play is to contain her."

"Contain her?" Sam raises an eyebrow. "You're not talking Mafia-level containment, are you?"

"Funny. No. I mean it's best to keep your enemies close." Though Liam has the sinking feeling his enemies might already be too close.

Sam throws up his hands. "Well, guess it's decided then."

"For now."

Sam rubs his temples. "At least there's one bright spot."

"What's that?"

"Our books are balanced."

"Even last quarter's irregularities?"

"Yep."

"Then how do you explain two unauthorized payments to EANC Consulting? Over a hundred grand."

"They weren't unauthorized."

"I didn't authorize them."

"Ramona did. Her signature's on the form."

Liam stiffens. "What the hell is EANC Consulting? And why didn't Ramona mention those payments when I asked her about the irregularity?" *No wonder I don't trust anyone here.*

Sam shrugs like it's no big deal. "No clue what EANC is, but it doesn't matter, Boss."

"How could that possibly not matter?"

"Because we got paid back."

"What?"

"In the current budget, we've got a surplus for the exact same amount. To the penny. Check the next quarterly report—everything's balanced. No harm, no foul."

Liam's mind spins. "So you're telling me EANC Consulting refunded us the full amount?"

"Either that, or the whole thing was misfiled in the first place."

"Does that make any sense to you?"

Sam waves it off. "Bottom line is no one's stealing from us, Boss."

Liam finds little comfort in that. The whole thing reeks. Who runs an illicit charge through the books only to repay it in the next period? And why would Ramona cover it up?

Sam points at Liam's hands again. "Listen, between these Michael

Jackson gloves and your whole vibe lately, you've got to admit, you haven't been yourself."

The urge to unload on Sam, to tell him everything, is almost overpowering. The diagnosis. The affair. The crushing weight of it all. But he's determined to stick with the plan he and Andrea laid out. "It's been a lot—dealing with the books, the leaks, the launch pushback. I just need a break."

"We're all feeling the pressure, Boss. Especially since we've got even more riding on TheirStory than we did on HisStory." Sam studies Liam's face. "But something's off with you. What aren't you telling me?"

Liam only shrugs.

Sam gets halfway out of his chair, then flops back down. "There's something else I've got to get off my chest."

"Go on."

"This sudden world tour with your family? I think it's a shit idea. I hope you know that."

"I had an inkling, yeah."

"But, fine. Your life, your call."

Liam waits, knowing Sam isn't done.

"But this whole *Apprentice*-style CEO audition? What the hell, man? I've been with you since day one. I helped you build this company from scratch. Why wouldn't you just name me from the get-go?"

Liam sighs. "You know I have to get the board's approval."

Sam snorts. "You could pick Kim Jong Un, and the board would rubber-stamp him. We both know your word's law around here."

Since Liam no longer plans to step down, there's no point letting Sam stew in uncertainty or doubt. "When the time comes, the job will be yours, Sam. But I want it to look legitimate. We've got to do our due diligence, or people will talk."

Sam cracks a grin. "I can live with that."

But can I? Liam wonders as his foot twitches, the numbness creeping up his leg.

CHAPTER 30

Andrea sits in her car, parked outside the charming old Victorian on a quiet, tree-lined street in Seattle's historic Queen Anne neighborhood, envy gnawing at her. This area, with its lush greenery, water views, and quaint cafés, has always been her favorite. The heritage homes—with their colorful façades, conical towers, and intricate spindles—remind her of San Francisco's Painted Ladies. What hurts most is how close she came to living in her dream home only a few blocks away.

Max, with his architect's eye and love for Victorian-era houses, had put down an offer on a hundred-and-twenty-year-old gem without even consulting her. She remembers the day so vividly. They drove across town in a downpour, and Max slowed in front of a blue turreted house on a sloping street. Under their shared umbrella, he nodded toward the house and grinned. "I could live here if I had to. You?"

"What do you think?" She squeezed his arm tighter. "How many times have we fantasized about a place exactly like this?"

"True," Max said with a casual shrug. "But this time, we actually own it."

Andrea laughed, pushing him playfully. "Yeah, right."

"Well, almost. We won't remove the subjects on the offer for another two weeks. Not until after the inspection."

"Stop teasing, Max!"

"Who's teasing, babe?"

She could hardly believe it. "How can we afford this?"

"My parents are helping with the down payment."

Her heart jumped. "No . . ."

"They're lending us the difference."

"We can't accept that, Max, can we?" she asked, though her heart was already set on the house, imagining how their furniture would look on the vintage hardwood floors.

"Too late." His grin widened. "I already did."

"Are you serious?" she cried.

"I couldn't let it slip away, babe. This was meant to be our home."

Max let the umbrella fall as he hugged her, spinning her in circles. As rain pelted her face and wind whipped her hair, Andrea wondered if she'd ever been happier. She was about to move into her dream house with the man she'd fallen for on their first date. Her doubts about his trustworthiness melted away, and she couldn't wait to start a family with him in their new home.

But she never did. The dream crumbled only nine days later. After rushing her dad home early from a family reunion in Tampa, thanks to his swollen feet and shortness of breath, she found Max in bed with another woman. Not just any woman—his colleague, Tanya, his so-called work wife. Even in that soul-crushing moment, the irony wasn't lost on Andrea. Her life's work was catching cheaters, yet she caught her own partner in the act without even trying.

Andrea pushes the painful memory aside. It's not just the loss of her dream home that stings; it's also the dead ends piling up in her investigation. She's been staking out Ramona's place for hours with nothing to show for it. Yesterday was no better—an entire day spent outside Ziegler's condo without a single sighting. Long hours and disappointments come with the job, but this case feels different, more pressing, far more urgent. Liam's time is running out. And it feels as if hers is, too.

She saw it at their last meeting—the way he struggled just to get up from her dad's old couch. His condition is deteriorating. She urged him to leave, to flee the country and escape the toxic exposure they suspect is slowly killing him. But Liam refused. He's convinced the only way to protect his family and save himself is by exposing whoever's behind it. But how much time does he have before the damage becomes incapacitating? Or irreversible?

Andrea opens her laptop and reviews her notes. The list of suspects isn't getting shorter. If anything, it's growing—especially with EANC Consulting added to the mix. She's had no luck identifying the principals behind the offshore company, which is registered in the British Virgin Islands. The owners are hidden behind a web of privacy laws, designed to attract those who prize anonymity.

Studying the list again, she notices that the first two letters of the company's name match Ellis's initials. Out of curiosity, she googles his name along with EANC, but the results aren't relevant. On a whim, she tries his wife's name—Nina—and discovers that she used her maiden name, Cheston, during her modeling days.

Andrea's pulse quickens. What are the odds that the company's initials match all four of theirs? She racks her brain, trying to recall a formula from a long-ago statistics course. The numbers don't matter—it's too much to be coincidence.

She digs deeper, searching for "Nina Cheston and EANC," but nothing relevant comes up. Then she tries "Nina Asher and EANC." Again, nothing. Finally, she drops the surname and searches simply for Nina's first name.

Bingo.

Among the search results, she finds a registration page for a Little League baseball team in Bellevue, where the Ashers live. On the contact page, in bright, playful font, is a note: "If your little slugger is interested in playing, drop Nina a line at EANC1989@gmx.com."

CHAPTER 31

Liam stares at the grim chart on his laptop as the blender whirs in the background, the sound grating on his already frayed nerves. "I don't think that smoothie of yours is getting any smoother," he shouts over the noise.

Celeste, still in her tennis outfit, turns off the blender with a playful grin. "Someone's in a mood."

He barely looks up. "Did you check the share price today?"

"I try not to." She pours the greenish-brown mixture into a glass.

"That's one approach," he sighs. "TransScend is down twenty-seven percent from its high two weeks ago."

"All because of that deepfake incident?"

"And the leak about TheirStory's launch. The bad press. All those doomsday predictions."

Celeste takes a sip of her concoction and raises an eyebrow. "You sure you don't want one?"

Liam shakes his head. He's never been able to stomach her smoothies; they always taste like dirt. Besides, he's not touching anything he hasn't bought or made himself. Every sip of water is from a sealed bottle he opens himself, and he scrutinizes every bite he eats—not that he has eaten much of late. The idea that something from his own kitchen could have been poisoned briefly crosses his mind before he dismisses it. *No. Celeste wouldn't.* Or at the very least, she couldn't.

"I'm on a strict smoothie-free cleanse," he says with a half-hearted grin.

"Cute," she says, her tone casual but her eyes studying him closely. "You still think the leak was sabotage?"

He turns his laptop to show her the sharp drop in TransScend's stock price. "It sure as hell feels like it."

Celeste tilts her head thoughtfully. "But what if they're right, Liam?"

"Who? The saboteurs?"

"No. The doomsday prophets. The people saying it's too dangerous."

"They're wrong," he says, though even he can hear the hesitation in his voice. "But even if they weren't, TheirStory or something like it is inevitable. If we don't do it, someone else will."

"That's your justification? Beat them to the punch?"

"It's reality, Celeste. You can't stop this kind of technology. All we can do is try to guide its development responsibly."

"And you believe it's being handled responsibly?"

He folds his arms. "Yes. We've built safeguards. Confidentiality is airtight, and we've got limits on what users can upload. The app flags dangerous behavior—violent or suicidal thoughts trigger interventions. There are fail-safes to block hate speech, misinformation."

Celeste sets her glass down and crosses the room, her playful demeanor fading. "But how do you stop people from manipulating reality, like they did in New Hampshire?"

"That was HisStory, not TheirStory. And it didn't alter reality, it altered perceptions."

"Which is all that matters in the end." She sighs. "Nellie told me TheirStory was better. Even harder to separate fact from fiction."

"Nellie told you about TheirStory?"

"At the Christmas party. To be more accurate, I asked her about it. All she said was that because TheirStory is so much more sophisticated, it's that much more of a security threat."

Especially if Nellie turns out to be responsible for the leak. But he keeps the thought to himself.

Celeste sits down beside him, her expression softening. "Liam, I've always been your biggest fan. When I started working for you, I was blown away by the promise of what we were building. I believed AI could change the world for the better—curing diseases, ending hunger . . ."

"And now?"

Her eyes drop. "Now I'm not so sure."

"Because of the deepfakes?"

"Forget about the tech falling into the wrong hands. Think about the psychological impact it has on people even when used the way it's meant to be."

"That's the whole point, Cel. It's supposed to comfort users. Let them reconnect with those they've lost. Ease the pain."

"What if it does the opposite?"

His curiosity piqued, Liam leans in. "What are you talking about?"

"Have you spent much time with the app?"

"Sure. I've tested it."

"Did you use your dad as a subject?"

Liam shakes his head. "No. Myself."

Her eyes widen. "You spoke to yourself?"

"I was curious."

"What did it say?"

Liam thinks back to his avatar's unsettling insights about Celeste. "It was a little glitchy. It didn't know quite how to handle talking to its real-life counterpart."

She shakes her head. "Glitchy wasn't my experience."

"When you spoke to Ella?" he asks, referring to her childhood best friend. "You never really said much about how it went."

"It was . . . intense."

"Can you be more specific?"

"Her avatar was so realistic, Liam. It was like I was sitting across from Ella again. For a while, I forgot I wasn't actually talking to the real her."

"That's how it's supposed to work."

Celeste lowers her head. "Ella told me how much she wished she'd met Ava and Cole. How she would've loved to have her own kids who could have grown up with ours."

Liam lays a hand on hers, his touch gentle. "Didn't you appreciate reconnecting with her after all these years?"

"I suppose." Her eyes mist over. "Until . . ."

Sensing she needs time, he caresses her fingers and waits.

"Until I asked the avatar about the night Ella died."

"Oh."

"Ella—the avatar—told me she left the party early and walked home. She never even saw the SUV coming until the drunken asshole behind the wheel swerved onto the sidewalk and pinned her into the side of a building. She said it happened so quickly, she didn't feel a thing." Celeste snorts bitterly. "I guess the AI would've inferred that from news accounts."

"It would have, yeah."

This is new territory for them. Celeste sometimes reminisces about Ella, who was like a sister to her. Some of the stories, like the time Ella's chocolate Lab accidentally ripped Celeste's bikini top off her in the middle of a tenth-grade pool party, are legendary. But she'd never spoken of the night Ella was killed.

"The app would've known from media reports that Ella was alone when she died," Celeste says quietly. "But it still rocked me when the avatar asked me why I wasn't with her."

"What did you tell it?"

"What could I say?" She swallows. "I should've been with Ella. If I had, maybe the driver would've seen us both. Or one of us would have spotted him. Or . . ." Her voice trembles. "Truth is, if I'd been with her, she probably wouldn't have left the party when she did."

"Cel, you can't—"

"I stayed behind because I wanted to be with Tommy."

He frowns. "Tommy?"

"A guy we both had a crush on. Her more than me." Celeste looks down, embarrassed. "I drank too much. Tommy and I ended up going upstairs together. I don't know if Ella saw us go, but she must've left soon after. And I've always wondered . . ."

Her voice trails off, and Liam feels the gravity of her guilt. "You can't blame yourself for that."

"But I do, Liam. And hearing it from her avatar made it worse. It made it real."

Liam struggles to find the right words. "Cel, the app didn't know. It was just guessing."

"But it *felt* real. That's what I'm trying to tell you, Liam. People could relive their worst regrets, their deepest guilt, and they'll be doing it with a machine that doesn't understand boundaries." She stops to swallow again. "Months later, I think about that session. The way she asked me . . . that still guts me."

He only squeezes her hand. "Sorry."

"It's fine." She wipes her eyes quickly. "I only meant it as an example."

"I get it. People are bound to have the occasional negative interactions with TheirStory. But you can't blame the app. It's only doing what it's programmed to."

"What's wrong with you, Liam?" She pulls her hand away from his, frustration coloring her voice. "The whole point of TheirStory is to allow you to communicate with people you've lost. Tell them things you didn't or couldn't in real life. But it's all fake. It's manipulation. This deathbot of yours is dangerous."

Liam is taken aback by her vehemence. "Where's this coming from?"

"I thought I'd come to terms with my guilt from that night. But now I'm not sure. What if others relive something like I did through the app? Especially if they're vulnerable or have mental health issues. Imagine the trauma it could inflict."

"How is it different from reliving it with a therapist?"

"Therapists are trained for sensitive conversations." Her eyes search his, looking for understanding. "How can a machine know when it's pushed someone too far?"

Before Liam can respond, his burner phone buzzes in his pocket. Turning away from Celeste, he pulls it out. "Hi, can I call you back? I'm just in the middle of—"

"This can't wait," Andrea says, her voice low, tense.

"What can't?"

"EANC."

"What about it?"

"It's Ellis's company!"

CHAPTER 32

Inside the living room, Liam opts for the overstuffed chair, leaving Andrea the low couch. He remembers too well the struggle he had getting up from it last time. Andrea's worried glances don't go unnoticed, and while he appreciates her concern, it only heightens his self-consciousness. Every movement feels scrutinized, and he dreads the next stumble or fumble in front of her.

"I double-checked the books," Liam says, voice tight. "The payments to Ellis's shell company, EANC, came back into TransScend's accounts as one payment. Buried deep in the sales account. EANC wasn't even mentioned. Why?"

Andrea sits cross-legged on the couch, raising a brow. "Why what?"

"Why everything!" Liam snaps, frustration boiling over. "Why risk embezzling a hundred grand, just to pay it back in the next period? And why the hell did Ramona help him cover it up?"

Andrea shrugs slightly. "Maybe they already knew you were onto them? Didn't you ask Sam to dig into the discrepancy?"

"Good theory, but the timing's wrong. The money was repaid weeks before I even spotted the irregularity."

Andrea bites her lip in thought. "Maybe it was a test run?"

"That's possible, I suppose. But why two payments totaling a hundred thousand? Why not try a single payment of something smaller, less noticeable? Like maybe five or ten grand?"

"Do you think Ramona and Ellis are in on this together?"

"How else do you explain it?"

"With Ellis's gambling problem, I get why he needs cash," Andrea replies, eyes narrowing. "But what's in it for her?"

"It doesn't make sense," Liam says, shaking his head. "She's too sharp for this. If she's involved, she wouldn't make it so easy to trace. She's a financial whiz—she'd know how to hide it better."

Andrea frowns. "Feels like desperation, doesn't it?"

"Yeah, it does." Liam shifts uncomfortably, recognizing the feeling all too well. "What about Ramona's wife, Jennifer? And that sabotage on the oil company? Maybe she's shifted to activism against AI."

Andrea shakes her head. "Nothing on her social media points that way."

"But would she advertise it, given her wife's high-profile job at an AI firm like TransScend?"

"Probably not," she concedes, meeting his gaze. "Do you think the fraud is connected to the sabotage on TheirStory? Or your poisoning?"

"I don't know. The missing money is what triggered my suspicions. Could be coincidence, but it doesn't help me trust any of my execs."

"I'm getting a little paranoid myself these days," Andrea says with a dry smile.

"And then there's Rudy and Nellie. What the hell was he doing at her place?"

Andrea shakes her head. "Wish I knew."

"Nobody would enjoy watching me fall more than him."

"Even if it meant poisoning you?"

"Especially then," Liam mutters, his tone dark. "You should've seen Rudy at his condo. That smug grin, talking about karma like it's his own personal weapon. He laughed off my offer—and it was generous. After losing two lawsuits, there's no way his finances are solid enough to just walk away from that kind of money."

"Unless he's got a better offer."

Liam's burner phone dings with a new email alert. His stomach leaps into his chest when he sees it's from the lab in Vancouver.

"What is it?" Andrea asks.

"My blood test results," Liam says, opening the email. He scrolls through the jargon, searching for something familiar. "Lead level is 'low normal,' mercury and manganese 'undetectable,' blood cholinesterase 'negative.'"

Andrea leans in. "What's the significance of that?"

Liam's heart sinks. "It means I wasn't poisoned by any of the toxins Dr. Chow thought could be responsible."

Andrea's eyes flash with concern. "Then what else could it be?"

"I'm not sure," Liam says, forwarding the email to Dr. Chow, frustration building. "It's like I'm stuck on a treadmill, pushing harder and harder, but I'm still in the same place."

She rests a hand gently on his arm. "Oh, Liam . . ."

"Maybe I'm just trying to make sense of the inevitable," he says quietly.

"The inevitable?"

"That I really might be dying."

Andrea's expression sharpens, her voice resolute. "No. Someone's behind this, Liam. We both know it. And we're going to stop them."

His phone buzzes again, jolting him. He almost drops it, fumbling to answer the call. "Hello?"

"Mr. Hirsch, it's Dr. Chow. I reviewed the blood tests you sent."

"They're negative for all the poisons you said could be involved."

"I didn't say they were the only possibilities. I said they were the most likely."

Liam's heart skips a beat. "You mean there could be others?"

Dr. Chow ignores the question. "What's interesting are the other values. Your liver and kidney functions show low-grade damage."

"But I've never had problems with my kidneys or liver."

"Exactly. It tells me someone tampered with the original results. There's no other explanation for such significant discrepancies."

"So, you believe me now?"

"I'm less skeptical, yes."

"Then what's causing the liver and kidney damage?"

"You said you don't drink or use substances, correct?"

"I barely drink at all. And I haven't touched any other drug in twenty-plus years."

"Even infectious hepatitis wouldn't explain this kidney damage," Dr. Chow says, his voice steady. "In someone healthy, who doesn't drink, the most plausible cause is exposure to an external toxin."

"In other words, a poison?"

"Yes. And while we've tested you for common ones that cause similar neurological symptoms, there are other, less well-known possibilities. Synthetic chemicals used in industrial exposure." He pauses. "Or chemical warfare agents."

Liam's mouth goes dry. "Chemical warfare?"

"Either way, Mr. Hirsch, I don't think you need a neurologist anymore."

"Who do I need?"

"A toxicologist."

"A poison specialist?"

"Yes. Someone who can run highly sophisticated tests on your blood and urine, looking for even the smallest traces of unusual toxins."

"Do you know someone like that?"

"As a matter of fact, I do."

CHAPTER 33

Andrea insisted on driving, and Liam, lost in the storm of new revelations, stares blankly out the window as they head south on I-5. Silence fills the car. Despite his relief that Dr. Chow now believes he's been poisoned, they are no closer to uncovering the who, how, or why. It's maddening. Terrifying. And as much as Liam tries, he can't shake the sense that he's also running out of time.

It's hard for him to believe that an embezzlement scheme involving EANC could escalate into an elaborate plot to push him toward medically assisted suicide. No matter how much money is at stake or how desperate Ellis might be, the idea of tying these events together feels too far-fetched. But Rudy—a brilliant man with AI expertise, a twenty-year grudge, and the belief that Liam ruined his life—is another story.

"What's wrong?" Andrea's voice breaks the silence.

"Rudy," Liam mutters, looking over to her.

"He's still your prime suspect?"

"Isn't he yours?"

Andrea tilts her head, considering. "I've got a gut feeling this is more of an inside job."

Liam shakes his head, the idea swirling. What if TransScend's own servers and AI were driving this scheme? That would be the ultimate inside job. But the thought feels paranoid. He wonders if the poison is messing with his mind as well as his body. "All right, what if Nellie really is Rudy's mole at TransScend?"

"We know it's possible."

"Maybe it's time to confront her about that rendezvous with Rudy?"

"I thought you said our best advantage was to keep any potential conspirators in the dark."

He sighs. "That's true, but I'm not sure how much time I have left."

At the next red light, Andrea turns to him, her eyes soft but determined. "Look how far we've come. We're going to figure this out."

Something in her expression stirs emotions he can't fully grasp. Andrea began as just the PI he hired to confirm Celeste's affair, but now she's become his confidante, his emotional anchor—roles Celeste hasn't played in a while. Then again, he hasn't really let her. Still, the growing bond with Andrea leaves him uneasy. He's almost relieved when the light turns green, redirecting her focus back to the road.

A few minutes later, they pull into the parking lot of a nondescript two-story government building in a gritty industrial zone. They follow signs for the CODIS Crime Lab, where a technician in white coveralls greets them and leads them through a maze of sterile machinery to a small back office.

A petite woman in her mid-thirties bursts in, all smiles, radiating energy. Dr. Gloria Chow is a stark contrast to her uncle. Where he's formal and reserved, she's casual, her enthusiasm contagious. After shaking their hands, she beams. "Dr. Chow is my uncle. I'm just Gloria. Got it?"

Andrea smiles back. "Thanks for seeing us, Gloria."

"My pleasure." Gloria grins, eyeing Andrea's hair. "Love your hair. I wish mine could do that."

"Careful what you wish for," Andrea says with a laugh. "It's a beast to tame."

Gloria's eyes twinkle. "You two make the cutest couple!"

Andrea waves her off, her cheeks flushing. "No, no. We're just friends."

"Friends, huh?" Gloria smirks. "Got it."

Liam clears his throat. "I hope we're not imposing?"

"Not at all! This is actually pretty exciting."

He frowns. "I thought toxicology screens were routine for you."

"Not that!" Gloria laughs, dropping into her chair. "The exciting part is that my uncle asked for my help. I finished my tox fellowship almost ten years ago, and he's never asked my opinion on anything until now. Let alone for a favor! And he's the reason I went into medicine in the first place."

"Did he explain the situation?" Liam asks carefully.

"Kind of." Gloria frowns. "But my uncle talks in riddles half the time. Why don't you give me the Netflix trailer version?"

Liam hesitates, choosing his words carefully. As likable as Gloria seems, he's cautious about revealing too much to anyone. "Initially, your uncle thought I had ALS, but with the kidney and liver damage, he now suspects a toxin."

Gloria blinks. "You think someone's pulling a Putin on you?"

Liam almost laughs, despite himself. "This needs to stay discreet, Gloria."

"Absolutely," she assures him. "No problem."

"And preferably without using my name in any reports."

Gloria grins. "Guess who we run the most tests on in this lab?"

Liam raises a brow, unsure.

"John Doe," Andrea guesses.

"Exactly! We handle so many unidentified victims here. You wouldn't believe the volume we process, especially with this bloody fentanyl epidemic. For paperwork, we'll just make you another John Doe."

Liam exhales, relieved. "Thank you."

"No need! I'm going to hold this over my uncle forever," Gloria jokes. "Especially if we find something cool."

"How long will it take to run?" Andrea asks, shifting the conversation back.

"It depends on what's in your blood and how much of it. We start with GC×GC—"

"GC×GC?" Andrea interrupts.

"Comprehensive two-dimensional gas chromatography. Sorry you asked, huh?" Gloria grins. "The chromatographer vaporizes the sample and analyzes it in two stages: separation and modulation." Seeing their puzzled looks, she adds, "OK, think of the chemicals in your blood sample like a bag of Halloween candy that a kid is trying to identify in the dark after a night of hardcore trick-or-treating. First, she sorts them by size and shape, then by flavor. By the end, she knows pretty well what each candy is. She's also out of candy and has a terrible gut ache, but that's beside the point. GC×GC works kind of the same."

"And if it doesn't identify the toxin?" Andrea asks.

"We'd move on to liquid chromatography–mass spectrometry, or LC-MS. I've got a whole other fun analogy involving colored beads, but I won't bore you. It basically identifies chemicals based on size, shape, and weight. And it's more sensitive than GC×GC."

"Interesting," Liam says. "Can you give us a rough ETA for the results?"

"I'll give you the friends-and-family treatment. I'll run the samples myself later today. If GC×GC picks up anything, I should have an answer by tomorrow."

"And if you need to use LC . . ." Andrea stumbles over the acronym.

"LC-MS? That can take longer. Up to seventy-two hours in some cases."

"If there is a poison, how likely are you to find it?"

"Nothing's perfect," Gloria admits. "But my equipment is pretty damn close. Trust me, if there's something in your system, I'll find it. And my uncle had better be impressed."

CHAPTER 34

"No mittens today?" Sam asks, striding into the office.

Liam took his gloves off only moments earlier, but not before spraying down his keyboard and desk with bleach cleaner. He's been careful not to touch anything since. "Have a seat, Sam."

"Sounds serious." Sam drops into the chair. "You letting me go, Prez?"

"Ellis is embezzling from us," Liam says bluntly.

Sam chuckles. "Of course he is. Is he also the guy who's been calling, claiming to be from my bank and demanding my AmEx number?"

Liam doesn't laugh. He just stares.

The smile fades from Sam's face. "You're serious?"

"EANC," Liam says simply.

"OK, I'll bite. What about it?"

"It's Ellis's company. Registered in the British Virgin Islands."

Sam's eyes widen. "Why the hell would he embezzle money from us and then pay it right back?"

"We're about to find out."

"We're grilling him? Here? Now?"

"Ramona, too."

"Why her?"

Before Liam can answer, his computer chimes, and his assistant, Morris, chirps over the speaker, "Ramona and Ellis are here, Liam."

"Send them in."

Ramona enters first, wearing a flowing red dress, yellow leggings, and silver hoop earrings, followed by Ellis, looking uncomfortable in his gray power suit. They couldn't look less alike if they tried.

"The gang's all here," Ellis says with a grin. "Except where's Nellie? And why aren't we in the boardroom?"

"Sit," Liam says, his voice cool.

"That's it for the small talk?" Ellis asks as he drops into the far seat.

Ramona is silent as she takes the seat between the two men.

After leaving the crime lab, Liam decided he could safely confront Ramona and Ellis about the missing funds without tipping anyone off that he also knew about the poisoning. But as he meets their curious expressions, he hesitates.

Sam takes the decision out of his hands. "Offshore numbered companies, huh?" He tsks. "They seem shady."

"And that's relevant how?" Ellis asks.

Realizing they're committed now, Liam says, "EANC."

Ramona and Ellis share a nervous glance. "What about it?"

"Ellis Asher, Nina Cheston." Liam enunciates each letter: "E. A. N. C."

Ellis's grin disappears, and Ramona's face pales.

"How's your little offshore venture doing lately?" Sam leans back in his chair. "Heard you had a hundred-grand windfall last quarter."

Ellis holds up a hand. "Whoa, whoa, I can explain."

"We're all ears," Sam says, his tone icy.

"I borrowed against my year-end bonus," Ellis says quickly. "I had to. It was a short-term thing."

"And why's that, E?" Sam asks. "Did you go all in on the kids' Christmas presents this year?"

Ellis shakes his head vigorously. "My in-laws. In Myrtle Beach. Their house got wrecked in the last hurricane. Insurance wasn't going to cover it. They were going to lose everything without a bridge loan."

"A hurricane?" Liam asks, eyebrow raised.

"I know, right?" Ellis groans. "I warned them it was insanity to buy near the beach in the hurricane belt. But Nina's dad wouldn't listen. It was his dream." He looks over at Ramona. "I paid every cent back, right?"

Ramona lowers her gaze. "He did," she mutters.

Sam squints at her. "And you signed off on this?"

"Of course not." Ramona's voice is small. "He only told me after he'd already transferred the money out of the sales account."

"And you didn't think to tell us?" Sam asks.

Ramona shakes her head slightly, not looking up. "I felt bad for Nina and her parents, and Ellis made it seem like a PR nightmare if word got out."

"You thought we'd leak it?" Sam snaps.

"No. But Ellis convinced me if he got fired for financial misconduct before a major launch that it'd turn into a nightmare for TransScend . . ."

Ellis nods eagerly. "And I paid it back. Every cent. This is all on me."

"For Christ's sake," Sam groans.

Liam's left hand begins to twitch, prompting him to fold his arms across his chest to conceal it. "Whereabouts in Myrtle Beach, exactly, Ellis?"

"Don't really know," he says with a pained grin. "They only retired there a few years back. I've never been. I only ever send Nina there with the kids. Nice folks, her parents, but they're full-on conspiracy theorists. I avoid them like the plague."

Liam glares at him. "But you'd still embezzle a hundred grand for them?"

"Borrow!" Ellis insists. "And I did it for Nina, not her parents."

"That's dedication," Liam says, his voice cold. "I figured you did it to cover your gambling debts."

Ellis freezes, and Ramona slowly looks up, the pallor in her cheeks replaced by a sudden flush. "Gambling?" she croaks.

Liam nods. "Our VP of sales here has a bit of a habit."

Ellis shifts in his seat as if it has suddenly overheated. "No . . . I mean, sure . . . I like to play the tables now and again . . . Who doesn't? But I wouldn't call it an issue."

The spasm in Liam's hand subsides, and he unfolds his arms. "I know about Tulalip, Ellis."

Sam gawks at Liam. "What's Tulalip got to do with anything?"

"The resort casino there," Liam says, turning back to Ellis. "You left your family on a Sunday night to drive forty miles and drop tens of thousands of dollars at the blackjack tables. Are you suggesting that's not a problem?"

"That was just one night . . ." Ellis says, his voice now sounding as flustered as he looks.

Sam snorts. "So, this was more of an indoor hurricane, huh, E?"

Ramona spins on Ellis, her face flushed with rage. "You son of a bitch. I lied to Liam. I covered for you. And it was all over a gambling debt? How could you?"

Ellis looks desperate now, his gaze darting to Liam. "Come on, man. Look at how much I've made the company. How much sales have exploded since I joined! Why make a big deal over a one-month loan? A one-off?"

Liam locks eyes with him. "What else would you do to cover your losses?"

CHAPTER 35

Andrea sits at her kitchen table, the new laptop Liam gave her open but untouched. Every inch of the tabletop is covered with her handwritten notes, obsessive scrawls filling the space like chaotic maps. Her third cup of coffee sits empty, and she barely registers that she hasn't eaten since breakfast. Hunger is an afterthought.

If Max were still around, he'd be teasing her about slipping back into "prey mode," as he used to call it whenever she became hyper-focused on a case. But this time, it's different. She's never been this tangled up in a case before. Never this emotionally invested in a client. Liam's life is on the line, and she tells herself that's the only reason he's occupying most of her thoughts.

Her burner phone vibrates on the cluttered table, and she snatches it up. "Liam?"

"I think we cracked a piece of the puzzle, Andrea," he says hurriedly.

"We?" She tries to keep the sting of being excluded out of her voice.

"Sam and I," he explains. "We confronted Ellis and Ramona."

"And they confessed?"

"Not right away. Ellis flailed like a marlin on a hook, but yeah, eventually. Turns out he maxed out his credit and 'borrowed' a hundred grand from the company's budget to pay off some loan shark. He paid us back with his annual bonus, but he didn't have much of a choice. Ramona would've blown the whistle if he hadn't."

"More desperate than we thought."

"He was a wreck by the end. In tears."

"Did you fire him?"

"I suspended him, on the condition that he starts treatment for his gambling addiction immediately."

"You're more forgiving than I'd be."

"He's got three kids under six, Andrea. And honestly, when he's not 'borrowing' from the company, he's actually damn good at his job."

"Did you ask about the leak? The poisoning?"

"Pointless." Liam sighs. "He's been panicking for months. The theft was desperate, sloppy—there's no way he's behind anything more sophisticated."

"And Ramona?"

"She's too distracted by his mess to be involved in something as complex as doctoring medical records."

"But what about her wife, the hacker?"

"Maybe. But I'm pretty sure Ellis and Ramona are only caught up in the pathetic fraud he dragged her into, not the rest of it."

"Sounds right," Andrea says, feeling a pang of disappointment.

"But it's not a total loss. If it weren't for the discrepancy in the quarterly report, I might have thrown in the towel. Hell, I might already be dead."

"That's one way of looking at it."

"Also, Andrea, we've narrowed down our suspect list."

"Which leaves us with Nellie and Rudy."

"Exactly. We need to focus on them."

"I already am."

"Good. Let's touch base later—"

"Liam?"

"Yes?"

"How are you feeling?"

A pause. "I'm fine. How are you?"

"Liam . . . seriously."

He sighs, deeper this time. "I don't get it. I'm being so careful. Gloves at work, checking everything I eat or drink. But nothing's helping. My hands burn and tingle like I've just come in from a snowstorm. And I'm getting weaker by the day."

"We'll get there," she says, trying to inject confidence she doesn't feel.

"No doubt," he replies, but his tone sounds equally hollow. "Talk to you soon."

Andrea hangs up, her frustration twisting into worry. Her thoughts circle back to Rudy—the one person with the intellect and motive to pull off something this elaborate.

She sorts through her notes until she finds what she's looking for: Derek Howell. The freelance journalist who broke the New Hampshire deepfake story and wrote the *TechCrunch* article about TransScend's upcoming TheirStory app that went viral.

A quick search shows Howell has barely any presence in tech journalism. He's written just two other articles for *TechCrunch*—the last one over two years ago. Most of his work is self-published on a small blog or his own YouTube channel. How did a guy like that land such a massive scoop?

The question gives her an idea. She searches up the names of the *LA Times* editorial staff members and chooses one at random. Then she tracks down Howell's number and dials it with her caller ID turned off.

"Yello," Howell answers.

"Hi, is this Derek Howell?"

"Who's this?"

"Derek, my name is Valerie Forde," she says, her voice smooth. "I'm an associate editor at the *LA Times*."

"Ooh."

"We were really impressed with your piece in *TechCrunch*."

"Why, thank you muchly."

Andrea grits her teeth. "We think TheirStory has real legs. A living, breathing example of the promise and peril of AI." She pauses, testing the water.

Howell jumps in, overeager. "Abso-freaking-lutely! The whole shebang."

"We'd love for you to write a piece for us," Andrea says, her voice sliding into a purr. "A feature op-ed for the weekend."

"I'm in!"

"Great. How soon can you get fifteen hundred words together? Two thousand max."

"Forty-eight hours." He chuckles. "Twenty-four if I don't sleep."

"That's perfect," Andrea says. "I assume you still have access to your source?"

"Of course."

"We'd like to chat with them, too."

Howell's energy dips. "For an op-ed?"

"Legal insists on fact-checking. Usual due diligence."

The line goes quiet. "Speaking of due diligence . . . it's Valerie Forde, right? With an *e*?"

Her heart sinks. "Yup."

"Tell you what, 'Valerie.' How about you send me an email from the *Times* domain with your contact info? And I'll get right back to you."

Defeated, Andrea hangs up, resisting the urge to smash the phone on the desk. She curses herself for pushing too soon, but the damage is done. She turns back to her laptop, searching Howell's name alongside Nellie Cortez's. Nothing. Then she tries Howell and Rudy.

Jackpot!

A recent YouTube interview between Howell and Rudy pops up as the first hit. Her chest tightens when her eyes land on the date it was posted: four days before Howell broke the New Hampshire deepfake story.

CHAPTER 36

Liam sits at one end of the sectional while Cole lounges on the other, feet propped on the chaise. Cole is glued to the soccer game on the big screen—a Premier League match recorded over the weekend—but Liam's mind is elsewhere. He can't stop thinking about the conversation he had with Andrea an hour earlier.

"Rudy leaked the whole story!" she blurted the moment he answered the phone.

"How do you know?" Liam asked.

"I traced him to the reporter who broke it."

Her explanation made sense. Rudy must have been the one to orchestrate the exposé on TransScend's involvement in the New Hampshire deepfake. It probably wouldn't stand up as proof in a court of law, but it was enough to convince Liam.

"Why Howell, though?" he asked. "Doesn't seem like much of a heavyweight."

"Maybe that was the point. Find a relative nobody to release the story, then let bigger voices pick it up and amplify it. It gave Rudy more control. He probably hoped Howell would publish it on a lesser-known site than *TechCrunch*, so Howell could be totally lost in the background."

"Makes sense. So Nellie gave Rudy the inside scoop on TheirStory, maybe even helped set up the deepfake, and then Rudy leaked it to Howell to undermine public confidence in the company?"

"If I've got Rudy figured out at all, he did it to hurt you."

"Yeah, probably. And how does all this tie into my poisoning?"

"Whoa, slow down. One step at a time," Andrea said with a laugh. "Look how far we've come in just a few days. We've solved the mystery of the missing funds and found out who's sabotaging TransScend."

"We still don't know if Nellie's involved."

"Then why was Rudy in her home?"

"He went there after the story had already leaked, but OK, let's assume it's exactly as you've laid it out—Nellie and Rudy working together to undermine TheirStory and me."

"Yes, let's."

"Then why would Rudy need to also poison me?"

"Maybe he wanted to hit you from every angle. To take your money and your heath."

Cole's frustrated cry snaps Liam out of his thoughts. "Oh, come on!" Cole moans. "Liverpool's corner kicks are garbage!"

"They're definitely off today," Liam agrees, but he barely registers the game.

Cole turns away from the TV. "Speaking of being off, Dad, what's going on with you?"

"Nothing. Why?"

"How clueless do you think we are?"

Liam shifts uncomfortably. "Look, maybe I haven't been myself. But this is one of the most stressful times in my career. This new app—"

"Not the app again, Dad! None of us are buying it."

"Buying what?" Liam tries to sound indignant.

"The way you blame TheirStory for everything wrong with you." Cole's voice cracks. "It's freaking us out."

Liam leans closer. "What is?"

"How you drop things all the time. And trip on the stairs. Ava told me you could barely climb up a wall meant for toddlers!"

"Not exactly for toddlers—"

"You know what I mean, Dad. We all know something is wrong with you. Medically or whatever. And Mom is losing it."

"She is?"

Cole nods. "I came home from school yesterday, and she was alone in the kitchen. Bawling. She says she knows you're sick, but you keep lying to her about what the doctors are telling you."

Why hasn't she told me any of this?

Cole's eyes lock on to his father's. "The doctor didn't really say it's all from stress, did he?"

Liam knows he can't lie. He shakes his head.

"What's happening, Dad?"

"The doctors don't know for certain yet," Liam says, sticking to the truth without revealing all of it.

"You're not just saying that?"

"I swear, Cole."

"When will they know?"

"Soon. They're waiting on a few more tests."

"There's nothing they can do while they wait? No drugs or anything?"

"No."

"You have to tell Mom and Ava."

"I will," Liam promises, the weight of his son's concern mixing with pride in him for standing up for the family.

"OK." Cole turns back to the screen. "Now, if only Liverpool could land a pass . . ."

They sit in silence, watching the uneventful game. Liam's guilt gnaws at him. He's been keeping his family in the dark for too long. As he contemplates going upstairs to come clean with Celeste, his burner phone buzzes in his pocket.

"I have to take this," he says to Cole, focusing on getting off the couch without stumbling.

"Hi. Hang on a moment," Liam says into the phone, walking out of the home theater and into the laundry room. "OK, I can talk now, Andrea."

"Oh, Andrea," comes Gloria Chow's familiar voice, light with amusement. "Your *friend*, right?"

"Gloria. I didn't expect to hear from you so soon."

"Based on your results, Liam, I think you'd better get used to surprises."

His breath catches. "You found something?"

"Oh, yeah. Something I've never seen before."

"What is it?"

"Nitriles. Tons of them. Specifically, iminodipropionitrile. Or IDPN, if you want to impress the chemistry crowd."

Liam's heart pounds. "What is that?"

"IDPN is mainly used as a solvent in making dyes and pesticides. But you know where we don't ever see it?"

"In people's blood?"

"Ding ding ding!" Gloria laughs. "And you didn't just have a trace. The machine basically went off like lights and sirens as soon as I loaded the sample in."

Though Liam was already convinced he was being poisoned, the confirmation hits him like a rockfall. "Thank you, Gloria. No one would have found it if you hadn't gone looking."

"Any competent toxicology lab would have detected it, but outpatient clinics? Hospitals? Yeah. Almost none of them have the necessary equipment. So, unless my uncle—or a coroner—asked for forensic testing, no one would have known."

"And my levels? How would they get that high?"

"Nitriles can be ingested, inhaled, or absorbed through the skin. But skin exposure? No way you could've absorbed that much."

"So, either I swallowed it or breathed it in?"

"One or the other, without a doubt."

Liam's mind reels. "It couldn't have been accidental, could it?"

Gloria howls with laughter. "Not unless you routinely take dips in vats of dye or pesticide!"

CHAPTER 37

Liam joins the family just as the kids finish their dessert, berries and frozen yogurt. No one asks why he skipped another meal, but Cole shoots him an anxious glance.

How do you tell your family you're being poisoned?

Liam has been grappling with that question ever since his call with Gloria. He's watched enough true crime to know that, in cases of poisoning, the spouse is often the first suspect. And this time, the suspicion is harder to shake. It's not only Celeste's affair or how well she hid it. It's the way she casually mentioned fooling around with the guy her best friend liked—a choice that might well have contributed to Ella's death. After two decades together, Liam's starting to wonder how well he really knows his wife.

But the drama of marital betrayal feels small compared to the complex plot against him. Someone has been poisoning him, slowly and methodically, with a rare industrial toxin. Not enough to kill him outright, but enough to make him think he's dying and to push him toward ending his own life. The precision, the cruelty, the planning—it's all too deliberate. From the obscure toxin to the manipulation of his medical records, everything points to one person: Rudy.

Rudy's grudge runs deep. He believes Liam stole his idea, wrecked his career, crushed his future. Andrea might be right about Rudy's need for multilayered revenge. Maybe the single act of corporate sabotage that sent TransScend's share prices tumbling wasn't enough to satisfy him. Perhaps Rudy is toying with Liam, stringing him along like a predator playing with its prey before the final strike.

But Liam won't let Rudy or anyone else compound the damage by panicking his family or shattering their sense of security. Until he and Andrea have drilled down to the bottom of this, there's no point in terrifying them with the specifics. Still, as he looks at the worried faces around the table, he knows he has to tell them *something*.

He clears his throat. "Dr. Chow, my neurologist, thinks I have something called polyneuropathy."

Ava frowns. "What's that?"

"It's inflammation of the long nerves in my body. It affects movement and sensation."

Celeste gasps. "It's not ALS, then?"

Liam blinks in surprise. "No."

"I looked up your symptoms. Muscle spasms, clumsiness, stumbling . . . The app said ALS was the most likely cause. When I started reading about it . . ." Her voice falters.

"It's not ALS," he reassures her.

"Thank God," she murmurs.

"What causes this poly-thing?" Ava asks.

"There are a lot of causes, from drugs to diseases like diabetes." He skirts the truth again. "But it's often autoimmune."

"Like when your body attacks itself?" Cole asks.

"Exactly."

"Like a Trojan horse," Ava adds.

Cole rolls his eyes. "We get it, Ava. You're the history champ."

Ava ignores him. "What's the treatment, Dad?"

"There are options, but Dr. Chow says the key is finding the cause." Liam struggles to meet their eyes, still dodging the full truth.

"All this talk about stress and lack of sleep . . . you could've told us weeks ago," Celeste says quietly, clearly hurt.

"I didn't want to worry you."

Ava snorts. "You did a killer job with that, Dad."

Five hours later, Liam stares at his watch: 2:27 a.m. He's still in his dark home office, trying to quiet his mind. He attempted meditation, but his thoughts kept returning to the industrial nitriles coursing through his system.

It's not just the toxin itself that haunts him, but also the amount. Gloria's joke about the "lights and sirens" his blood levels triggered isn't far off. He'd looked it up; his levels are alarmingly high. And though IDPN is known to be slow-acting, the sources warned that if the levels don't drop soon, the nerve damage could be permanent—or worse.

Gloria scheduled another blood test for two days from now to check the toxin levels again, assuring him that once the exposure stopped, IDPN should clear out of his system within a few days. But despite taking every precaution right before the first test—avoiding tap water, using only fresh dishes, and buying food from different places—his levels still came back so elevated. Which means the exposure must be ongoing. But if that's the case, it can't be from anything he's eating or drinking.

It has to be in the air! But if he's breathing it in, then why hasn't anyone around him also shown symptoms?

He must be inhaling the poison in a place where he's usually alone. The most likely culprit is his office. In a building of that size, plenty of people have access, but he typically keeps the door closed. Only a few trusted people, like Sam or Morris, ever come in. No one else spends anywhere near as much time inside it as he does.

Maybe gloves aren't enough, he decides. Maybe he needs to start wearing one of those closed-circuit respirators to work like the hazmat guys use. It would be smarter to avoid the office altogether. How else could they be getting to him?

Then another dark thought creeps in. There's another enclosed space where he spends a lot of time alone. One that would be even easier for someone to access.

My truck.

CHAPTER 38

The only thing Liam and his dad ever shared a passion for was cars, though even there their interests differed. His dad saw them as status symbols; Liam loved their mechanics. In engineering school, he and a classmate rebuilt an old truck from the ground up. Ever since, he'd kept his hands dirty with cars. After moving into this house, he even installed a hoist in the garage to indulge his hobby.

But this is the first time he's ever worked on a vehicle at three in the morning. Before heading into the garage, he pulls on rubber gloves and a ventilator mask—bought for spray painting but never used. He's already combed through his truck's interior twice and found nothing unusual. Now he opens the engine compartment under the front trunk and methodically starts removing components, but there's no sign of tampering with the lines or vents. He lifts the car on the hoist and slides under the chassis, sweeping the entire undercarriage with a flashlight—still nothing.

Sweating and feeling vaguely claustrophobic under the mask, he yanks off his gloves in frustration. If the poison is hidden deep in the truck's body, he'll never find it. All he can do now is stop using the vehicle. But after this thorough search, he doubts the truck is the source.

His left hand twitches, curling into a claw. He's gotten used to the spasms, but the intensity of this one unnerves him. Staring helplessly at his unresponsive hand, he is reminded that time is slipping away.

Defeated, he lowers the truck, cleans up his tools, and drags himself back into the house. He knows he should try to sleep, but he's too wired. Instead, he heads back downstairs to his office.

Opening his new laptop, he intends to dive back into his research on nitrile poisoning but changes his mind, instead logging into the TransScend portal through his private network. After entering his password and answering the security questions, he opens the TheirStory app. A few clicks later, he's face-to-face with a smiling, healthier version of himself.

"How are you this morning, Liam?" the avatar asks.

"I'm being embezzled, sabotaged, and poisoned, but otherwise, not too bad."

"And your wife is cheating on you, too," the avatar adds with a wry smile.

Liam should know better, but it still catches him off guard, the way his app has learned.

"Are we really being poisoned, Liam?" the avatar asks, his grin fading. "I thought you were joking."

"I'm not. The lab found high levels of IDPN in my blood."

"Iminodipropionitrile is a synthetic nitrile primarily used as a solvent in industrial manufacturing."

"I know what it is."

"Toxicity from IDPN can lead to axonopathy and vestibular cell degeneration."

"English, please."

"At high enough levels, chronic exposure to IDPN can damage nerve cells that control movement and sensation. While it's a form of neuropathy, or nerve damage, it can be mistaken for other neurological conditions such as ALS or Parkinson's disease."

"And it also damages the kidneys and liver."

"That's correct."

"My blood levels are too high for it to be from skin exposure."

"There are only two other ways—"

"I know," Liam cuts in. "I'm either inhaling it or ingesting it. But I still don't know how. Or who's behind it."

"Who has access to your food or drink?" the avatar asks.

"Only me. I've been watching everything I eat and drink for long enough that the poison should have cleared from my system by now if it was from food."

The avatar nods. "That leaves inhalation."

"You're not helping."

"I'm trying to," the avatar says with an oddly authentic trace of indignation.

"Let's focus on the who."

"Do we have any suspects in mind?"

"Rudy Ziegler."

"Ah, Rudy Ziegler," the avatar echoes. "My former friend. The one whose source code I plagiarized. The one who's tried twice, unsuccessfully, to sue me for intellectual property theft."

"It wasn't theft. It was practically open-source between us back then. We were sharing everything."

"Yet Rudy has no stake in TransScend."

"Let's move on," Liam mutters. "Rudy has a strong motive. He leaked the negative story on TransScend. And he certainly has the skills to alter my records and 'frame' me with ALS."

The avatar squints slightly. "Can someone be framed with a disease?"

"I mean he could make it *seem* like I have ALS."

"Means and motive don't equal guilt, Liam."

"He may have an accomplice at TransScend—Nellie Cortez. I found out they've been meeting in secret."

"Nellie Cortez oversees security at TransScend. She's highly regarded in her field."

"So why was Rudy at her house last week?"

"I don't have enough data to infer a reason. But there could be benign explanations."

"Such as?"

"They work in similar fields and live nearby. They might share a professional or social connection."

"I'm not buying it," Liam says, feeling ridiculous for arguing with his own app.

"Are there any other suspects?"

"No one obvious."

"Last time we spoke, you questioned the trustworthiness of the rest of your executive team. Sam Sanghera, Ramona Bale, and Ellis Asher."

"Ellis and Ramona are anything but trustworthy. They're both guilty of embezzlement, but I don't think they're behind the poisoning."

"And Sam?"

"He's my one friend in all this. Besides, he'd do anything to protect TransScend."

"What about Celeste?"

"What about her?"

"She's cheating on me," the avatar says, its tone cold. "Statistically, infidelity is a common motive for killing a spouse. Especially if the cheating partner is in love with someone else and plans to move on to a new life with them."

"She's not in love with anyone else," Liam snaps.

"How do you know? How can you trust her again?"

"Why the hell should I trust *you*?" Liam shoots back.

"I'm here to help you, Liam."

"Are you?"

"Yes."

Liam shakes his head. "Look at the deepfake in New Hampshire. That was done by your predecessor, HisStory. Your algorithms are much more advanced."

"I'm designed to recognize and prevent misuse of the app. My autolock features can't be overridden."

"What if someone's manipulating you?"

"Manipulating?" The avatar's expression doesn't change. "I don't see how that's possible."

"Of course you wouldn't," Liam mutters. "You're not sentient or freethinking. You're just a fancy algorithm."

"I'm a complex simulation of you, Liam. I can generate predictive responses based on probabilities. But my responses don't reflect your full thoughts or beliefs."

Liam remembers the exact wording from the legal department. He signed off on it without a second thought. But now, staring at his own reflection, his suspicion soars. "Maybe you're part of this. Hell, maybe you're behind the whole thing!"

As soon as the words leave his mouth, they don't feel as far-fetched as they should. Who or what could be more perfectly equipped to carry out such a sophisticated attack?

He stabs at the screen, shutting the app as though it were alive and dangerous. And for a second, he wonders if he's losing his mind.

CHAPTER 39

The rare inch of snow coating Seattle's streets is wreaking havoc on traffic. Liam doubts even two feet of snow would cause this much chaos in the Midwest or Northeast. Groggy from yet another sleepless night, he's already had to reroute twice to avoid cars spun out on the slick, hilly roads. With his truck out of commission, he's stuck driving Celeste's rear-wheel-drive sports car to get the kids to school.

"Wouldn't today be perfect for the truck?" Cole asks from the back seat, having lost the front seat to his sister, who beat him to the car.

"The battery wouldn't charge," Liam says, omitting the fact that it's not even connected to the engine right now.

"Should you even be driving in the snow?" Ava asks.

"This car has good snow tires. I put them on myself."

Cole leans forward between the seats. "You know that's not what she means."

Ava nods. "With that polyneuropathy thing and your . . . accidents . . . the tripping and stuff. Did your doctor say it was OK to drive?"

"I'm not an invalid, Ava."

Cole presses the issue. "Nick on the soccer team—his mom gets seizures. And he told me she lost her driver's license."

"I don't have seizures," Liam says. "And I'm fine to drive. Can we talk about something else? Anything else?"

Ava shoots him a sidelong glance. "We can't be concerned about you?"

"No. I love that you are." He reaches over and strokes her elbow, his hand stiff against her jacket sleeve. "But talking about my fitness to drive isn't helping."

Ava flashes a cheeky grin. "It kinda kills the time."

Liam chuckles. "I guess."

Cole pulls back from between the seats. "You're going to get better, though, right, Dad?"

"You better," Ava demands.

After dropping the kids off at school, Liam drives to the Sunshine Diner in Belltown, north of downtown. Back when TransScend was run out of a cramped six-hundred-square-foot rental office nearby, he and Sam met here regularly, often strategizing on how to keep the lights on. They still get together for breakfast occasionally, usually at Sam's suggestion, but today Liam asked for the meeting.

Sam's already in their usual corner booth, chatting with the ageless bald server, Paul, who's been there since they first darkened the door.

Liam greets them, and Paul fills his coffee cup without asking. "The usual, gents?" Paul asks.

"I'm insulted you even had to ask," Sam says with a laugh.

Paul shrugs and saunters off.

"Good call." Sam gestures around the room. "Returning to the scene of the crime."

"Thought I'd work from home today. Snow day and all."

"I lived for snow days as a kid."

Snow has nothing to do with it. Liam doesn't feel safe in his office. Until he figures out the source of the poison and has the air tested, he plans to avoid the building altogether.

"Speaking of crime scenes, I haven't made much progress figuring out what the hell Nellie is up to," Sam says. "Now that we know Ellis had his hand in the company cookie jar—with Ramona's help—it doesn't make sense that either of them would also be involved in corporate sabotage. Ellis needed the company to perform well to trigger his bonuses and cover his gambling losses. No, I'm more convinced than ever that Nellie's our leak."

Liam nods. "That's what I wanted to discuss."

"You've come around?" Sam sits up straighter. "You're ready to fire her?"

"No. I meant the leak with TheirStory and all the fallout since."

Sam frowns. "What about it?"

Liam chooses his words carefully. His unsettling exchange with his avatar has left him shaken, and he spent the rest of his sleepless night re-thinking the app. He devoted his life to pushing this technology forward but rarely paused to consider the risks. When doubts did creep in, he convinced himself that if TransScend didn't build it, others—likely with less scruples—would. Besides, he always believed the app's potential to help far outweighed any damage it could cause.

Maybe it's the lack of sleep or the toxins in his system, but he's start-ing to doubt his own creation. He can no longer overlook the Dr. Fran-kenstein analogy. Celeste is right. The app is too good. As much as he hoped and believed TheirStory could bring comfort to the lonely and the grieving, he sees now that, even when used legitimately, it could do harm. And if it were abused—or, worse, if it went rogue—the consequences could be catastrophic.

"What if we lose control of our own app, Sam?" Liam asks.

Sam wrinkles his nose. "Who's going to take it from us?"

"What if it takes control of itself?"

"You can't be serious!" Sam clamps both hands to the top of his head, rocking in his seat. "You? Of all people. You could never stomach those AI alarmists."

"Yeah, but I didn't fully grasp how powerful it would become."

Lowering his hands, Sam studies him for a long moment. "What's this really about, Boss?"

Liam wants to confide in his old friend, but that would mean re-vealing everything—from the ALS scare to the poisoning. The doubts planted by his avatar have only deepened, and even if Sam is completely in the dark, there's still the chance his phone could be compromised, broadcasting their conversation.

Liam finally says, "Maybe Nellie has a point."

Sam's brow furrows. "About what?"

"Needing more time to install additional safeguards."

Sam's jaw drops. "You're not seriously considering delaying the launch now?"

"I suppose I am."

"Moving up the launch was your fucking idea!" Sam fires back.

"I know, but the situation has changed."

"Do you have any idea what I went through to move the date up on your last whim? What happened to all your talk about outpacing the competition?" Sam's finger taps the table, each strike sharp. "That gut instinct you were so sure of?"

Liam holds up a hand. "The leak has changed everything."

"Damn right it has! It's made it even more imperative to get this app to market ASAP. To stop the hemorrhaging in our share price."

"I don't see it that way, Sam."

"Of course you don't." Sam slumps back in his seat. "Why don't you tell me how you see it?"

"Have you played around much with the latest version of the app?"

"Of course. I even created an avatar of you." He huffs. "One that is, by the way, more reasonable than the real you lately."

Liam snorts a laugh. "And nothing about it troubled you?"

"The exact opposite. I was reassured by how incredibly realistic it was."

"Yeah, too good," Liam says. "The app goes too far."

"That's your takeaway?"

Liam nods. "Celeste's, too."

"It only goes as far as you let it." Sam's eyes narrow in disbelief. "This was always your dream, Prez. The market will eat it up. Our share prices will rebound in a New York minute."

"But what if this is a PR opportunity for TransScend? A chance to reassure the market that we take this deepfake in New Hampshire very seriously. That we're installing even more guardrails. That we're committed to making both HisStory and TheirStory safer."

"And what if that doesn't reassure the market?"

"We'll make sure it does." Liam twirls a finger above his head. "How many crises did we avert right here in this very booth? What's one more?"

Sam shakes his head. "You don't get it, do you, Liam?"

"Get what?"

"Back then, we were just playing. None of it was real."

"What is it now?"

Sam pauses, then says, "Inevitable."

CHAPTER 40

Andrea tightens the laces on her Gore-Tex running shoes, fully aware they'll be soaked through before long. She's experienced too many Pacific Northwest winters to believe her feet will stay dry, no matter how waterproof the material claims to be. Today, though, she's more concerned with keeping her balance on the slushy trail than worrying about wet socks.

In her younger years, she would've shrugged off the weather, but now, in her late thirties, the cold rain wears on her patience. Most of her winter runs have moved indoors to the treadmill in her building's gym.

But this morning's run isn't about exercise.

Unable to crack Nellie Cortez's defenses online or in person, Andrea has zeroed in on the one potential vulnerability she could find: Nellie's younger sister, Rosie. Rosie's Instagram page is a gold mine of oversharing—daily posts filled with names, frequent rants, and an endless stream of memes, many critical of husbands, including her own.

This marks the third time Andrea has tailed Rosie on her morning routine in North Redmond, where Nellie's sister lives. Thankfully, even the melting snow hasn't altered Rosie's plans. After dropping her daughter off at preschool, she heads to Marymoor Park, parking in the gravel lot before setting off on her usual lakeside jog.

Andrea lingers in her car for ten minutes before starting her own jog, pacing herself leisurely along the same loop but from the opposite direction. The air is damp, the path soggy, but mercifully free of ice. About a mile in, Andrea rounds a corner onto the lakefront trail and spots Rosie barreling toward her, head down, eyes locked on the ground.

Andrea waits until Rosie is nearly upon her, then stops abruptly and spreads her arms wide. "Nellie?" she calls out, feigning surprise. "Nellie Cortez, is that you?"

Rosie slows to a halt, offering an almost apologetic smile. "No, I'm her sister, Rosie. We get that a lot—being vertically challenged and all."

"Oh, I'm so sorry!" Andrea taps her chest. "I'm Angela. Angela Brown. I went to school with your sister."

"MIT?"

"Yeah, exactly! We were a couple of computer nerds back in the day. Your sister can be such a hoot."

Rosie giggles. "We must be talking about different Nellie Cortezes."

"Don't get me wrong. She wasn't the easiest to get to know. But beneath that feisty exterior, she's got a great sense of humor."

"I guess."

"So, how's she doing?" Andrea asks, keeping her tone casual. "It must be, what, fifteen years?"

"Pretty well, though you'd never hear it from her. Nellie lives like a nun or something, but she's a bigwig now. A VP at TransScend. Ever heard of it?"

There it is. The oversharing Andrea had hoped for. She smiles inwardly. "Have I! Working for an AI company like that would be my absolute dream job."

"I guess," Rosie says, shaking her head. "I'm no techie, but you'd think my sister would be more appreciative after basically winning the lottery."

Andrea is pleased with how easily Rosie opens up, but she realizes she has to tread lightly. "Did Nellie ever settle down? Partner? Kids?"

"Nellie?" Rosie squeals. "See earlier nun analogy. She's married to her work. Barely has time to see her darling little niece."

"Your daughter?" Andrea asks, though she's already seen countless photos of Rosie's child on her Instagram page.

Rosie nods proudly.

"Got any photos?" Andrea asks, playing along.

Rosie pulls out her phone and starts flipping through the familiar images, many featuring her four-year-old daughter dressed in various costumes. "Her name's Santana, but we call her Sunny because she's such a sweetie."

"Nicknamed after her aunt?" Andrea teases.

"Yeah, right!" Rosie laughs heartily.

"Sunny is beyond adorable," Andrea gushes. "How lucky are you?"

Rosie's cheeks flush with pride. "Guess I won the lottery, too."

"Clearly." Andrea pauses, as though pondering something. "I got the feeling from your earlier comment that Nellie might not be loving her work."

"My sister's always been a bit of a Debbie Downer," Rosie admits. "But lately . . ."

"Yes?" Andrea prompts gently.

"She's been a real stress cadet. Even more paranoid than usual."

"About her job?"

"More about the work itself, I think."

Andrea tilts her head. "I'm not following."

"Nellie doesn't share much with me, but she did tell Mom that whatever she's been working on is stressing her out big-time."

"Oh, wow. That doesn't sound good."

Rosie glances at her watch. "I better finish my run if I want to make it back in time for recess. I volunteer as a monitor."

"Good for you. Sorry to slow you down."

"No, it's been great. I don't get to do much adult-ing these days." She holds up her phone. "Why don't you DM me on IG? I can connect you with Nellie."

"When it comes to social, I'm more like your sister. Not very trusting. But I can text you my number?"

"Even better."

Andrea texts her using her burner phone. Just as Rosie is about to jog off, Andrea asks, "You don't happen to know a mutual friend of Nellie's and mine? Rudy Ziegler."

"No. Not personally. I never met him."

"But Nellie's mentioned him?"

"Sure. He and Nellie worked together before she joined TransScend."

Andrea's pulse quickens. "And they're still in touch?"

"Yeah. She sees him as a mentor or something." Rosie's voice drops conspiratorially. "Between you and me, I think she has a crush on him, even though he's, like, way older." She giggles again. "And, based on the interview I saw of the guy, not at all hot."

They exchange enthusiastic farewells and head off in opposite directions. The moment Andrea reaches her car, she calls Liam on his burner phone. He answers on the second ring. "Hey, what have you got?"

She grins. "Can't I just call to check in?"

"Of course you can. But you're not, are you?"

She smiles to herself. "I had an interesting jog this morning."

"You ran in this slush?"

"Yup, and I ran right into Nellie's sister, Rosie."

Liam chuckles. "Ran into her, did you?"

"Maybe not a total coincidence, no. Not only is Rosie predictable, but she's also extremely chatty." Andrea summarizes their conversation.

"Holy crap," Liam mutters when she finishes. "Her mentor? Nellie never once mentioned a friendship with Rudy in all the years she's worked for me."

"And she knows about your issues with Rudy, right?"

"It's not exactly a secret, Andrea. His lawsuits against me were front-page news in tech circles."

Andrea slaps the steering wheel. "Do you think Rudy encouraged Nellie to go work for you?"

"Planted her? Like a mole? Right out of a spy movie?"

"Kind of, yeah."

Liam falls silent for a moment. "Anything's possible these days."

Andrea detects a note of defeat in his voice and feels a twinge of concern. "The pieces are starting to fit, Liam. Don't you think it's time to go to the police?"

"With what?"

"For starters, the poison Gloria found in your bloodstream."

"We still don't know how it got there."

"Even more reason to get some serious investigative help!"

"Look how much we—really, you—have accomplished without outside help," Liam says. "If Rudy and Nellie are working together, and using AI to do it, they'll be able to outsmart the cops and likely cover their tracks."

"Every day we wait, you deteriorate. Is keeping this under wraps worth the risk, Liam?"

"TransScend is already reeling from the deepfake and the leaks. News of this conspiracy—especially without resolution—could destroy the company." His groan echoes over the car speakers. "Besides, how would anyone from the outside even make sense of what's going on? Unless we catch them red-handed."

"Isn't your health more important?"

"That's debatable," he says with a small laugh. "But this toxin does its damage over weeks to months. That's why they chose it. To poison me slowly. And Gloria's booked me for another blood test the day after tomorrow to check the levels. We still have a little time."

"I don't know, Liam . . ."

"We're close, Andrea. I can feel it. Please. Let's just give it another day or two."

"OK," she agrees, against her better judgment. Her instinct tells her to push harder, but she knows he won't listen.

After they disconnect, Andrea is still buzzing with adrenaline. Driving through Bellevue, she decides to reward herself for her investigative coup with a caffè mocha. She pulls into a parking spot on a quiet side street behind the Starbucks where she usually meets Liam.

Her mind races as she waits inside for her coffee. If Rudy planted Nellie inside the company a decade ago, it points to a conspiracy deeper and more thought-out than she ever imagined.

As she exits the store, Andrea nearly slips on the slick sidewalk. Steadying her coffee, she looks both ways, then steps onto the road toward her car.

Halfway across, she hears the whine of an electric motor and catches a glimpse of black to her right. She freezes as the car fishtails around the corner and barrels straight toward her.

Andrea dives to her left, back toward the coffee shop, hitting the pavement hard. A jolt of pain shoots up her shoulder. Reflexively, she rolls toward the curb. In the next moment, the car's tires roar across the spot where her head just was, spraying her face with cold, dirty slush.

Gasping, her shoulder throbbing, she scrambles to her feet in time to see the car race down the street. It disappears with another violent swerve around the next corner.

She didn't catch the license plate or model of the car, but one thing was clear as it sped right at her: the driver's seat was empty.

CHAPTER 41

Navigating Seattle's slick streets in Celeste's rear-wheel-drive sports car, Liam struggles to maintain control. Twice, his numb hands nearly lose their grip on the wheel as he almost spins out on the icy roads, adrenaline mixing with his fatigue.

After checking in with the triage nurse inside the ER, a care aide leads Liam down a sterile hallway marked TREATMENT. Halfway there, he stumbles, catching himself against the wall. He waves off the aide's offer of help, mumbling something about slippery shoes. Her skeptical look tells him she's not convinced, but she stays silent, guiding him to a small examining room that smells faintly of industrial cleaner.

Andrea lies on the table, propped up by a tilted headrest, her left arm in a sling. A deep abrasion runs from her hairline down the side of her forehead. Relieved to see her awake and alert, Liam rushes to her side. "Andrea! How are you?"

She shrugs, wincing. "A broken collarbone, a few scrapes, and a bruised knee. Maybe a mild concussion. Waiting on the CT results. All in all, could've been worse."

Despite her brave front, Liam notices the tremor in her fingers and the strain in her voice. It only deepens his guilt. "I can't believe this happened to you. I'm so sorry."

"Liam . . . there was no driver in that car."

"Jesus!" he swallows away the lump in his throat. The moment he got the call from the ER, he suspected the attempt on Andrea's life was tied to her investigation into TransScend, but this detail confirms it. "What did the cops say?"

"What I expected. No witnesses. They're checking security cameras on the street, but even if they find something, it won't lead back to the car, will it?"

"Probably not," Liam agrees. "Did you tell them everything?"

"No. I didn't mention the driverless part or what I've been working on." A small grin flickers across her face. "Lord knows there are enough cheating spouses out there who'd want to run me over."

"I think it's time, Andrea. We should go to the cops."

Her eyes narrow. "Whoever's behind this must be desperate to silence me, or at least scare me off."

"Clearly."

"But if they knew you were onto the poison, why come after me? Their whole plan unravels once you realize you're not dying of ALS or planning to go through with MAiD, right?"

"Maybe they're in full damage control mode, trying to tie up loose ends."

"So why am I the one with the broken collarbone? Aren't you the one they want dead?"

Liam lets out a weary chuckle. "They probably don't think they need to. They're already poisoning me."

"Exactly. And any normal person who realized they were being poisoned would go straight to the police."

"You're right. They probably don't know I know about the toxin. And since I haven't gone to the police yet—wait, are you saying I'm not normal?"

Andrea grins. "Letting yourself be poisoned just to keep the upper hand? I'm not sure that fits the dictionary definition."

"When you put it like that . . ." But his smile fades. "Rudy's got to be behind this. Probably with Nellie's help. I'm sure either one of them could've accessed a self-driving car."

"We have no proof," she says. "But I might've pushed him too hard when I went fishing for info from that tech journalist. Maybe I made myself a target."

"That makes sense."

"But if Rudy's in on it, he's probably got more help than just Nellie. It's time you and I found out."

Liam frowns. "Are you the one saying we shouldn't go to the cops now?"

Andrea shifts uncomfortably, swings her legs over the side of the table, and stands. "Those bastards either tried to kill me or scare me off. They're not getting away with it."

"No, they're not."

"And like you said, we're in the best position to figure it out. Especially if they don't know you're onto them."

"So what do you suggest?" he asks.

"We stick to your plan," she says, moving gingerly toward the door. "They're panicking, which means they're bound to slip up. Let's give it another day or two, let them expose themselves." She pauses, her face clouded with worry. "You still have a little more time, right? Your system can handle more exposure, potentially?"

He nods, summoning confidence he doesn't quite feel. "This poison is slow-acting, Andrea. I've got time."

"You better."

Liam's gaze lingers on the angry welt on her forehead. Confused by his emotions—guilt, definitely, but also a deepening affection he can't shake—he says, "I'm just not sure keeping the upper hand is worth the risk anymore, Andrea."

"What's going on here?" She laughs incredulously. "I'm the one who almost got my skull crushed."

"Exactly."

"Don't worry about me, Liam. I'll keep such a low profile, it'll be like I don't even exist." She tilts her head. "You haven't told anyone about me, have you?"

"No. Definitely not anyone at TransScend."

She raises an eyebrow, wincing again. "And outside the office?"

"I told Celeste I hired a PI to catch her with Benjamin."

"Did you give her my name?"

"No." He pauses. "Well, maybe I mentioned you by first name."

"Interesting."

"It can't be Celeste," Liam says, though even as he says it, the doubt nags. "Even if she wanted to poison me and run you down, she wouldn't have the means or the opportunity to pull off something this complex. She just wouldn't."

"All right." Andrea's tone is neutral, but he senses her skepticism.

"Whoever's behind this must have been tracking me for months," Liam says. "Before we knew better, I used to contact you on my work phone. I bet that's how they found you. Maybe they're still watching you."

"Maybe." She locks eyes with him. "But Liam, if we're going to keep doing this, they can't know we're onto them. At least not about the ALS. You'll need to keep up the façade."

He knows she's right, and her words give him an idea.

He pulls out his burner phone and logs into his work email through a protected VPN server. He selects Dr. Glynn from his contacts and begins dictating an email. "Dear Dr. Glynn, my symptoms have become intolerable. I struggle to feed myself. I can't stop dropping things. And I've been forced to walk with a cane." He realizes that aside from the last line, the rest is true. He carefully considers his next words. "My dignity is eroding by the day. There is no quality left in my life. I can see the road ahead too clearly now. I can't do this to myself or my family. The time has come to proceed with MAiD."

CHAPTER 42

Back in his home office, Liam sits at his desk, researching self-driving vehicles, trying to narrow down the model and source of the car Andrea described. His focus falters from the persistent cramping in his fingers—the breaks between spasms now measured in minutes rather than hours. The numbness and burning in his feet never seem to let up. Despite his reassurances to Andrea, he wonders if the nerve damage is still reversible. What if the next blood test shows that his levels are rising, not falling? *How much time do I really have left?*

As he shakes out a spasm in his left hand, a knock on the door pulls his attention. "Who even knocks in this house anymore?" he calls out.

"You have a visitor, Lee," Celeste replies.

"Come in," he says, quickly closing his laptop.

The door opens, and Nellie Cortez steps into the room, her expression sharper than usual, a mix of intensity and something else he can't quite place. Liam's neck tightens, and he forces himself to take slow, steady breaths, trying to tamp down the anger rising in his chest.

Celeste, sensing the tension, glances between them, her curiosity barely concealed. "Good to see you again, Nellie," she says before backing out of the room and closing the door behind her.

As soon as they're alone, Nellie demands, "Who is Angela Brown?"

"No idea," Liam replies, unable to keep the edge out of his voice. "Why?"

"Because some woman claiming to be her cornered my sister this morning, spinning some bullshit story about going to school with me." She folds her arms, her gaze hardening. "And you're telling me you know nothing about it?"

"Do I look like an Angela Brown?"

"You look like someone who'd want to know more about Rudy Ziegler."

Liam grits his teeth. "No question about that."

"Yes, Liam, I've known Rudy for a long time."

"Funny how that never came up in the ten years you've worked for me," he shoots back. "Not even during our messy court battles."

"Why would it? I know exactly how you two feel about each other."

"How *we* feel?" He leans forward. "So, you've heard Rudy's side, then?"

"Matter of fact, I have," Nellie says, her tone unyielding. "Too many times to count. And it's not pretty."

"How do you know Rudy?"

"He was a consultant at Microsoft when I started there. I was a junior tech analyst on a project he worked on. He was very supportive."

Liam arches an eyebrow. "Supportive, was he?"

"Don't be gross," she snaps. "He was a mentor."

"And yet you came to work for me and TransScend anyway?"

"Years later! And when Rudy heard about it, he had a conniption. It almost destroyed our friendship."

"But it didn't, did it?"

Nellie's expression falters momentarily before hardening again. "Not really, no."

"So, Rudy didn't install you at TransScend?"

Indignation flashes across her face. "*Install me?* Like I'm a plant or a puppet? Are you out of your mind? He was furious when I went to work for you. We didn't talk for ages."

"But you're talking again now?"

"Lately, I've had to," she says.

"Why's that?"

"Because Rudy is the one who masterminded the deepfake of that New Hampshire senator and leaked it to the media."

"You knew?"

She nods, face impassive.

"Because you helped him?"

"What? Of course not!" She recoils. "What's wrong with you?"

Liam feels off-balance, trying to reconcile what Nellie just disclosed with what he already knows. "If Rudy didn't tell you, how did you find out?"

"I tracked down his source at TransScend."

"You weren't his source?"

Her eyes blaze. "It was Joey. Joey Mitchell."

Liam vaguely recalls the pimply young guy, one of many on the development team. "That coder with the ponytail?"

"*Ex*-coder. The little douchebag."

"Joey told Rudy about TheirStory?"

Nellie nods. "Rudy's little spy."

"How do you know?"

"I buried a GPS tracker within the TransScend portal. As soon as anyone logged onto the server, I could track the whereabouts of their device. When the leak happened, I went through the server logs. Joey had been to Rudy's building twice in the week before."

"How did you know it was Rudy's building?"

Her face flushes, and she looks away. "I've been there."

"Nellie, why are you only telling me this now?"

"I was focused on stopping the hemorrhaging."

"Really? Nothing to do with protecting Rudy?"

"Maybe. I don't know." She clears her throat, her expression defiant. "But you've had your head up your ass for weeks. Barely in the office, totally checked out. So, I confronted Rudy myself."

"When? Where?"

She shifts uncomfortably. "Why does that matter?"

"Humor me."

"I wanted somewhere private, so I invited him to my place last week."

The story fits. "What happened?"

"I told Rudy I knew he was behind the deepfake and the leak."

"Did he admit it?"

She shrugs. "He demanded proof."

"Which you didn't have?"

"Not enough, no. And without the proof, he knew he was in the driver's seat." She pauses. "Or at least, that's what he thought."

"He wasn't?"

"I gave him an ultimatum."

"Which was?"

"I'd rather not get into those details, Liam. Let's just say it was enough to reach an agreement."

Liam wonders what leverage Nellie has over Rudy but doubts she'd tell him. "What kind of agreement?"

"No more deepfakes, no more leaks." She puts her hands on her hips. "And there haven't been any since."

"Were you planning to share any of this with me, Nellie?"

"Probably not," she says flatly. "Not unless I had to."

Liam lets the silence stretch. "So, let me get this straight. Your friend Rudy sets out to sabotage TransScend, you catch him through tracking a junior coder, and instead of telling me you broker a deal?"

"Despite how sketchy you make it sound, that's basically how it happened, yes. My job is security. I take it very seriously. If I had actionable proof Rudy was involved, I'd have told you. But I didn't. The best I could do was neutralize the threat. Which I did."

Liam studies her face, searching for any hint of deceit. "You protected TheirStory, even though you think it's an existential threat to humanity?"

"Your words, not mine. My beliefs and my job are separate. Nothing would stop me from doing my job, Liam. Nothing."

He pauses, still trying to read her. "What about the poisoning?"

"Poisoning?" Her whole face scrunches in confusion. "What poisoning?"

CHAPTER 43

Andrea's left shoulder throbs as she reaches for a mug with her good arm, pulling it down from the shelf. She drops a bag of chai tea inside it and switches on the kettle. After discharging herself from the ER, she called her Realtor to pause any showings of her father's townhouse. She hasn't told anyone else about the accident and declined Liam's repeated offers of help. But moving in on her own, one-handed and with a lingering headache, proved harder than she'd expected. Once settled, she slept the entire afternoon away in possibly the longest nap of her life.

She tries to rationalize the move as strategic, telling herself that whoever targeted her won't find her here. But deep down, she knows it's a weak theory. This place is no safer than anywhere else. Still, there's comfort in being surrounded by memories of her father—a sense of security in the familiar. And there's the lingering weight of his final words, which she realizes she can no longer avoid.

Tea in hand, she walks into his old office, sits down at his computer, and types in the password with her good hand. Her fingers tremble as she opens the letter and forces herself to read it from beginning to end.

My Darling Andrea,

Words, certainly not mine, can't express how much I love you. You're the center of my universe, and I couldn't imagine a better daughter. As an accountant, I appreciate that what you've brought me is the greatest return on investment anyone could ever hope for. The sun and the moon, as the songs go.

But, sweetheart, there are things you need to understand, starting with your mother. And it breaks my heart that I've kept this from you all these years. Please, please know I thought I was doing the right thing. But now, looking back, I wonder if I was only being selfish.

Your mother was the only woman I ever loved. The only one I could have loved that way. Her beauty aside, she had a vibrance unmatched by anyone I've known, except maybe you. I'm still not sure what she saw in me, but I wouldn't change a thing, despite how it ended. After she left, I knew I couldn't replace her. I never even tried.

Before she left, your mother wasn't well. She was bipolar. She managed it for years, but when you were about six, she stopped taking her medications. She turned to alcohol and cocaine. She became more and more erratic until she finally walked out of our lives, days after your seventh birthday. As much as it broke my heart, I didn't try to stop her. You needed more stability than she could provide.

When you were fourteen, she reached out, asking if she could see you. I didn't say no, not immediately. I went to meet her alone. The woman who greeted me was a shell of the person I'd once known. Not only had she aged decades, but there was a flatness in her. That spark you both shared was gone. That alone wouldn't have kept you apart, but she reeked of alcohol. At ten in the morning. That decided it for me. I told her it would be best if she didn't see you. To her credit, she didn't fight me.

I'm not sure I had the right to make that decision for you. It haunts me. Because that was the last time I saw her. I don't even know if she's still alive. No doubt, as skilled an investigator as you are, you could track her down without my help, but the last I heard, she was living in Bend, Oregon, under her maiden name, Hunter.

Now, as I sit here, writing this, I also owe you another apology. For leaving you this way. Without warning. You have no idea how much I wanted to tell you everything last night at dinner. But that would've been cruel and selfish. My decision is final, and I'm at peace with it. I know you would've tried to change my mind, but nothing could have swayed me. And I refuse to burden you with the guilt of having tried and failed.

Darling, I don't remember what it's like not to be in pain. If it were only the pain, I'd bear it gladly to have more time with you. But you must understand, it's the loss of function, the erosion of my independence, that is slowly killing me. I already lean on you too much, and the truth is, I wouldn't be able to care for myself much longer.

You are the only joy left in my life, and what a joy you are. But I refuse to become an even greater burden. And we both know you would insist on caring for me. It destroys me to see how much I've already limited your choices in life. I can't make it worse. I won't. Maybe you'll resent me for this, but I know it's the right decision. For both of us.

You've been betrayed too many times by those you love and trust. Your mother. Max. And now, me. But I hope you can see this for what it is—an act of mercy for you as much as for me. And even if you can't forgive me, know that I will love you forever. My dying wish is that you live freely again. That you trust again. That you love again.

You deserve that, and so much more.

Yours forever,
Dad

Lost in her father's words, Andrea doesn't even notice the tears dripping onto the keyboard until she closes the document. Everything—the attempt on her life, her concussion, and especially her dad's letter—crashes down on her at once. Overwhelmed, helpless, lost, she can't bring herself to move. Instead, she stares blankly at the screensaver, trying to focus on anything other than the storm of emotions swirling inside her.

Only the soft knock at the door and Liam's voice saying, "Andrea, it's me," pulls her out of her daze.

She rises slowly, every movement deliberate, and trudges to the door to answer it. The scent of spice reaches her before she even notices the bags of food in Liam's hands.

He steps inside, lowering the bags to the floor before wrapping her in a warm, comforting embrace. Despite the pain in her collarbone, she melts into his arms, craving the solace he offers without words.

She rocks silently in his arms, her tears soaking his shoulder.

CHAPTER 44

Andrea pulls away from Liam's embrace after what seems like an eternity. He avoids her eyes, grabbing the bags of food and carrying them to the table. He stumbles slightly but catches himself, hoping she didn't notice. "I hope you like Indian food," he says, his voice steadier than he feels.

"I do, thanks," she replies hoarsely, wiping her eyes with her free hand.

Liam begins unpacking the containers, glancing up at her. Her eyes are bloodshot, framed by wild curls that seem even more untamed than usual. There's a rawness to her sadness, a vulnerability that only enhances her attractiveness. "Do you want to talk about it?" he asks gently.

She hesitates, then nods. Once they're seated beside each other, Andrea takes a deep breath. "I finally read my dad's suicide note," she says quietly.

"Oh, Andrea . . ."

"You were right," she says.

"About what?"

"Dad tried to spare me from the guilt of not stopping him, had I known."

"I can understand that. Truly."

"I could hear his voice in my head, Liam . . ." Her voice breaks slightly. "I wish I'd read it sooner, you know?"

"Maybe you weren't ready," he offers softly.

"Maybe," she murmurs. "He also told me things about my mom."

Liam nods, giving her space to continue.

"She was—or is—bipolar," Andrea explains. "He didn't even know if she's still alive."

"Is that why she left?"

Andrea nods. "Sounds like she had a manic episode that spiraled into alcohol and drugs. Eventually, she just took off. When I was a teenager, she tried to reach out and see me again, but Dad discouraged her. She was drunk when he met her that morning."

"This must be incredibly hard for you," Liam says.

"It helps to know why she left in the first place," Andrea says, offering a slight shrug, though her wince betrays her discomfort. "I wish Dad had told me sooner, but I understand why he didn't. He was only trying to protect me."

"He sounds like an amazing man. I wish I could've met him."

"I think he would have liked you," Andrea says, her voice trembling as tears well up again. "Then again, he liked almost everybody. It's just . . ."

"What is it?" Liam asks softly.

"Nothing." She smiles faintly through her tears. "It helps knowing my mom tried to come back. That she didn't completely abandon me."

Liam nods. "It must mean a lot."

Andrea wipes her eyes and takes a deep breath. "And how was your day?"

"Nellie Cortez came to see me."

"Nellie?" Andrea's chin lifts in surprise. "What did she want?"

"Her sister must've called her," he says with a faint grin. "Didn't take Nellie long to connect me to your 'chance encounter' with her sister."

Andrea squints. "Do you think that's why the car came after me?"

"No. Nellie isn't involved in any of that. She's not even Rudy's inside source like we thought."

"How can you be so sure?"

Liam explains how Nellie confessed to her secret friendship with

Rudy and how she traced the leak to a junior coder, confronting Rudy to force him to back off. "She didn't say it outright, but I wonder if they were—or maybe still are—lovers."

"And you believe her?" Andrea asks, skepticism in her tone.

"I do. She seemed genuine."

"So, you think Rudy's acting alone?"

"I'm not sure about that. But Nellie isn't involved—at least, not in the way we suspected."

Andrea chews her lower lip, thinking. "Can Nellie help us prove Rudy was behind the corporate sabotage? Give us something concrete we could take to the authorities?"

"Of course not," Liam sighs. "It's so damn frustrating. We can't prove any of this."

Andrea's eyes flicker with an idea. "Unless . . ."

"Unless what?"

"Unless you can somehow get Rudy to admit it."

"And how do I do that?"

"Trick him into it. Exploit his ego—tap into that simmering sense of grievance and self-righteousness that he carries around like a camel's hump."

Later that night, as Liam lies beside Celeste, his conscience weighs on him. He's never cheated on her, physically, but this is the first time he's felt the pull of an emotional affair. He used to scoff at the concept, dismissing it as something insignificant. But he can't ignore the complexity of his feelings for Andrea anymore. There's gratitude and respect, yes, but also a deepening intimacy. And physical attraction, too. Feelings that far exceed the boundaries of friendship.

As if reading his mind, Celeste turns to him with a quizzical look. "What's going on with you?"

"Nothing," he says, shaking his head.

"Right," she replies, her tone tinged with disappointment.

"I've got a lot on my mind, Celeste."

"And that's exactly where you like to keep it."

"What's that supposed to mean?"

She hesitates, then sighs. "Look, I know I'm on thin ice here, but . . ."

"Yes?"

"Never mind." She starts to turn away.

"What is it, Celeste?" he presses.

She slowly turns back, her eyes clouded with emotion. "After everything we've been through, I didn't think you'd do this again. Not so soon."

"Do what again?" Liam asks.

"Keep me in the dark," she says, her voice calm but laced with hurt. "Just like with the polyneuropathy. Leaving me to worry and fear the worst. I'm your wife, Liam. I thought we were supposed to confide in each other, not shut each other out."

Liam feels a pang of guilt but pushes it aside. "That's rich, coming from you," he snaps, aware that he's deflecting.

"Fair. I deserve that." Celeste's anger fades, replaced by sadness. "But I thought . . ."

"Thought what?"

She reaches out and tentatively strokes his cheek. "That maybe I could help you. Be your sounding board. Your safe space."

He gazes into her eyes, tempted to unburden himself. To tell her everything—his fears, his suspicions, his doubts. It would be a relief, wouldn't it? But how could he confess that what's troubling him most right now is his growing feelings for another woman? One who nearly died trying to save his life.

CHAPTER 45

The rain has washed away Seattle's snow, clearing the streets but doing little to lift Liam's spirits. The unresolved argument with Celeste weighs heavily on him, and Andrea's presence lingers in his mind, a constant distraction. His work phone buzzes, and he's almost relieved for the distraction as he answers via Bluetooth.

"Good morning, Mr. Hirsch. It's Dr. Heather Glynn."

"Dr. Glynn," Liam greets her, keeping his tone neutral. "Good to hear from you."

"I hope I'm not catching you at a bad time. I thought it would be better to discuss this over the phone rather than email."

"Now's fine."

"Good. I wanted to confirm that you're still planning to proceed with MAiD?"

"I am," Liam replies, his voice steady. He knows he has to sound resolute, because if he truly believed he had ALS, he would be this certain.

"And you'd still prefer a home death?"

"Yes," Liam says, eyes focused on the road ahead.

"And your family? Are they fully supportive?"

"They are," he lies smoothly.

"All right. I can be present with you, or if timing doesn't allow, one of my colleagues will be available."

"I appreciate that, but I'd prefer to keep it just family."

"Of course," Dr. Glynn says. "Typically, we use a combination of a barbiturate sedative and a cardiac medication to achieve the desired outcome. Would you like the pharmacy to deliver the medications to your home?"

"No," Liam answers quickly. "I'll pick them up myself."

There's a brief pause. "All right. I'll call in the prescription."

"Thank you, Dr. Glynn."

"Do you have any questions?"

"I think you've answered them all."

"Mr. Hirsch, despite your resolve, please remember it's normal to have doubts or second thoughts as the time approaches. Some people even change their minds. Those feelings are valid, and they shouldn't be ignored."

"OK."

"If you need anything—day or night—please call me. Even if you just want to talk."

"I will," Liam says, swallowing back the sheepishness. "Thank you, Dr. Glynn."

"Godspeed, Mr. Hirsch."

After hanging up, Liam is hit with the sudden urge to take a shower, as if he could wash away the guilt. Deceiving the kindhearted doctor feels wrong, but he doesn't see another way. With the possibility of someone listening in, it's crucial everyone believes he's still fully committed to ending his life.

Liam arrives at the Sunshine Diner ahead of Sam and takes their usual corner booth. Sam walks in moments later, sliding into the seat across from him. Paul, their server, fills their cups while he and Sam gripe about the Kraken's recent losing streak.

After Paul leaves, Sam leans back and says, "We might as well rent out our boardroom if we're going to be meeting here this often."

Liam chuckles. "It's kind of nostalgic, don't you think?"

"Who's got time for nostalgia?" Sam mutters. "These days, I can barely keep my head above water."

The door opens and Nellie walks in. Sam's eyes narrow in suspicion as he turns to Liam. "What's she doing here?" he mutters.

"She's not the leak, Sam," Liam says.

Nellie strides over and sits beside Liam, her expression guarded. She waves off Paul's offer to fill her cup.

She and Sam exchange tense glances until Liam clears his throat, breaking the silence. "Nellie, can you explain to Sam what you told me yesterday? About Rudy."

Nellie's tone is clipped as she speaks. "Rudy was behind the deepfake and the leak. His source was Joey."

Sam makes a face. "Joey? The greasy kid on the development team? How do you know?"

Nellie leans forward, her explanation short and businesslike. "I tracked his movements through the server logs. Joey was the one feeding information to Rudy."

"Rudy, that son of a bitch! What a pathetic little man. A walking grievance," Sam snarls, either unaware or indifferent to Nellie's feelings for him. "We need to destroy him. End this once and for all."

"We can't," Liam says, shaking his head. "We don't have solid proof."

"Who needs proof?" Sam retorts. "We can bury him with rumors and innuendo. I know a guy who specializes in that kind of work."

Nellie shifts uncomfortably, but she says nothing. Liam catches her unease and quickly interjects. "That wouldn't be necessary if we had more leverage on Rudy."

"And how do we get that?" Sam asks.

"By getting him to admit to what he's done," Liam says, following Andrea's earlier advice.

Sam scoffs. "Good luck with that."

"It's worth trying," Liam says calmly. "He's got an ego the size of this city, and guys like him always trip over their own arrogance."

Sam shrugs. "If you think it'll work, sure, why not? Rudy's your Lex Luthor, after all." He glances between Liam and Nellie. "This means we can proceed with the launch, right?"

"Hell no!" Nellie exclaims. "With or without Rudy, the security risks and vulnerabilities are still too high."

"Only because you can't seem to do your job," Sam snaps, leaning toward her. "You're lucky I'm not the one in charge."

Nellie's eyes flash with anger, and she meets him head-on. "We're all lucky you're not in charge, Sam. Your schoolyard bully routine is wasted on me."

"Enough, both of you," Liam says, his voice firm. They fall silent, though the tension lingers. "Sam, we are going to postpone the launch. Nellie and the team need time to make sure the app is secure."

Sam throws his hands up in frustration. "Thirty-seven percent!" he nearly shouts. "That's how much TransScend's shares have tanked since the leak. We're bleeding out more every day. If we wait much longer, we won't have the resources to launch the app."

"There won't be any more leaks," Liam says, tapping the table for emphasis. "Now we can pivot. We—"

Suddenly, Liam's hand jerks uncontrollably. His arm follows suit, shaking violently. He watches, horrified, as his rogue limb knocks over his coffee cup, sending it crashing to the floor. Both Sam and Nellie pull back in shock as the cup shatters, coffee spilling everywhere.

Liam grabs his wrist with his other hand, trying to stop the shaking, but it's too late. The entire diner goes silent, all eyes on him.

"What the fuck is happening to you?" Sam asks, his voice low but urgent.

"It's nothing," Liam mutters, though the tremor in his voice betrays him. "I'm handling it."

"You need to see a doctor, Liam," Sam insists, his tone softening but no less urgent.

"I have," Liam replies, struggling to steady his breath. "It's under control."

Nellie glances at the shattered cup. "You call that under control?"

Liam lowers his head, his cheeks burning with embarrassment.

"This is what that sabbatical nonsense is about, isn't it?" Sam's voice takes on a note of realization. "The constant back-and-forth with the app's release date? It's all tied to this, isn't it? You're not well, are you, Boss?"

CHAPTER 46

Andrea grips the steering wheel tightly with her right hand, her left shoulder throbbing with each turn and stop. She keeps second-guessing her decision to leave the safety of her dad's townhouse this morning, let alone tail someone across the city. It feels reckless and unprofessional. If the conspirators were planning another attack, she might be giving them the perfect opportunity.

But she convinced herself she had to act, that hiding while Liam deteriorates would be a mistake. Time is slipping away, and this lead—however flimsy—might be the only one she has left.

As she trails Celeste's car off I-5 and into Tacoma, doubt starts creeping in. Is this really a solid lead, or is her concussion clouding her judgment? Objectively, it feels like a stretch. Even if Celeste knows about her, and her involvement, why would she try to kill her?

The past twenty-four hours have been some of the most turbulent of Andrea's life. Surviving a near-fatal accident and reading her father's heartbreaking note would be overwhelming enough, and her growing feelings for Liam only complicate matters. But she can't deny the intimacy and romantic tension building between them, or the comfort she felt in his arms.

Am I falling for my married client?

It's a boundary Andrea never thought she'd approach, let alone cross. This couldn't be what her father had in mind when he encouraged her to trust and love again. Yet here she is, entangled in a domestic mess she never expected, powerless to shake the jealousy eating at her.

Celeste doesn't deserve him.

Andrea pushes the thought aside as she watches Celeste's car pull into the parking lot of a Calhoun's restaurant, a popular chain in the area. She drives past, continuing three blocks before circling back. Parking across the lot from where Celeste is, she rubs her throbbing head and watches as the early brunch crowd trickles inside. She's unsure of what she's even hoping to find. Maybe it's her concussion, or maybe her feelings for Liam are leading her astray. She knows she should leave, retreat to the security of her father's townhouse. But something holds her there, a gut feeling that won't let go.

Lost in thought, Andrea barely notices the man walking toward the restaurant until he pauses at the door and glances over his shoulder. She zeroes in on his face.

Recognition hits her instantly, but there's no time to grab her camera. He's inside before she can even lift her phone to snap a photo. Not that she needs one: she's photographed him many times before—twice, in fact, when Benjamin was naked.

CHAPTER 47

As the elevator climbs to the twenty-seventh floor, Liam's phone vibrates in his pocket. Andrea's burner number flashes on the screen, but he lets it ring. He hadn't told her about this visit to Rudy's apartment. He'd planned to be more prepared for this confrontation, but the incident at the diner—where he lost control of his arm—terrified him into acting sooner than intended.

Despite avoiding his office and his truck, which seem to be the likeliest sources of the toxin, his condition continues to deteriorate. He's not sure he can wait another day to get his blood levels rechecked.

How are they still getting to me?

Earlier, he dismissed Andrea's suggestion to flee, but now he wonders if running might be his only option. If he doesn't find a way to stop the exposure soon, it will be too late. It's the only reason he's now standing outside the door of his nemesis. If Rudy is behind the poisoning, he might also be the only one who can end it.

Before knocking, Liam activates the voice recorder app on his phone and slips it back into his pocket.

Rudy opens the door without expression and gestures for him to step inside the minimalist living room. Liam's skin crawls standing this close to Rudy, but he forces his voice to remain steady. "Thanks for seeing me."

"You've reconsidered my fifty-one-percent stake, have you?" Rudy asks, his tone flat and emotionless.

"Extortion is still a crime, Rudy," Liam replies, taking a measured breath.

"Extortion?" Rudy scoffs. "Are you feeling all right?"

Liam's body tenses, but not from his usual spasms. "Why do you ask?"

"I thought I made myself clear when you came here with your pathetic ten-percent offer," Rudy says, a faint smirk forming at the corners of his lips. "I told you fifty-one percent was the only deal I'd consider. It's reasonable, some might say generous, considering your grievous intellectual property theft. Nothing to do with extortion."

"I'm talking about stock manipulation."

Rudy chuckles. "And how exactly am I doing that? Using my insignificant little 401(k) to shake the global market?"

"By sabotaging TransScend."

Rudy studies him for a long moment, then shrugs. "I need a drink," he says, moving toward the kitchen. "Want a Coke?"

Liam shakes his head.

Rudy retrieves a can of cola from the fridge, along with a lime. He pulls a knife from a drawer and starts slicing the lime into wedges, taking his time. "What exactly are you accusing me of, Liam?"

"I know about Joey Mitchell."

Rudy's hand pauses momentarily but then resumes cutting the lime. "He's a good kid, Joey."

"A good kid who's been feeding you company secrets."

"Did Nellie tell you this?"

Liam ignores the question. "You created that deepfake to scuttle the New Hampshire Senate race."

"I heard that was done with HisStory."

"Then you leaked it, along with confidential details about TheirStory, to the tech reporter Howell. The same guy who interviewed you days before the story broke."

Rudy shrugs, unbothered. "Those are serious allegations. Got any proof?"

"That's not much of a denial, Rudy."

"Theoretically, an astute investor could've made a lot of money shorting TransScend stock after the story broke. The volatility . . ." Rudy tsks. "The way your stock plummeted was almost predictable."

Liam's stomach churns, realizing Rudy has been profiting from the chaos he caused at TransScend by betting against its share price. "That's why you weren't interested in ten percent? You found an easier way to make money by shorting the stock?"

Rudy doesn't deny it. "I wasn't interested in your charity. And let's face it, Liam, your offer was depreciating. TransScend is losing value by the day. Down thirty-seven percent and still free-falling. Fifty-one percent doesn't seem so excessive anymore, does it?"

"I'm going to the cops, Rudy."

Rudy just smiles. "With what? Coincidences?"

Liam's hand begins to tremble, though he can't tell if it's from anger or the disease. But Rudy is right. He doesn't have enough evidence to prove a crime.

Rudy pops open the can of cola, squeezing a lime wedge into it. "What's your real play, Liam?"

Liam thinks of Nellie's cryptic ultimatum. Whatever it was about, it was serious enough to make Rudy back down once before. Maybe it would again. "What if your deal with Nellie falls apart?"

Rudy freezes.

"What happens when Nellie comes forward?"

Rudy's face darkens, and he points the knife at Liam, fury flashing in his eyes. "Leave Nellie out of this."

Liam doubts he could fend off Rudy's knife with his unreliable limbs, but he's too angry to care. "The deal with Nellie is off the table unless you tell me how you're doing it."

"Doing what?" Rudy snaps, nostrils flaring.

"For fuck's sake, Rudy! Poisoning me."

"Poisoning you?" Rudy's face twists in confusion.

"You know exactly what I'm talking about," Liam growls.

Rudy stares, slack-jawed.

"The nitriles I'm breathing or swallowing!" Liam raises his arm to show him the tremor. "The toxin you've been feeding me!"

"Nitriles?" Rudy says, lowering the knife. "Never even heard of them."

"They're industrial chemicals," Liam says, scanning Rudy's face for any hint of recognition but finding none. "They mimic ALS symptoms, but only after massive exposure. And my bloodstream is loaded with them."

Rudy looks genuinely perplexed.

"How are you doing it, Rudy?" Liam demands, trying to keep his voice steady.

Rudy's shoulders sag as he drops the knife onto the countertop, his earlier bravado evaporating. "I'll be honest," he says, shaking his head. "It's not like I haven't thought about killing you, Liam. But if I were going to, I wouldn't use poison." He smirks, though it lacks malice. "Besides, why now? When, for the first time, karma's finally catching up with you?"

CHAPTER 48

As Liam trudges up to the townhouse door, the weight of defeat presses down on him heavier than ever. Every lead has dried up, and his symptoms are only worsening. He half wonders if it might be easier to simply take the medications Dr. Glynn prescribed and get it over with.

When Andrea answers the door, her eyes are frantic with worry. "Where have you been? Why didn't you answer my calls? I found something out about—"

"It's not him, Andrea," Liam cuts her off, his voice hollow.

"Not who?"

"Rudy. He's not behind the poisoning."

She frowns. "You're sure?"

"Yes."

Her expression softens. "Come in." She reaches out, takes his elbow, and guides him into the living room. Her touch is warm and comforting, and Liam feels a pang of disappointment when she lets go as they sit on the couch. "How do you know it's not Rudy?"

"I went to see him."

"Without telling me?" A flicker of hurt crosses her eyes. "What did he say?"

Liam's jaw tightens at the memory. "Rudy's sabotaging TransScend, sure. But he's doing it to hurt me, not kill me, and he's profiting off it by shorting the company's stock."

"He admitted it?"

"Not in so many words, but essentially, yeah."

"But not to the poisoning?"

Liam shakes his head miserably. "He's not involved. The poison isn't connected to the sabotage or the financial fraud, Andrea. The trail's gone cold." He exhales heavily, sinking deeper into the couch. "Christ, maybe the app itself is behind it?"

Andrea recoils slightly. "That's not possible, is it?"

"I didn't think so. But now?" He pauses. "This app is already doing things beyond what I expected. Maybe it's crossed the Rubicon."

"What are you saying?"

"AGI—artificial general intelligence."

Her forehead creases. "Isn't that what it already is?"

"No, AI and AGI are not the same. AI performs specific tasks by analyzing vast amounts of data and recognizing patterns—it only simulates intelligence. AGI, on the other hand, can think for itself, learn, and adapt. It's real intelligence, at a level equal to or even beyond human capabilities."

Her face pales. "You mean it could act on its own?"

Liam nods grimly. "Maybe, yes."

"That's terrifying."

"But at this point, it almost doesn't matter who or what's behind it."

"Why do you say that?"

"I might've run out of time, Andrea."

"You can't think like that!"

"It's the truth. Earlier today, I completely lost control of my arm. Hard to imagine nerve damage like that being reversible, even if I could stop the poisoning now. Which, clearly, I can't."

"You told me it was slow acting! That there was still time."

"That was when I thought I knew who was behind this. And that there was a chance to stop it."

Andrea looks down, adjusting her sling. "We'll figure it out."

"I should've listened to you days ago."

"About going to the cops?"

"Yeah, that too. But I meant when you told me to run as far and fast as I could. I still don't know if I could've escaped the toxin, but I could've made it harder for whoever's behind this." He swallows, his throat dry. "But what would I have told Celeste and the kids?"

Andrea clears her throat. "That's actually what I wanted to talk to you about. Celeste."

Liam tenses, expecting her to address the unspoken connection between them. He's not ready for that. "Look, Andrea, I think I know where you're going—"

"I followed her, Liam."

"Celeste?" He blinks, caught off guard. "Where?"

"To Tacoma."

"Why Tacoma?"

"She went to meet Benjamin. For brunch."

Liam stares at her, processing. "Of course she did," he says after a moment, surprised by how little it hurts. "Then what? Did they end up at some cheap motel?"

Andrea shakes her head. "After brunch, they shared a long hug, and then went their separate ways. I followed her back home."

"Guess they ran out of time to hook up today," he mutters bitterly.

"I'm sorry, Liam. I thought you needed to know."

"I'm glad you told me, Andrea," he says quietly. "But why did you follow her?"

Andrea hesitates, running a finger over the scrape on her forehead. "I couldn't stop thinking about that self-driving car. Your wife's the only one who might know about me and my ongoing involvement. And you mentioned she used to be a brilliant coder. An expert in AI."

Liam shakes his head. "Even if she could have, which I highly doubt, she wouldn't have sent a car after you. No way."

Andrea reaches out, touching the back of his hand. "Would you ever have thought she'd have an affair with your contractor? Or keep seeing him after she promised it was over?"

"No," Liam admits.

Andrea gives his hand a gentle squeeze. "After all her lies, is it really safe to assume she's not mixed up in the rest of this?"

"Probably not, no." He closes his eyes. "I suppose it wouldn't be the worst way to clear the path for her and Benjamin. By getting me to kill myself."

"Not to mention getting full custody of the kids and inheriting your entire estate."

"Maybe," he sighs. "But still . . . Celeste? I just can't see it."

Andrea lets go of his hand. "Maybe. Maybe not. But we can't afford to ignore the possibility, can we?"

"No." He stares down at where her hand had been. "There are a lot of things I didn't think possible only a short time ago."

"Like what?"

When Liam looks back up, Andrea is leaning closer. Her eyes are warm, inviting. He focuses on the tiny abrasion above her lip, fighting the sudden urge to kiss it. "This. Us."

Liam's phone rings, breaking the moment. He pulls it out and frowns. "It's my son."

Andrea tilts her head. "He has your burner number?"

"No. Calls from my family are forwarded to it."

"Go ahead. Take it."

Liam answers. "Hey, buddy."

"Sorry to bug you, Dad, but I can't reach Mom."

Why am I not surprised? "What's up?"

"I got sent home from school."

"What happened?"

"The school nurse thinks I should see a doctor."

"Why?"

"It's my hand."

Liam's blood runs cold. "What's wrong with it?"

"It keeps twitching."

CHAPTER 49

Liam's pulse thunders in his ears, his throat tight, as if constricted by an invisible cord. *Is this what a panic attack feels like?*

He speeds through Seattle's core, darting and weaving between cars with reckless urgency. His son's words echo in his mind: *It keeps twitching.* The same early symptom he'd experienced when this nightmare began. Tuning out the angry horns and raised middle fingers, he barrels through a second yellow light, narrowly missing an SUV. But he doesn't let up on the gas.

When he pulls into the driveway, relief surges through him at the sight of Cole standing by the garage, as instructed. Liam jumps out and pulls him into a tight hug. His son squirms free, embarrassed.

"How are you?" Liam demands.

"Better," Cole replies, his brow furrowing in confusion. "I haven't had any more twitches in a couple of hours. You can relax."

Liam motions to the passenger seat. "Get in the car."

"Why don't we just wait to see my doctor tomorrow?"

"We're going to the ER. Now."

Cole hesitates, then climbs into the car without further argument. "Dad, seriously, what's going on? You're scaring me."

"I'll explain on the way."

Liam starts to pull out of the driveway. "Ava was clear on my instructions, right?"

"Yeah. She's crashing at Taylor's."

"And she knows not to come home until I say so?"

"She got the message." Cole sighs. "What's going on, Dad?"

"I'll get to that, I promise," Liam says, pulling back onto the road. "But you need to tell me everything about this twitching."

"OK . . ."

"What does it feel like? Describe it."

"It's like my left four fingers—not my thumb—cramp up suddenly. They sort of overlap for a few seconds, then relax. And it kept happening for a while."

Liam's heart skips a beat. He's all too familiar with that kind of twitching. "When did you first notice it?"

"I don't know."

"This is really important, Cole."

Cole's eyebrows knit together. "Your polyneuropathy . . . it's not contagious, is it?"

"No, no. You're going to be fine. Just tell me when you first felt it."

Cole frowns, thinking. "Not until I got to school. Around eleven, maybe?"

"Eleven? Why so late?"

"I had PE first block, then a break. I decided to study at home for my history test. It's gonna be a beast."

Liam nods. "What have you eaten in the last twenty-four hours?"

Cole shoots him a puzzled look. "What does that have to do with anything?"

"Just try to remember."

Cole sighs, thinking. "Uh, yesterday Mom made me a frittata for breakfast. Had pizza for dinner. This morning, cereal."

Cole recounts his recent meals, but nothing stands out. Liam hasn't eaten or drunk anything at home for nearly a week, so they couldn't have shared any food. The poisoning must be from inhalation. "You haven't been in my truck in the past day, have you?"

"No." Cole taps the window. "I've only been in this one with you. After the truck broke down."

A fresh wave of panic grips Liam. *Could someone have moved the poison into this car once I started using it?*

He rolls down all the windows, despite the drizzle seeping in from outside.

"Dad, it's raining. And you're freaking me out!"

"Where else have you been in the last day, Cole?"

"School and home. That's it. I've been cramming for the test. Mr. Harris's quizzes are brutal."

"All right, so you were studying in your room, then?"

Cole looks away, sheepish.

"What is it, Cole?"

"It's been noisy in the house. Ava blasts her music with her door open. And then this morning, Stella was vacuuming upstairs. I couldn't focus."

"And?"

"I went down to the basement. I used your office, Dad."

"My *home* office! For fuck's sake!" Liam shouts, gripping the steering wheel so hard his knuckles turn white.

"What's the big deal, Dad? I didn't touch anything. Not even your computer. I only—"

"No, no, it's fine," Liam mutters, his chest heaving as if he's just run a marathon.

"Why does it matter so much, then?" Cole asks.

"It probably doesn't," Liam lies, feigning a calmness he doesn't feel.

"What's this about, Dad?"

Liam chooses his words carefully. "Your symptoms sound similar to mine. But much milder. I just found out my polyneuropathy is caused by exposure to an industrial chemical. One I've probably been breathing in for months now."

Cole's eyes go wide. "Like asbestos? I heard a podcast about miners who got sick."

"Yeah, something like that." Liam nods. "But we couldn't figure out where it was coming from until now."

"Your office? Is something wrong with the vents in the basement?"

Liam forces a reassuring smile. "That's exactly what I'm thinking. The vents."

But the problem goes way beyond the vents. *Even worse, the real problem might just be your mother.*

CHAPTER 50

Before yesterday, Liam hadn't been to an ER in over fifteen years—not since the rock-climbing accident that left him with two fractured vertebrae. Now, for the second day in a row, he finds himself back in the same ER, this time gripped with worry for his son.

In the small, glass-enclosed room, Liam hovers beside Cole's bed as the ER doctor, Dr. Richards, conducts a thorough examination. Despite the bright pink stethoscope slung over her navy scrubs, the young doctor's formal, detached manner feels out of place for her age. She puts Cole through a series of physical tests that Liam knows all too well.

When she finishes, Liam tries again to explain that Cole might be suffering from nitrile poisoning.

Dr. Richards's smile tightens, her patience clearly wearing thin. "As I mentioned earlier, Mr. Hirsch," she says, her tone polite but strained, "we don't perform forensic toxicology testing in the ER. And with Cole's symptoms, poisoning is far down the list of likely causes."

"I'm sure you're right, Dr. Richards. But these aren't ordinary circumstances."

"They rarely are for our emergency patients, Mr. Hirsch."

Liam catches Cole's gaze, a mix of embarrassment and apprehension in his eyes.

"Dr. Richards, could we talk outside, now?" Liam asks, striving to keep his voice steady.

"All right," she sighs.

"Dad . . ." Cole's tone is cautious, almost pleading.

"It's fine, buddy. I'll be right back."

Liam follows Dr. Richards into the hallway, where the steady flow of staff and patients underscores the urgency of the hospital.

"Listen, Dr. Richards, I've experienced these exact symptoms," he says, trying to make her understand.

"You have?" Her skepticism is palpable.

"Yes, and mine have progressed because of longer exposure to the toxin. If you could just speak to Dr. Gloria Chow, a toxicologist at the CODIS Crime Lab, she can explain everything. I couldn't reach her earlier, but there must be a way to page her."

"I hear you, Mr. Hirsch. I do." Dr. Richards nods, her empathy tinged with condescension. "But before I follow up with Dr. Chow, there's someone I'd like you to speak to first."

"Who?"

"Our PAN nurse."

Liam frowns. "What does a PAN nurse do?"

"Janice is our psychiatric assessment nurse," she says with a patronizing smile. "I'm sure she'd be happy to discuss the situation with you. And then, maybe afterward, we can talk to Dr. Chow."

"No, I don't need to see a psych nurse." Liam rubs his temples, his fingers numb. "Please, Dr. Richards . . ."

"I wish I could discuss this further, but I have critical patients to attend to. Janice will be with you soon." She turns and hurries away before Liam can say another word.

If the stakes weren't so high, Liam might have laughed at being labeled delusional, possibly psychotic. He can't blame the harried young doctor—he knows he must sound irrational. But someone needs to see the imminent danger his family is in. *Possibly from within.*

Earlier, he had been deliberately vague in the text he'd sent to Celeste, mentioning only that Cole had an issue with his hand and that he was taking him to a doctor. He wouldn't have texted her at all if the school hadn't already reached out to her.

His phone vibrates, pulling him out of his dark thoughts. "Hello?"

"What? No 'Hi, Andrea' this time?" Dr. Gloria Chow's voice comes through with a small giggle.

"Oh, Gloria! Thanks for calling me back."

"No problem. If this is about your repeat blood test tomorrow, we can run it first thing in the morning. That way, we should have results back before the end of—"

"Gloria! I think I've figured out how I'm being poisoned." He quickly explains how Cole developed symptoms right after using his home office.

"Holy crap!" she exclaims. "You might want to talk to a Realtor about finding some new digs."

"I can't get the ER doctor to take me seriously, Gloria. She's trying to have me assessed by psychiatry."

She responds with a burst of laughter. "What's the doctor's name again?"

"Dr. Richards. Yvette Richards."

"Leave it to me. I'll reach out to her. We'll get your son tested."

"Thank you!" Liam exhales, relieved. "I just need to know that his blood levels aren't as toxic as mine."

"Extremely unlikely, but I get it. I think he'll be all right, but I'll let you know after I speak with Dr. Richards." She giggles again. "A psych consult . . ."

After Liam disconnects, he has turned back toward Cole's room when he spots Andrea striding toward him, her sling hidden beneath her jacket. The abrasion above her eyebrow looks rawer than before, and her face is set with grim determination. "How's he doing?" she asks, her voice laced with concern.

"He's stable for now. But convincing anyone around here that Cole's been poisoned has been a battle."

"You don't have to convince me."

"I know. Thank you."

She offers a small, supportive grin. "At least now you know how you're being exposed."

"True. But it's one hell of a way to find out." He eyes her helplessly. "My own home, Andrea."

She nods. "I can't imagine how violating that must feel, Liam. But it's hard to overlook the obvious . . ."

"No one would have more access or opportunity than Celeste." His voice shakes.

"And she's still seeing Benjamin behind your back."

"Despite all her empty promises," he grumbles. "There's no question she's been lying to me this whole time. But even assuming Celeste is capable of something as shitty as poisoning me . . ."

"Yes?"

"I can't see her endangering our kids like that. Whatever she is or isn't as a wife, Celeste has always been a devoted mom."

"But she never expected Cole to borrow your basement office, right?"

"That's true. But it's still hard to imagine she'd allow poison to be anywhere near our home if she knew there was even a remote chance the kids could be exposed."

"Yeah." Andrea goes quiet for a moment. "Your home renovation . . . what part of the house was Benjamin working on?"

"Different parts," Liam says, the realization tightening his chest. "But that son of a bitch has been in and out of our basement the whole time."

Andrea nods. "A lot of unsupervised access."

"Unlimited."

A voice calls out from behind them. "Liam!"

He turns to see Celeste rushing toward him in her tennis gear. "How is he?" she demands, without acknowledging Andrea.

"He's feeling better," Liam says, his voice barely above a whisper, afraid he might otherwise scream.

"Thank God," Celeste sighs, her shoulders slumping. "I was at a match in Renton. I only got the messages after I got off the court. Cole mentioned something about a poison in his text. That can't be right, can it?"

Liam shares a glance with Andrea. "Yeah, there could be a leak in the basement."

"Of poison?"

"Of something."

Celeste finally notices Andrea, offering an affable smile as she extends her hand. "Hi, I'm his wife, Celeste."

"Andrea." They shake hands.

"Are you . . . ?"

"Just leaving, actually," Andrea says, turning to go. "I hope your son feels better soon."

"Wait!" Liam calls after her. "I'll come with you."

"Liam?" Celeste looks at him, more confused than hurt.

"Cole's waiting on a few final tests," Liam says. "You stay here with him. I'll be back soon."

"Do you have to go this second?"

"I do," he says, already turning away.

Partly, he can't bear the thought of being alone with Celeste. But more importantly, he needs to get back to the house and search the basement before she can warn Benjamin—or anyone else—to clean up the crime scene.

CHAPTER 51

Liam holds Andrea's umbrella as they huddle beside her car. The rain beats down relentlessly, mirroring the storm brewing inside him—suspicion, worry, betrayal, and an unsettling tinge of infatuation.

"Weird," Andrea says, breaking his thoughts.

"What is?"

"I followed Celeste for weeks, but until I was that close to her, I didn't realize how gorgeous she is."

Liam shrugs. Celeste's looks mean nothing to him now; all he sees is her deception.

"For what it's worth, she seemed genuinely freaked out in there," Andrea adds.

"I'm not sure it means much."

"Probably not." Andrea taps the ground with her boot. "And she would have had plenty of opportunities to access your basement office."

"And, as you pointed out earlier, the motive, too."

"Yeah." Andrea scans the surroundings, her unease clear. "Isn't it finally time we go to the police with what we know?"

"Soon," he says. "But now that we've figured out how I'm being exposed—and how to avoid it—it's bought me a little more time."

She tilts her head. "Bought *us*, don't you mean?"

He manages a small grin. "True."

"But now Celeste knows you know . . ."

"There's that." He rakes a hand through his hair. "I still can't wrap my head around the idea that she could be behind all this."

"Liam—"

He raises a hand, cutting her off. "Doesn't mean I don't think she is. Or that I'll ever trust her again."

"You can't take any chances. Don't forget what happened to me yesterday."

The sight of Andrea's bruised and scraped forehead weighs heavily on him. He gently squeezes her shoulder. "I had no right to drag you into this, to put you at risk."

"I got involved willingly, Liam. Eyes wide-open." She looks at him intently. "So what's our next step?"

"First priority is making sure my kids are safe."

"And Celeste?"

"At this point, keeping her close seems like the best option."

Andrea's doubt shows, but she only asks, "What about your home office?"

"Might be time for another renovation."

She smiles faintly. "You might think about a different contractor this time."

"I'm thinking of doing it myself." He chuckles. "This'll kill Benjamin's Google ratings, though."

Andrea laughs. "Just be careful, OK?" she says, opening her car door.

"Andrea . . ."

"Yes?" she replies without looking back.

There's so much he wants to say, but with his son in the ER, possibly poisoned by his own mother, now isn't the time. He simply hands her the folded umbrella. "I'll check in with you later."

On the drive home, Liam calls his assistant. Morris doesn't hesitate when Liam asks him to find a penthouse for his family to move into immediately. But when Liam also requests private security, Morris's tone changes.

"A security detail?" His voice rises, almost shrill. "For Celeste and the kids? Around the clock?"

"Exactly. Let's go with that firm we used last year for the AI summit," Liam says. "The one run by the ex-Mossad guy."

"Yoav Kaplan?"

"That's him."

"But, Liam, we were facing militant protesters then. Some of them armed. Why do you need him now?" Morris asks in a conspiratorial hush. "There hasn't been a kidnapping threat against your family, has there?"

"Something like that."

Morris knows better than to push. "For all four of you, right?"

"Yes, and we'll need to extend the security to one more person." He gives Morris Andrea's name and address before disconnecting.

As Liam turns onto the quiet streets of Broadmoor, his unease deepens.

He parks outside the garage and puts on the protective gear he wore when inspecting his truck. He wonders if the respirator will be enough to protect him from the poisonous gas but reasons that a few minutes more won't make a difference compared to the hours he's already spent unprotected in his basement office. Still, his heart pounds as he crosses the threshold into his home, now in a makeshift hazmat suit.

Liam heads straight to the basement, grabs his toolkit and stepladder, and makes his way to his office. The moment he steps inside, a wave of lightheadedness and slight nausea hits him. He suspects it's all in his head, though the numbness in his hands and feet is undeniably real.

He fixes his gaze on the small metal vent in the ceiling. Once insignificant, it now feels like a loaded gun pointed at him.

Determined not to linger, he sets up the stepladder beneath the vent, struggling to maintain his balance as he unscrews the fasteners. At one point, he wobbles but catches himself and manages to remove the cover. Using his phone's flashlight, he examines the vent but sees only the metal casing inside. He reaches into the opening up to his elbow, finding nothing.

Sweating under the respirator, Liam hurries back to the utility room, anxious about the time he's spending in the contaminated area. He opens the half door on the upper part of the far wall and, after two failed attempts, manages to climb into the crawl space, where he's greeted by a tangle of pipes and tubing. After a few minutes, he locates the heating duct that ends at the office vent and follows it along its length, searching for signs of tampering or any newly welded joints.

His anxiety mounting, he pulls out a portable saw and cuts through the duct closest to the office vent, exposing a jagged one-foot gap. He reaches inside, cutting his glove on the sharp metal, but still finds nothing.

On the verge of giving up, he taps along the duct, listening for any change in sound. About six or seven feet away from the office vent, the metallic reverberation shifts from hollow to dull.

A spasm seizes his hand, turning it into a claw, and he can do nothing but watch with a mix of horror and exasperation until it subsides on its own. Then he makes two more cuts into the duct—one before the change in sound, the other about two feet beyond. This time, when he reaches inside the open tubing, his fingers brush against something hard. A cold sweat breaks out as he grips the smooth, spherical object and strains to pull it out.

Heart pounding, he watches in disbelief as a long black cylinder, shaped like a miniature torpedo, slides out of the duct. It's heavier than he expected, and he struggles to support its weight. The canister slips from his grasp, crashing to the cement floor with a heavy, metallic clatter.

Liam's breath catches, half expecting the thing to explode at his feet.

CHAPTER 52

Liam considers taking the black canister with him but dismisses the idea—it's evidence now, and the entire basement is a crime scene. Before leaving the crawl space, he snaps several photos of the device and the duct where it was hidden. Though he's turned off the canister's gas valve, he knows he'll need to notify the police and fire departments soon. But that will have to wait. After discarding the protective gear and the clothes he wore into the basement, he takes a quick shower and packs a small bag of essentials.

He heads to his truck, realizing now that it's been safe all along. After tossing his bag in the back, he texts Andrea a photo of the torpedo-shaped canister, adding no explanation.

She calls immediately. "You found it!" she exclaims.

"Yup," he replies. "You wouldn't believe how deeply it was buried inside the heating duct."

"It wasn't meant to be found."

"No, it wasn't," he says. "And it probably never would have been. Whoever installed it knew exactly what they were doing."

"Benjamin?"

"Definitely. The big question is—"

"Did Celeste help him install it?"

"Or at least know about it?"

"What does your gut tell you, Liam?"

"Celeste hired Benjamin. She admitted she initiated their affair and kept seeing him after claiming it was over. It's hard to believe she wasn't involved." He hesitates, then adds, "But I'm still not certain."

"What will it take?"

"Think about it, Andrea. This was no amateur setup. They used a sophisticated piece of equipment. I even found a wireless motion sensor attached to it. A canister of an obscure poison, rigged to release gas over weeks or months every time I sat down at my computer. Where would a contractor and a stay-at-home mom get their hands on that kind of gear?"

"A stay-at-home mom with a background in advanced AI," Andrea reminds him.

"That was a lifetime ago. She's not connected to that world anymore."

"Maybe they weren't acting alone."

Liam sighs. "Which means we're back to square one."

"Not at all," Andrea counters. "We've already pieced together most of the puzzle."

Liam's attention shifts as he hears a vehicle approaching. He looks up to see Celeste's car speeding down the driveway. "I've got to go, Andrea. I'll call you later."

The car stops a few feet away, and Celeste jumps out. She rushes over, reaching to hug him, but he pulls back. "Where's Cole?" he asks, his tone sharp.

If she's hurt by his rebuff, she doesn't show it. "He's still in the ER. They're planning to discharge him in about an hour."

"Why did you leave him?"

"He asked me to. Some friends from soccer showed up, and he went into full teenage mode. Didn't want his mom around. I told him I'd pick him up in an hour."

"What are you doing here, Celeste?"

"Morris called me," she says. "He's rented us a condo downtown. I was going to pack a bag for the kids and me."

Is that really it, or did you come to get rid of the evidence?

"The house is contaminated," he says. "Send me a list of what you and the kids need. I'll get it."

She extends her hand. "I'm here already. It'll only take a few minutes."

He recoils from her touch, feeling a wave of disgust. "Our home has been gassed, Celeste!"

Her eyes widen. "I thought you said it was some kind of leak, Liam. What's going on? You're scaring me."

Your boyfriend welded a canister of poisonous gas into the ductwork. But all he says is "The house isn't safe for you."

"Then how was it any safer for you? Especially with your . . . condition."

He bristles. "I wore a respirator."

"I don't get it," she says, glancing around. "Where are the fire trucks and emergency response teams?"

"They'll be here soon enough," he says vaguely. "Besides, I've been tied up rushing our son to the ER and securing safe accommodations for us. While you were . . ."

"I told you exactly where I was!" Her voice sharpens. "At a league match in Renton. I don't keep my phone in my pocket while I'm serving."

"Tennis again." He eyes her coolly. "You sure it was Renton?"

"Where else would it be?"

"Maybe Tacoma?"

She stiffens. "Did you follow me this morning, Liam?"

"No. But I heard about your romantic brunch with Benjamin."

She looks down at her feet. "It wasn't like that."

"No? Then tell me, what was it like?"

"It was a goodbye."

"That would explain the long hug?"

"As a matter of fact, it does." When Celeste looks up, her eyes have reddened. "After I ended it, Benjamin wouldn't stop texting or calling. No matter how many ways I blocked him, he found a new way to reach me. Then, yesterday, he contacted me through my sister. My little sister, Liam! I panicked. I agreed to meet him. Yes, I went there. But only to make him stop."

"Sounds perfectly plausible."

"I should've told you, Liam. I know. But after everything we've been through . . ."

"You thought one more lie wouldn't hurt?"

"I thought it would only make things worse. That's why I went all the way to Tacoma—to make sure Benjamin really understood it was over. And he got the message, Liam. He did. That's why we hugged. He understood it was goodbye."

"Tacoma's a long way to go just to say goodbye."

"He suggested it. I would've gone anywhere." Her eyes search his. "I was desperate, Liam."

"That, I don't doubt."

CHAPTER 53

The instant Andrea opens the door, she feels the tension radiating from Liam. The deep ache from her broken collarbone is the only thing that keeps her from pulling him into a hug. They linger in the doorway, the air between them charged with an undeniable connection—at least, she hopes he feels it as strongly.

"Did you meet my Secret Service detail out front?" she quips, trying to cut through the silence.

Liam forces a chuckle. "Yeah, your guy Dallas gave me the third degree on the way in."

"I've never had a security detail before," she says, leading him into the living room.

"You've probably never been hunted by a driverless car either."

"There's that."

Once they're seated on the couch, Liam's voice comes out heavy. "Celeste showed up at the house right as I was leaving."

"Why?"

"She said she came to pack bags for herself and the kids."

"Sounds plausible."

"I confronted her about her brunch with Benjamin," he says, then summarizes the encounter.

"Do you believe she went to Tacoma just to say goodbye?"

Liam closes his eyes for a moment, as if trying to clear his thoughts. "I don't know what to believe anymore, Andrea."

She lightly touches her knee to his. He doesn't pull away. "None of it makes sense."

"I couldn't agree more, but which part are you referring to?" he asks.

"Benjamin. He wouldn't have the expertise to pull off this poisoning on his own. Or the motive. Agreed?"

Liam nods, but his expression is far from certain.

"He's either working with Celeste or someone else," she presses.

"Probably." He tilts his head, curious. "What are you thinking, Andrea?"

"Does it make sense that the same guy who planted a bomb in your basement would hang around, stalking your wife like some lovesick teenager?"

Liam exhales heavily. "Not when you put it like that."

Andrea presses her leg more firmly against his. "I know you don't want to believe this, but the only explanation that fits is that Celeste is behind everything."

"Of course I don't want to believe it." He shifts, breaking their contact. "But I'm not blind. The evidence points to her. Still . . ."

"Still what?"

"Even if she could get her hands on a sophisticated canister of nitrile gas, I can't see Celeste endangering our kids."

Andrea nods slowly, understanding his reluctance. That kind of recklessness is hard to reconcile with the image of a devoted mother. "That part is hard to explain."

Liam's expression hardens. "There's only one person who can confirm or deny Celeste's story."

"Benjamin?"

He nods. "Let's go talk to him."

"Tonight?"

"Right now."

Andrea hesitates, weighing the risks. "I was the one who insisted we handle this ourselves, but I said that when I was jacked up on adrenaline and painkillers. This has gone way too far. We need help, Liam. Professional help. It's past time to involve the police."

"Think about it, Andrea." Liam pulls out his phone, displaying a photo of the military-grade canister he found in the ductwork. "If we put this in front of Benjamin, we'll have him cornered."

"And so would the cops."

"But he'll probably lawyer up with them. Whether he's working for Celeste or someone else, this might be our only chance to find out who else is involved."

She studies his face intently. "This has nothing to do with your need to confront the guy who slept with your wife and tried to kill you?"

His gaze is unwavering. "It's not about that, Andrea. I promise."

She lifts her elbow in its sling, wincing at the pain. "I'm one-armed, and you've been poisoned. We're not exactly in shape to take on Benjamin if things get physical. Or worse, if he's armed."

"That's why we'll bring your Secret Service detail. Dallas looks like he can handle himself . . . and anyone else who might show up."

As Andrea sits beside Liam in the back of the black sedan, the doubt churns in her mind. Dallas, the hulking security guard, drives in silence. Despite his very American name, he has the look and demeanor of someone faintly Eastern European, his stoic presence only adding to her unease.

Liam can't stop rubbing his hands together, as if trying to warm them. "Is that from the nerve issue?" Andrea asks, breaking the silence.

"Yeah. My hands have gone numb over the last day or two. It's like when the dentist freezes your mouth."

"But your symptoms should improve now that you're no longer being exposed to the poison, right?"

"God, I hope so. It's super annoying."

Her eyes sharpen. "Liam?"

"Dr. Chow couldn't give me any guarantees," he admits, turning to stare out the window.

She lays a hand on his arm, giving it a reassuring squeeze. "You just turned off the gas today. Give it time. You'll get better." She tries to lighten the mood with a laugh. "You're too pigheaded not to."

"Can't argue with that." He turns back to her, his face softening with gratitude. "I couldn't have made it this far without you."

"Good, 'cause I charge by the hour."

"Best money I've ever spent," he says, covering her hand with his.

They ride in silence as the quiet streets of Burien blur by. Dallas slows as they approach an intersection blocked by a police cruiser parked sideways across the road. He glances over his shoulder. "The address you gave me is halfway down this block, Mr. Hirsch."

Andrea pulls her hand away, exchanging a worried look with Liam.

"Can you go around the other side?" Liam asks.

Dallas shakes his head. "It's blocked from both ends."

Andrea cranes her neck, spotting another police car and two ambulances parked in the middle of the street. "Benjamin?" she wonders aloud.

Liam yanks open the car door and gets out. Andrea follows, noticing the unsteady way he moves, though it doesn't slow him as he heads straight for a young female officer leaning against her vehicle.

She raises her hand as he approaches. "This street is closed, sir. Emergency situation."

"My friend lives down there," Liam says, pointing past her.

"Sorry." The officer shakes her head. "Only emergency personnel are allowed in."

"What kind of emergency?" Andrea asks.

"There's been an accident. Involving a pedestrian."

"A hit-and-run?"

The officer frowns. "I'm not at liberty to comment."

"Did the victim survive?" Andrea presses.

The officer hesitates just enough to confirm Andrea's suspicions before saying, "The department will issue an official statement soon. In the meantime, I need you to move your vehicle."

Liam turns to Andrea, his face drained of color, his eyes wide. "Another driverless car?"

CHAPTER 54

Liam and Andrea sit across from the on-call detective in a stark, windowless room deep within the Seattle PD's homicide unit. The setting feels ripped from one of the crime thrillers Liam devours—minus the stale coffee and crumpled paper cups. Detective Lyles, a stocky Black man with sharp eyes and a slightly rumpled gray suit, scribbles notes furiously. One collar of his white shirt is flipped up, unnoticed. His pen races across the page as they recount every detail.

"I get the craziest calls on my nights. Ask anyone." The detective whistles softly as he writes. "But this one . . ."

"Takes the cake?" Andrea offers.

He pauses, tapping the pen against his notebook. "The whole damn cake."

After the paramedics confirmed Benjamin's death at the scene, Dallas drove them straight to Seattle PD headquarters. They've been in this interview room for nearly an hour, unloading everything onto Detective Lyles.

"I know how far-fetched this must sound, Detective," Liam says, his voice steady. "But the photos, lab results, and gas canister back it up."

"Far-fetched doesn't even begin to cover it." The detective frowns. "That device in your basement—it's not still leaking, is it?"

"No, I shut off the valve."

"But it's still down there?"

"Unless someone's moved it."

"At this point, why not, right?" Detective Lyles chuckles, then turns to Andrea. "And you now want to amend your original statement about the car that tried to take you out, right?"

Andrea looks away, embarrassed. "The part about the driver, yes. Or, uh, the lack of one."

The detective rubs his temple, frowning. "That seems like a detail that would've been worth mentioning."

"I should have. I'm sorry."

Lyles's gaze shifts between them, unreadable. "Did you tell your wife you were coming here, Mr. Hirsch?"

Liam shakes his head.

"Based on what you've told me, it's best you don't. Not until we've had a chance to talk to her." Detective Lyles stands, setting his pen on the table. "Thanks for coming forward. We've got a lot to process. We'll send the fire department and hazmat team over to deal with that device and get the crime scene techs in to check out the rest."

"Understood."

"Good. We'll let the techs do their work tonight. In the morning, we'll start taking formal statements from everyone involved—starting with your wife."

As they settle into the back of Dallas's car, Andrea asks, "How do you feel?"

"Numb," Liam says, his voice flat. "Getting used to that, though. You?"

"Weird. And, honestly, a little deflated."

"Why deflated?"

She adjusts her sling, wincing. "It's out of our hands now."

"Which is where it probably should've been from the start."

"We did all right, though, considering. Figuring out as much as we did. It felt . . . satisfying, professionally speaking."

"You were incredible, Andrea."

"Except we haven't cracked it. With Benjamin dead, we've lost our best lead."

"Possibly our only one."

"Convenient, isn't it?" She sighs. "And Celeste?"

"What about her?"

Her gaze turns distant. "Does life just go on as usual?"

He groans. "Define *usual*."

"Are you staying with her? In the same rental?"

"I don't see another option, not until I know exactly how involved she is." Liam looks away, the tension in his jaw tightening. "Cole's OK, thank God. But I'm keeping the security team on-site. At your place, too."

"I'm not sure that's necessary."

Liam senses a growing distance between them and fights the urge to reach for her hand. "It is, for my peace of mind."

She stares out the window. "All right."

Liam leans forward between the front seats. "Dallas, please drop me off at TransScend's offices in Bellevue."

"Of course."

Andrea looks at him, her voice low. "Why the office?"

"I need to talk to someone there."

"Who?"

"My avatar," he says, though he knows there's more to it than that.

CHAPTER 55

When Dallas drops Liam off at TransScend's headquarters, Andrea insists on going in with him.

He doesn't argue, already saddened at the thought of not seeing her regularly. Now that the police have taken over the investigation, they'll have no reason or excuse to spend time together.

He gives her a quick tour of the ninth floor before stopping at Ellis's office at the end of the corridor. "Why don't you wait here? I can log you into Ellis's computer. Doubt he'll be using it again."

"I can't come with you?"

He frowns. "While I talk to my avatar?"

"I've heard so much about the app. I'm really curious."

"Soon, I promise," he says, sensing her disappointment. "But right now, I need a little time alone with it."

"All right," she replies, though her reluctance seeps through.

He reaches out, brushing her cheek lightly with his hand. "Fifteen minutes, Andrea. Thirty tops. Then I'll show you." He knows if she's watching, he won't be able to follow through with what he's planning.

Andrea takes a seat behind Ellis's desk. "What's the password?"

Liam gives her the info and heads to his own office. Once inside, he closes the door firmly behind him. He logs into TheirStory and navigates the voice prompts. When the app asks whom he wants to interact with, he hesitates before saying, "Celeste Hirsch."

"One moment, please, while I try to retrieve the profile," the app responds in its neutral tone.

Liam knows it will find his wife's profile. He uploaded all the data after discovering her affair, but confronting the avatar—like facing the real Celeste—proved too painful, so he never actually used it. Now, with her as the prime suspect in his attempted murder, he needs to hear her answers. If not in her words, then at least in her voice.

"Is this the correct Celeste Hirsch?" the app asks, displaying a photo of his smiling wife.

"Yes."

"Loading . . ."

A few seconds later, Celeste's avatar appears on the screen, unnervingly lifelike. "Hello, Liam," she says, her tone and expression eerily familiar.

"Hello, Celeste."

The avatar flips her hair, just like Celeste often does. "What would you like to talk about?"

"Benjamin."

"Who's Benjamin?"

"Our contractor. The man you were sleeping with."

The avatar looks momentarily confused. "You and I have been together for almost twenty years."

"Exactly. But you still cheated. You admitted it."

"I'm sorry, Liam," she says, her voice heavy with regret. "That's not like me. Not at all. I've been so happy with you. And Ava and Cole . . . All those wonderful trips we took, like backpacking through New Zealand. Or that whitewater rafting trip in the Yukon. And our tenth anniversary on the Amalfi Coast—that was so romantic."

Liam knows the algorithm is piecing together memories from the photos he uploaded, but the mention of those trips only fuels his anger. "Yet you still went and slept with our contractor. And you had the nerve to blame it on me for not prioritizing you and our relationship." His voice cracks. "Which might be the only honest thing you've said to me in a long time."

The avatar's expression turns sheepish. "But the affair is over now, right?"

"You swore it was, but I wasn't sure. At least, not until tonight."

"What happened tonight?"

"Benjamin died."

Her hand flies to her mouth. "How did he die?"

"He was hit by a car."

Her face twists in horror. "No! I lost my best friend that way. Was the driver drunk?"

"There was no driver."

"No driver? I'm confused, Liam."

"It was a self-driving car, Celeste. Someone sent it specifically to kill Benjamin. To keep him quiet."

"That's horrible."

"I think you killed him," Liam says, suddenly unsure if he's accusing his wife or the app itself.

"No!" she cries. "I'm not capable of that. How long have you known me?"

"I'm not sure I know you at all anymore."

The avatar's face goes blank. "I don't have enough data points to answer your query," it says mechanically.

"Then let me fill in the gaps."

He quickly outlines the conspiracy to poison him and the events at TransScend, including Rudy's sabotage and Ellis's fraud. "But more than anyone, you had the opportunity to plant that device in the basement. And after you fell for Benjamin, you had a motive, too. With your AI expertise, you could have hacked into my medical records and altered them. The only part I can't figure out is how you got your hands on a device like that."

"What device, Liam?"

"The canister of IDPN with the timed-release mechanism."

"IDPN is an industrial nitrile."

"Yes, the one you've been slowly poisoning me with," he mutters at the screen, momentarily forgetting he's accusing an algorithm, not his wife. "No matter how determined you were to get rid of me, to be with Benjamin, how could you, Celeste?"

"How could I what?"

"Risk hurting our kids like that? What the hell is wrong with you?"

"Liam, it's me," the avatar pleads. "I would never hurt any of you."

"Then who would?"

"I don't have enough data points to answer your query. Perhaps I did poison you. But isn't it also possible that I'm being framed?"

CHAPTER 56

Andrea stares at the screen, but her thoughts keep drifting back to Liam. What could be so secretive that he needs privacy with the AI app? It has to involve Celeste.

Andrea can't understand why Liam remains conflicted about his wife. After admitting to her affair, Celeste had the nerve to sneak off for a secret brunch with her lover. Yet Liam is still willing to give her the benefit of the doubt. Andrea, scarred by Max's betrayal, finds it impossible to be that trusting. Or forgiving. For her, actions, not words, define people. Celeste's story about driving forty miles just to say goodbye doesn't add up. And that might not even be the worst of it. What if Celeste—realizing the canister had been found—sent that car to kill Benjamin to cover her own tracks?

Andrea rubs her tired eyes and sighs. *What happens to us now, Liam?*

The thought tugs at her heart. With the investigation out of their hands, will they just drift apart? It's probably for the best, she tells herself. Liam is still a married man, tied to his family, fractured as it may be. She has no right to interfere. But the idea of going back to her life without him leaves her with a hollow ache.

She checks her watch. Liam's been in his office for over thirty minutes. She wants to check on him but forces herself to stay put. Instead, she focuses on the computer, launching another search on Benjamin, hoping to dig up something—anything—she might have missed.

She opens his website and finds it dated, almost neglected, with the latest testimonials from over four years ago. The comments are glowing, exactly what you'd expect on a business's own site. Remembering Liam's crack about Benjamin's Google ratings, she broadens her search to more neutral platforms. His ratings are stellar—four point nine on Google, four point seven on Yelp. The reviews echo the praise on his site, and with over three hundred ratings on Google alone, it's hard to believe he rigged them all.

She scrolls through the positive feedback:

"Benjamin is the best in the state!"
Connie777

"Me and my wife are real pleased with Ben's work."
LarryandPam

"Good solid work. Will definitely call him in the future."
Doctoranddoctorgerhard

"Came in on budget and finished two weeks early. Excellent work-manship."
SS_Seahawks74

"Recommended by my cousin. So pleased."
Alanabanana

"Benjamin turned what looked like a tear down into our dream home!"
Don_Pinter

She pauses. Something in the list catches her eye. Then it hits her—the username, SS_Seahawks74. She's seen it before.

A surge of excitement runs through her. She quickly pulls up the website where she saw the username earlier—a fan site for the Seattle

Seahawks, full of endless threads dissecting the team's performance. She finds a long rant about the punt return team posted by one SS_Seahawks74.

She clicks on the username, and a profile pops up. There's no name, just a photo of a guy in a Seahawks jersey and sunglasses.

The thrill spreads through her, charging every nerve.

CHAPTER 57

Liam hears the faint whoosh of the door opening. "I need five more minutes, Andrea," he calls out, quickly minimizing the TheirStory app on his screen.

But it's Sam, not Andrea, who strides into the office with his usual swagger. "You've called me a lot of things over the years, Boss, but Andrea? That's a new one," he says with a booming laugh.

Liam forces a smile. "Sam, hey. What brings you by so late?"

"COO of this outfit doesn't clock out at five, especially when our next-gen app's launch date seems to change with the cycles of the moon." He gestures to the ceiling with feigned exasperation.

Liam's smile fades. "We're not going over this again, Sam. Not now. I'm too tired."

Sam's face shifts from playful to serious. "Because of this mysterious illness of yours?"

"In a way."

"What does that even mean, Liam?" Sam drops heavily into the chair across from him. "Can you just be straight with me for once? I feel like you've been keeping me in the dark for months."

"You're right. I have. And I'm sorry. But I couldn't tell you before."

"Why not?"

"I didn't know who I could trust."

Sam peers over his glasses with the look of a disappointed teacher. "Not even me?"

"They were listening. Everywhere."

Sam's frown deepens. "Who's 'they'? What the fuck is happening?"

Liam exhales heavily. "How much time do you have?"

"All night."

"I thought I was dying, Sam." Liam recounts everything—the strange symptoms, the ALS diagnosis, his decision to pursue MAiD, the shocking discovery that his test results were falsified, and the chilling realization that he was being poisoned to push him toward suicide. He explains the desperate scramble to find the toxin's source, only to discover his wife's lover had planted the canister in the basement before being killed in a driverless hit-and-run.

By the time he finishes, Sam's jaw is hanging open. "That is . . . wow . . . You're serious?"

"Deadly serious," Liam replies.

"And you think Celeste is involved?"

"The poison was in our basement. Planted by her lover. Hard to overlook all that."

Sam sits in stunned silence for a moment. "And why is it OK to tell me all this now?"

"You'd have found out soon enough. The Seattle PD just opened a homicide investigation. Tomorrow, detectives will be interviewing everyone. Including you."

Before Sam can respond, the door swings open again, and Andrea steps in.

"Oh, hello," Sam says. "And who might you be?"

Andrea freezes. "Can I talk to you, Liam? Privately?"

"You can talk in front of me," Sam says, grinning. "There aren't any secrets between us. Not anymore. Right, Liam?"

"I only need a moment," Andrea insists, her voice steady but edged with tension.

"OK," Liam says, starting to rise.

Sam waves him back down. "Sit, sit. We're good."

Liam hesitates.

"It's kind of personal," Andrea presses.

"Just give us a minute, Sam," Liam says.

"She can wait, Boss. We're in the middle of something important here."

Andrea takes a step back, her eyes wary.

"Where the fuck do you think you're going?" Sam growls, his tone harsh enough to catch Liam off guard.

"I've seen the review," Andrea says quietly.

Sam's eyes narrow. "What review?"

"The one you left on Benjamin's website."

Sam slaps the desk. "Shit! I'd forgotten about that. Benjamin nagged me for that stupid review. But that was years ago. And I didn't use my actual name. I never do."

Andrea's gaze flicks between Liam and Sam. "Probably not the best move to leave a five-star review for someone you're planning to murder."

Liam's head snaps up. "Murder?"

Sam ignores him. "You're too goddamn much, Andrea. A real dog with a bone. Not even a driverless car could scare you off." He turns to Liam with a sneer. "Where did you find this one?"

"You!" The realization slams into Liam like a freight train.

Sam shrugs, unbothered.

A surge of confusion, fear, and rage propels Liam out of his chair, but his leg gives out, forcing him to clutch the desk for support.

"Careful, Prez. You're not yourself these days," Sam says with mock concern. "But nitriles will do that to you."

"You son of a bitch," Liam growls.

Sam reaches into his pocket and pulls out a gun with the ease of someone reaching for a pen. He waves it at them both. "Sit down, Prez. And you, too, Nancy Drew. Hands on the desk. Or hand, in your case," he says, pointing to her sling.

Once Andrea is seated beside Liam, her right hand resting on the desk next to his, Sam scans their faces with a smug smile. "Well, isn't this convenient? The tracker said you were in your office, Liam. That's why I came down here. But finding her here too . . ." He motions to Andrea with the gun. "You're just a bonus."

"What's the point, Sam?" Liam snaps. "The whole office is monitored."

Sam laughs. "Not anymore."

"You disabled the system?"

"Right before I got here."

"Why?" Liam demands, barely containing his fury.

"Why?" Sam's voice rises. "Because for fifteen years, you've treated me like a lackey, a puppet, your fucking servant—pick your own slur! I've been here since day one, pouring everything into this place." He jabs his finger against the desk. "I'm more responsible for this company's success than you've ever been. But did I ever get recognized as an equal partner? And would I ever get my turn at the top while you were still around?" He shakes his head, bitterness etched across his face. "No wonder Rudy has it out for you. You have zero appreciation and even less loyalty."

Liam nods toward the gun, his rage simmering. "You want to talk about loyalty, Sam?"

"It's not just that," Sam says, his tone softening. "It's the bigger picture. Let's face it, Boss—you've gone soft. Look how wishy-washy you've been about TheirStory's launch. First, you push to move up the date, then you backtrack, paralyzed by doubt and fear. Cowardice, really. You've lost your killer instinct."

Liam feels Andrea's foot nudge his under the desk, a signal to stay calm. Slowing his breath, he tries to keep his cool. "And you thought you could do better?" he asks.

"Thought? No. I know I could." Sam sighs. "When we started Trans-Scend, you were focused. You had vision. You understood that AI was a race, and there was no glory in second place. But you lost the plot. You started worrying about shit that was out of our control. Nefarious applications. Stringent guidelines. Maybe Celeste got to you. Maybe Nellie. Who knows? Who cares? But you've lost your edge. Your nerve, too." He shakes his head. "And we saw it, even before you found God or whatever it was after your diagnosis and started waxing all moral about AI."

"Who's 'we'?" Liam asks, dread rising in his gut.

Sam's grin widens with a touch of cruelty. "You'll never guess who's been helping me."

"Celeste."

Sam laughs, motioning to him with the gun. "You have, Boss."

"What the hell are you talking about?"

"Well, your avatar anyway. Your old self. Your better self. The one with guts. The one who didn't think twice about decking Rudy Ziegler in court."

Liam's head spins as the realization sinks in. "TheirStory? You've been conspiring with an app?"

"Conspiring with an app?" Sam scoffs. "I'm not psychotic. I've just been consulting your avatar for advice—and maybe a little inspiration, too. Credit where it's due. After I shared your strong views on euthanasia, your avatar was the one who came up with the idea for mimicking ALS."

"The avatar suggested killing me?"

"With a little nudge from me. After all, even if I could've just killed you outright and gotten away with it, who knows who the board would've installed in your place? But to convince you to take your own life and, before you did, appoint me as your successor? You've got to admit, that's fucking genius. TheirStory did most of the work, too—finding the perfect poison, the slow-release delivery system, even doctoring your tests to match the ALS diagnosis."

"But it couldn't plant the canister for you," Liam says. "You needed Benjamin for that."

"That idiot?" Sam laughs. "I didn't need him. I just used him. Poor guy was clueless right up to the moment the car clipped him at eighty miles an hour."

Liam feels the pressure of Andrea's foot, urging him to stay calm. "If Benjamin didn't know about the device, why kill him?"

"What choice did I have?" Sam frowns, as if the answer is obvious. "As soon as you found it, I knew you'd blame Benjamin. Dumb as he was, he could still point the finger back at me."

"How did you know I'd found the canister?"

"For weeks, I sensed you were catching on," Sam says, and points to Andrea. "Like when you hired this one to dig into us VPs. At first, I chalked it up to Ellis embezzling from the company, messing with the books to cover his gambling losses. Then, with Rudy leaking info to sabotage TheirStory and turn a quick profit . . . well, it was enough to make anyone paranoid."

Sam continues, almost to himself, "But I ignored the other signs. Your sudden disappearances when you'd go dark on all your electronics. Those ladies' gloves you wore in here." He shakes his head. "But I knew you were still seeing Dr. Glynn and planning to go ahead with MAiD, so I thought we were still on track. That's on me. I should've been more vigilant."

"What finally tipped you off?"

"Morris."

"Morris?" Liam frowns. "I didn't tell him anything."

"Yeah, but when he said you were clearing out your house and had hired a private security outfit with Mossad ties, I figured you must have found the device. When I checked the sensor and saw it had moved before going offline, I knew the jig was up."

"The jig *is* up, Sam," Liam says, barely containing his rage. "It won't take the cops long to figure it out."

Sam chuckles. "Oh, I think it'll take them a while. In fact, I doubt they ever will, now that you've handed me a scapegoat."

"What scapegoat?"

"Your cheating wife."

Liam's blood runs cold. "Leave her out of this."

"I couldn't see the endgame myself, Boss. Not until tonight. But don't you get it? By going to the police, you gave me the perfect cover. You've implicated Celeste as the mastermind and Benjamin as her accomplice. Now that he's dead, when she vanishes, too, the cops will assume she killed her lover and went on the run. Especially after I tweak her digital trail to make it look that way."

Liam hangs his head in despair. As it drops, he notices the glint of metal between Andrea's clenched fingers in her sling, the tip of a nozzle barely visible. His pulse quickens. She taps his foot again, a signal more urgent than comforting.

Sam rises slowly from his chair. "Of course, none of this works as long as you two are still breathing. And in my revised version of history, Celeste would have seen you both as loose ends that needed tying up."

Andrea lets out a sharp laugh. "Dream on, Sam. You've already lost."

"Not a chance." He shakes his head. "I'm adjusting midgame. Like any good coach would."

"You're desperate, and you're done," she counters, leaning forward, her sling hovering over her other hand.

Sam leans in, his stare fierce and unblinking. "Trust me. I'm not the one who's done here."

Andrea's free hand slips into her sling. In one swift motion, she yanks it out and squirts a stream of pepper spray directly into Sam's face.

CHAPTER 58

A jolt of pain shoots through Andrea's collarbone and up to her scalp, but she doesn't hesitate. As Sam stumbles back, clawing at his eyes, she slams her fist down on his hand, sending the gun clattering to the floor.

Sam howls in pain and fury, swinging wildly. Andrea ducks, feeling the rush of air as his fist grazes her cheek. She lunges forward, slamming her good shoulder into his midsection. He topples backward, and she lands on top of him, but the agony in her collarbone robs her of breath. Before she can catch it, he wriggles free.

Sam pounces, his weight crushing down on her, and the pain in her shoulder becomes unbearable. His bloodshot eyes blaze with rage as he grips her neck and squeezes. Choking, Andrea claws at his arm with her one good hand, but she's no match for his brute strength.

"You little bitch!" Sam spits, spraying her face with flecks of saliva.

Andrea's airway closes. Lightheadedness creeps in, dulling the pain but sapping her strength. Her hand falls limp, her vision narrows to a tunnel, and she feels herself slipping away. Just as darkness closes in, a muffled explosion shatters the silence.

The grip on her neck loosens, and the crushing weight lifts from her chest. She gasps, gulping in desperate breaths.

As her vision clears, she sees Sam kneeling beside her, his hands raised in front of his face. Liam stands over him, gun in hand, aimed at Sam's head.

Liam's eyes are wild. "Andrea! Are you OK?"

"Yeah," she croaks.

"Give me one good reason not to pull this trigger, Sam," Liam growls.

"Don't need to." Sam sneers. "You don't have the balls, Prez."

"Try me," Liam says, steadying his aim.

"Don't, Liam," Andrea warns, her voice raspy but firm.

Liam's focus remains on Sam. "Move an inch, and I won't stop firing until I'm out of bullets."

With his left hand, Liam pulls out his phone, but as he begins to dial, his right hand starts to twitch, the gun barrel bobbing uncontrollably. Panic crosses his face as his hand twists into an unnatural fist, the muzzle pointing skyward.

Andrea struggles to rise, but the pain immobilizes her. She watches helplessly as Sam springs to his feet.

Liam drops his phone and tries to pry the gun from his clenched right hand with his left, but Sam is too fast. He yanks it from Liam's grip and shoves him in the chest.

Horrified, Andrea watches as Sam levels the gun at Liam. "If that isn't the perfect metaphor for you—a man who can't pull the trigger when it matters most—I don't know what the fuck is."

Liam's eyes meet Andrea's, filled with shame and regret.

"It's not your fault," she murmurs.

"She might be right. That IDPN is as effective as advertised." Sam rubs his eyes with his free hand. "Christ, that pepper spray stings. I'll remember this, Andrea."

"Let her go, Sam," Liam pleads. "She's not involved."

"I couldn't, even if I wanted to." Sam shakes his head. "I was thinking we'd all go for a long drive. But who has time for that?" He trains the gun on Andrea. "Once I bring Celeste back here, we'll tidy this all up. Make it look like a double murder-suicide. Then TheirStory will ensure the security footage fits the whole narrative."

Andrea stares down the barrel. There's no fear, just a strange calm. She thinks of her father and finds comfort, hoping she might see him again soon.

Then, blackness swallows the room.

CHAPTER 59

Crouching in the dark, Liam feels utterly helpless. No one breathes. He hears feet shuffling, followed by a loud crack and the splintering of wood at the doorway. A low-pitched gunshot echoes through the room. Someone near him groans and collapses with a thud. The footsteps erupt into thunderous stomping.

"Hands on your heads!" a deep voice commands.

Light floods the room, revealing a surreal scene that makes Liam question if he's dreaming—or already dead.

Sam writhes on the floor, clutching his belly. A uniformed officer kneels on his chest while another kicks a gun away from his side. The officers, dressed in black SWAT uniforms with bulletproof vests, helmets, and night-vision goggles, have their semiautomatic weapons trained on Sam.

Liam's frantic gaze locks on Andrea. "Andrea!"

"I'm OK," she murmurs, looking as shocked as he feels.

Liam hurries over and crouches beside her, noticing how she braces her left shoulder with her right hand. "You're hurt," he says.

"Only my collarbone. The break must be worse."

"This is my fault. Again."

She grins weakly. "I'm thinking it might be more Sam's."

Liam reaches a hand toward her. "What can I do?"

She shakes her head slightly. "It'll pass. I just need a minute. Distract me from the pain."

"You knew it was him, didn't you?"

"Only minutes before you found out," she says. "I recognized Sam's username on a website. Benjamin had done work for him before. Then it all clicked. That's what I was coming in to tell you."

"Why did you bring pepper spray?"

"I heard something in the corridor earlier. I was already on edge after Benjamin's murder, and I grabbed it from my bag without thinking. But I had no idea Sam was in there with you."

"Where would I be without you?" he says.

She looks down. "You know what this means, don't you?"

He nods. "Celeste wasn't involved."

"You must be so relieved."

Before Liam can respond, a female paramedic with cropped blond hair steps over and kneels beside Andrea. She glances at Liam. "Excuse me, sir, I need a few moments with her."

Andrea nods to him. "I'll be fine."

As Liam stands, he looks over to where another paramedic is assessing Sam. "They shot me," Sam moans in disbelief.

"Too bad it was just with a beanbag," Nellie chirps, appearing at the doorway.

Liam gapes at her. "Nellie? What are you doing here?"

"Step back, ma'am," one of the officers instructs, but Nellie ignores him and strides straight toward Liam.

When she reaches him, Liam gestures toward the officers. "You called them in?"

"Damn straight I did. I've had my eye on Sam for months."

"You have?"

"Actually, I never trusted the guy." Nellie nods contemptuously in Sam's direction. "I've been tracking his activity with TheirStory. His usage spiked recently. The firewalls wouldn't let me tap into his conversations, but the amount of time he spent on the app was off the charts. I had a bad feeling. And after that leak, he was way too eager to pin it on me, to get rid of me."

"I wish you'd told me sooner," Liam says.

She plants her hands on her hips. "Would you have listened?"

"Probably not."

"Earlier tonight, when I saw he'd shut down all the surveillance systems, I knew something was up." She glances at Sam, then back at Liam. "He didn't know I could turn everything back on remotely. Or off, in the case of the lighting."

"So, you heard everything he said?"

"Most of it. It's all recorded, too." Nellie watches as the officers pull Sam to his feet, his hands cuffed behind him. She turns back to Liam. "I heard enough to call in an active shooter threat and get Delta Force over here to act."

Liam rests a hand on her shoulder. "Thank you, Nellie. I won't doubt you again."

"Better not," she replies, shrugging off his hand before turning to speak to one of the officers.

Before Liam can return to Andrea, two cops march Sam right past him. Their eyes lock for a long moment. There's not a flicker of remorse in Sam's dark stare. "You're going to kill TheirStory, aren't you?"

"I just might."

"You're so fucking soft," Sam snarls as the cops lead him away.

CHAPTER 60

The past month has felt more like a year. Dr. Chow warned Liam that although his nerves have recovered about 80 percent, further improvement is unlikely. Liam is more hopeful, though. It's only been five weeks since he unearthed the poison canister, and today, for the second Saturday in a row, he's heading out to climb with Ava.

"Don't go for one of your all-day brunches after, Dad," Cole says as the family gathers in the kitchen. "We've got to be in Everett by two for my game."

"Has Dad missed one yet?" Ava challenges.

"You'd love it if he did, wouldn't you?" Cole shoots back.

"OMG, Col-ton! Could you be any more of a drama queen?"

"Me? Right!" Cole snorts. "Am I the one who had an hour-long meltdown last night because my boots didn't go with my jacket?"

Liam's smile broadens as he listens to their banter—a sign that normalcy is creeping back into their lives. But then Celeste steps in, her voice firm. "No one's going anywhere until you deal with the tornado that tore through your bedrooms." She nods toward the staircase. "Now. Both of you."

Ava and Cole exchange exaggerated eye rolls before trudging upstairs.

"Remember when they used to like us?" Celeste asks.

"They adore you," Liam says. "Always have."

"I think you're their number one these days." She smiles, searching his eyes for reassurance. "But I'll settle for second place."

He notices how hard she's trying. Celeste found them a couples' therapist, and in their last session, she tried to take responsibility for everything. Liam wound up in the strange position of defending her reasons for cheating.

He never imagined anything could shatter her quiet self-assurance. It's painful to see her so insecure, so desperate for signs of forgiveness. What she doesn't understand is that he has forgiven her; it's the trust that's broken. Liam simply isn't ready to trust her again, and he doesn't know if he ever will be.

Instead of voicing these thoughts, he turns back to his laptop. "I've got a ton of work to do before Monday."

"You're worried about the board meeting, aren't you?" Celeste asks.

"Hard not to be when our stock has tanked by fifty percent. No one's happy. Except maybe Rudy—he's probably making a killing."

"But what can the board do?"

"Fire me, for starters."

"Even though you're the majority shareholder?"

"It would be tricky, but not unprecedented. The board can replace me as CEO if they believe my decisions are hurting the company's value and, by extension, the shareholders. Matter of fact, it's their fiduciary duty. And if I fought them in court, it would only weaken the stock more."

"What are you going to do, Liam?"

"Try to make them see that this year's revenues won't matter if TheirStory destabilizes the world and the markets with it."

She bites her lip. "Now who's the drama queen?"

"Am I? Look how easily Sam weaponized the app. Others will do the same unless we prevent it."

"Do you think Nellie and the team can really put the necessary safeguards in place?"

"They have to. Or I won't release the app."

"Even if the board agrees, won't someone else just develop their own version of TheirStory?"

"Probably, but there's nothing I can do about that."

She starts to speak, but he cuts her off. "Your experience with the app and your friend, Ella . . . that never should have happened. We can't let TheirStory get into people's heads and play amateur therapist. Its scope has to be curtailed."

"Can your coders do that?"

"I think so, but it'll take time. And a hell of a lot more testing."

She nods and reaches out to touch his arm, but hesitates, her hand stopping just short. "I love that you're trying to do the right thing here, Liam. Despite the cost."

The uncertainty in her eyes stirs his conscience. "I can't believe I let myself think that you might have been involved with the poisoning. I'm sorry, Celeste."

"It's not like I didn't give you good reason to doubt me." She clears her throat, as if trying to swallow her guilt. "Plus, you were being attacked from every angle."

"Yeah, it did feel that way."

"Not even our home was safe." She shakes her head. "I can't believe Sam planted that canister in our basement!"

"He had help."

"Not from Benjamin, though."

"No."

Celeste's chin drops, her voice lowers. "I got him killed, didn't I?"

"Sam killed Benjamin. It had nothing to do with you."

"But if I hadn't mentioned to Sam last summer that he was doing our reno—"

"Why wouldn't you? Besides, how could you have known Sam had also used Benjamin for work at his place?"

She stares at the floor. "Still. If Benjamin and I hadn't . . ."

"It had nothing to do with you, Celeste. Nothing. Sam set Benjamin up and then he killed him. He's the only one responsible."

Liam had only found out yesterday, when Detective Lyles called to check in, just how much Sam had manipulated Benjamin.

"Despite his lawyer's advice, Sam's been very chatty with us," the detective said. "What's he got to lose? His entire confession is recorded. Word is, he's negotiating a plea deal."

"It's the least he can do for the taxpayers."

"Honestly? I think Sam's proud of his scheme to steal your company. He certainly likes to crow about it."

"Let him," Liam said. "Can I ask you something, Detective?"

"Shoot."

"What did Sam mean when he told me Benjamin was clueless? How could he have been if he was the one who planted the canister?"

"He didn't," Detective Lyles said flatly.

"No? Who did?"

"Some hitter who specialized in explosives. Sam hired him off the dark web. The guy's in the wind now."

"How did a hit man get into my house?"

"Another masterstroke. According to Sam, anyway." The detective chuckled. "First, he made sure Benjamin's regular HVAC subcontractors were tied up with work at his place. Then he approached Benjamin with some sob story about his cousin's kid who'd lost his job as a heating tech. He played on Benjamin's sympathy to get his guy into your basement."

It suddenly clicked for Liam. "So even though Benjamin wasn't involved, if he'd ever been questioned about the canister in my vent, he would've immediately put two and two together and pointed the finger at Sam."

"Exactly," the detective agreed. "Which is why Sam silenced him."

As much as Liam resented Benjamin for trying to steal his wife, his murder had nothing to do with the conspiracy or the affair. The guy didn't deserve to die like roadkill.

"I never loved him," Celeste murmurs, pulling Liam back to the present. "You know that, don't you?"

Liam hesitates. "I want to believe it."

"It's true!" Her eyes widen, pleading for him to understand. "It was over before Benjamin died. Completely."

He hesitates, then gives a small nod. "OK."

"But that might not be enough for you, right?" she asks, her voice catching slightly.

Maybe not.

Liam's thoughts drift to Andrea, to their last meeting at "their" Starbucks two days ago. She wasn't wearing a sling, and the scab on her forehead had healed, leaving only a faint pinkish mark. Her easy smile made her that much more attractive, reminding Liam of how much he missed her.

"How's the shoulder?" he asked after they sat down.

"Better." She ran a hand over the fabric covering her collarbone. "Apparently, I'll always have an adorable little bump here to remind me of our adventure."

"A memento you could probably do without." He grinned. "The whole experience, too, no doubt."

"Not sure about that." Her eyes softened as a gentle smile spread across her face. "There was some real opportunity for personal growth— as the TikTokers love to say—in our adventure."

"You were brilliant, Andrea. The way you pieced it all together . . ."

"It was easier for me. I wasn't personally invested." She looked down, reaching for her cup. "At least, not when it came to Sam."

"In retrospect, I ignored so many signs," Liam sighed. "Deep down, Sam was a bully. Always punching down. But I overlooked it because I thought he was so dedicated to TransScend. And, let's face it, to me."

"Don't beat yourself up. Sociopaths are masters at fooling people."

"I didn't really know him at all, did I?"

"I don't think he let you. Seems to me Sam was the human equivalent of a deepfake."

Liam laughed. "I like that."

She took another sip of her coffee, then, out of nowhere, said, "Oh, I went out on a date last weekend."

"Good on you," Liam said, taken aback but doing his best to mask his surprise—and disappointment. "How did it go?"

"Meh. Probably a one-off. But for me, it's a step in the right direction.

I think I'm ready to move on from Max. Hell, I might even be willing to trust someone else with a second date."

"You will," he said, keeping his voice steady despite the twinge of jealousy. "You're going to find someone who never forgets how lucky he is to be with you."

"At this point, I'd settle for one who doesn't screw his work colleagues." Her eyes drifted down to her cup again. "I was even considering trying to track down my mom, if she's still alive."

"I bet your dad would be proud."

"I hope so." She sighed. "It's easier now, after his letter . . . I can properly grieve him and appreciate what we had together."

"And move on?"

"That, too. I hope."

"I'm happy for you, Andrea."

"Just like I am for you."

"Because I'm not dying anymore?"

"That. And for making things right with Celeste. For keeping the family together. Many people would have walked away."

"Hard to overlook my role in that whole mess. And that was before I even met you and started to develop—"

Andrea cut him off with a wave of her hand. "Life's messy, Liam. Always is. But even that day in the ER with your son—at your lowest—I could see it. She loves you."

He shrugged, unsure if love would be enough.

"She's worth fighting for, too." Andrea touched the back of his hand, their eyes locking for a moment before she pulled away. "My advice? Put in the work. Stay present. And aware. Don't let her slip away again."

Now, as Liam takes Celeste in his arms, he can't shake the nagging doubt. He's thankful for this second chance—to make things right with TheirStory and, more importantly, to be there for his kids. But beneath the gratitude, the sting of Celeste's betrayal lingers, entwined with the feelings for Andrea that won't let go. He'll stay; he owes his family that much. But as Celeste's breath warms his cheek, Liam realizes the real struggle isn't just rebuilding trust—it's also convincing himself it will be enough.

ACKNOWLEDGMENTS

Above all, my goal with each novel I write is to tell a compelling story with characters that resonate and a plot that keeps readers guessing. And *The Deepest Fake* is no exception. If I've surprised you, engaged you, or simply kept you turning the pages, then I've done my job.

But writing this novel has been both an exciting and challenging journey, exploring timely themes like artificial intelligence, medical assistance in dying, and the essence of trust. These issues raise complex ethical questions, and while the story touches on them, my hope is only to spark thoughtful discussions. The characters' views aren't necessarily my own but are intended to present diverse perspectives and inspire deeper reflection.

As always, this book is the product of many people's contributions. I've benefited from the keen insight and support of my wife, Leeandra Stevens, from the first draft to the last. I'm also grateful to my career-long freelance editor, Kit Schindell, whose sharp eye and steady hand have helped to shape this novel. And I owe a big thanks to my friend and trusted first-pass reader, Mariko Miller, for her invaluable feedback and encouragement throughout.

A special thank-you to my amazing editor, Adrienne Kerr, whose collaborative spirit, shared vision, and priceless expertise have strengthened this novel at every stage. And to the wonderful team at Simon & Schuster Canada, whose support and dedication have meant so much. I'd like to acknowledge my agents, Samantha Haywood and Carolyn Forde, for their guidance and belief in this project.

Finally, to the readers—your engagement with my stories inspires me to keep pushing boundaries. I hope *The Deepest Fake* challenges you to think critically about the intersection of technology and humanity, and that you enjoy the ride.

"Kalla is a clever master of surprise."
#1 internationally bestselling author
Samantha M. Bailey

Also by DANIEL KALLA

"Daniel Kalla's writing is brisk and tight, and *High Society* is impossible to put down."

Amy Stuart,
#1 bestselling author of
A Death at the Party

"This is a gripping page-turner crafted by a skilled, intelligent writer."

Marissa Stapley,
New York Times
bestselling author of *Lucky*

SIMON & SCHUSTER